Trickster's Touch

Zohra Greenhalgh

ACE BOOKS, NEW YORK

*To the peacemakers of the next generation
and to the old guard of the Aquarian Age*

TRICKSTER'S TOUCH

An Ace Book / published by arrangement with
the author

PRINTING HISTORY
Ace edition / October 1989

Ace Books are published by The Berkley Publishing Group,
200 Madison Avenue, New York, New York 10016.
The name "ACE" and the "A" logo
are trademarks belonging to Charter Communications, Inc.

PRINTED IN THE UNITED STATES OF AMERICA

10 9 8 7 6 5 4 3 2 1

Acknowledgments

I WOULD LIKE to thank all of my teachers, known and unknown, who have helped me with this book—especially the Mevlevi in Turkey and Pir Vilayat Inayat Khan, head of the Sufi Order of the West. I would also like to thank the residents at the Abode of the Message, especially Hadi Hornik, who made it possible for me to bow out of the community kitchen and bow *to* the call of my typewriter.

In Milwaukee a special thanks goes to a silent sector of the Native American community who lent unseen support for this task. Old Man Coyote is a powerful medicine— thanks for letting me borrow him. Or did he borrow me? To Iman, who saw me through a scrapped draft and then some, thank you.

To the ubiquitous T.W., you opened the door in New York City for me in the first place: thank you.

In Maryland thanks go to my mother, whose enthusiasm is catching and whose financial support in the final month of preparation assured the completion of *Trickster's Touch* on deadline. To her friend Sue Ewald, thank you for inspiring me to redo the last draft. Sometimes the vagaries of my own life—and Trickster's incessant playfulness—make the task of writing for him both impossible and possible in the most peculiar ways. Of course.

Thanks go to my editor at Berkley, Susan Allison, for giving me time.

To Michael and Teshna of Delphi Chiropractic, amazed thanks for "straightening a few things out," especially to Michael, who took a special interest in seeing this tale come out right. True physicians are so very rare.

My final thanks go to the Sufi mystic and master, Hazrat Inayat Khan. I have borrowed extensively from his concept and practice of the *Universal Worship*. The words used in the funeral ceremony of this book are lifted nearly verbatim from the burial service used by the Sufi Order of the West and the Sufi Movement in Europe. Special heartfelt thanks go to Pir Vilayat Inayat Khan for permission to use them. To Amina Begum, Hazrat Inayat Khan's wife and friend, a woman who remains veiled even now, I say this: I know your name was Sharda and that you were the "tonic note" for the whole thing. May others come to know you as I have.

To Trickster, I say, "*Now* are you satisfied?"

And the hooligan just smiles . . .

Panthe'kinarok Prologue

THE GREATKIN WERE a motley, passionate family of twenty-seven. Since they had all sprung from the Presence at the same moment, each Greatkin was exactly the same age. Still, the Greatkin loved to play elaborate, sophisticated games of dress-up which involved the full spectrum of aging. One Greatkin was particularly good at this. His name was Rimble. He was the face of the Presence which represented the impossible, the unexpected, and the deviant. A mischief-maker without peer, Rimble was also called Trickster by many members of his large family. A master of disguise, Rimble might appear as a toothless hag one moment and a youthful, perfumed fop the next. Rimble excelled at many things: one of these was the art of making himself completely irritating to everyone in his proximity. When that failed to amuse him, Rimble would cause mischief on some world or other.

At present, Rimble and his brothers and sisters were all seated at a round table which had been elegantly set for a dinner party serving twenty-seven. This was the Panthe'-kinarok feast where everything the Greatkin said and did translated instantly into the known universes. The most idle conversation could have the most far-reaching consequences here. Spats or intrigues between dinner partners might cause wars—not to mention indigestion for the Greatkin themselves. Fortunately, Rimble was fond of his dinner partners, Phebene and Jinndaven. His affection for his sister and brother had spared the family the worst of his unusually abominable table manners. At present, Rimble had punctuated six of the nine dinner courses with only thirteen belches, eight farts, and twenty-six yawns. Great-kin Phebene was especially grateful to Rimble for behaving so well and said so.

"When you're polite, Rimble, dear, it makes eating so much more enjoyable." She was the Greatkin of Great Loves and Tender Trysts and tended to be a little on the syrupy side. Spectacularly beautiful, Phebene wore a rainbow-colored robe and a crown of green roses on her head. She beamed at Rimble now, her voice full of seductive pleasantries and good humor.

Rimble, who detested polite conversation, yawned for the twenty-seventh time and grinned as Phebene's smile turned into a reproving scowl. Picking his hooked nose (and eating its contents), Rimble said, "These Panthe'kinarok dinners go on forever. Hates them, I do. Boring, boring, boring."

Greatkin Jinndaven, who was seated on Rimble's right, groaned. If Rimble was feeling bored, he was apt to do something—anything—to relieve the tedium. Jinndaven tried not to think of all the ways Rimble might decide to entertain himself, but since Jinndaven was the Greatkin of Imagination he could not keep from imagining a thousand different scenarios, most of them disastrous. Dressed in mauves and small mirrors, Jinndaven literally sparkled when he moved. Leaning toward Trickster, the light of a nearby candle glinted off Jinndaven's robe and found an answering resonance in one of Trickster's pied eyes. Seeing this, Jinndaven hesitated.

"Well?" asked Rimble as nice as you please.

"I just hope you don't plan to make the last three courses of dinner as interesting as the first six."

"You still sore about the Jinnaeon?" Trickster asked incredulously.

Rimble referred to a sudden period of transition, a tricksterish *shifttime,* he had named for his imaginative brother, Jinndaven. In certain terms, this transition period could be seen as a mutation in time. This mutation (or fluctuation) had been necessary to throw space and time off balance for a while. If reality had remained on its usual track, Rimble couldn't have triggered a quantum leap of consciousness that the Presence wanted implemented through all the known universes. The Presence was the one great being to whom the Greatkin owed their allegiance. It was the Presence that all the Greatkin served, even Rimble.

It seemed the Presence thought the two-legged races in all the known universes, especially the world of Mnemlith, were too concerned with their day-to-day lives. They were missing the larger cosmological dramas that developed and exploded around them on a constant basis. In the past millennium or so, the Presence felt the two-legged races had grown unbearably small-minded. It was Rimble's task to make them large-minded again.

This task proved more difficult than Trickster could possibly have foreseen. Not only were the two-leggeds of Mnemlith out and out resistant to change, some of the Greatkin themselves acted in like manner, a few of them consciously thwarting Rimble's attempts to do the will of the Presence. Rimble thought this very small-minded of *them*, and said so often.

When Jinndaven didn't answer him immediately, Trickster repeated his question, "You still sore about me calling it the Jinnaeon?"

"Well—I—" Jinndaven shrugged. "Yeah. I'm a little sore."

"Jinnaeon sounds better than Rimblaeon."

"That may be," Jinndaven admitted. "But look at all the trouble you caused on Mnemlith. All in *my* name. You said it would be a teensy-weensy fluctuation of consciousness. You had drugs, torture, insanity, civil unrest—"

"Yes, yes," snapped Rimble hastily. "Well, it couldn't be helped. That was the resistance to change. Mattie's fault entirely," added Rimble with a sideways glance at another of his brothers, Greatkin Mattermat. This Greatkin was the Patron of All Things Made Physical: of everything that "mattered." At the moment, the ponderous fellow had his mouth full of salad. Dressed in earth colors, Greatkin Mattermat smelled richly of caves and loam and fir trees. Rimble grinned and added, "Mattie hates quantum leaps, see. Hates them and blocks them."

Swallowing swiftly, Mattermat glared at Rimble and said, "Did I hear what I think I just heard? Did you blame *me* for all the trouble on Mnemlith?"

Jinndaven pursed his lips and muttered, "At least Rimble didn't name an age of transition after *you*. The Jinnaeon. The worst period of history that Mnemlith has ever known." Jinndaven put his head in his hands and rolled his eyes.

Rimble returned Mattermat's glare with one of his own. "Trouble? That wasn't trouble. That was an experiment. An improoovement. A remedy for a stagnant situation—"

"Mnemlith was getting along fine until *you* interfered!" retorted Mattermat. Among other things, Mattermat was also the Patron of Inertia. Being the personification of change itself, Rimble had long ago decided that his divine charge included the subversion of entropy—i.e., Mattermat— wherever he found it. As a result, Rimble had earned the displeasure of his heavyweight brother on countless occasions over the millennia.

"I saved that world!" cried Trickster, his boredom vanishing as he warmed to the idea of having it out with Mattermat once and for all. "Furthermore and most importantly, I caused enough turmoil on Mnemlith to make folks start praying to us again. In order to pray to us, they have to remember our names. Remembering us makes them large-minded. And *that,* my dear brothers and sisters, is the point."

Moments before the Panthe'kinarok meet and feast were to begin, Rimble had decided that Mnemlith was the sleepiest world in the known universes. According to Rimble, only a quarter of that world's population could recite the names of all the Greatkin. Most had forgotten that the Greatkin had ever existed. And even less than a quarter knew which of the Greatkin lived in sunny Eranossa and which lived in the shadowy, subtle underworld called Neath. Can't have that, said Rimble. Such forgetfulness might spread to the *un*known universes. It would be a veritable plague of oblivion. So Rimble had taken Mnemlith by the shoulders and shaken that world. Hard.

Mattermat sipped his wine, his eyes never leaving Trickster's. There was a short silence while he drank. The tension in the room increased. Mattermat put his wine goblet down carefully. Before he could speak again, Sathmadd, the Patron of Organization, Mathematics, and Red Tape, interrupted.

"Rimble, I've had my fill of your turmoil, as you call it. Chaos and havoc would be more apt," she said primly. She was a bustling sort of Greatkin, fastidious and orderly to a fault. "I, for one, hope you keep your meddling to a minimum from here on out. We've got three more courses to get through. I vote to have them peaceful."

Several Greatkin nodded and clapped their hands politely in favor of Sathmadd's suggestion. Rimble noted that all of them hailed from tidy, cheery Eranossa. "Where all the *bright* ones live," muttered Rimble sarcastically.

Troth, a dark-skinned quiet fellow, cleared his throat. Like Rimble, Troth resided in Neath. The beautiful glass beads that adorned his braided hair swung forward now as he changed position. Troth was the Greatkin of Death; when he spoke everyone listened.

"Nothing is permanent, Mattermat. Not even us."

"Besides," said Trickster, "the Presence *told* me to meddle."

Mattermat snorted. "A likely story."

"Once a liar, always a liar," chimed in Sathmadd, wagging a finger at Rimble sternly.

"I don't lie," yelled Rimble. "I'm Trickster. I live in Neath. We're not like you day types. We don't tell everything we know all at once. It's not our nature."

There was a long silence. During it, Rimble slumped in

his chair. He crumpled the linen napkin in his lap with frustration. Would no one in Eranossa ever understand that *he* served the Presence same as the rest of them? He had a divine right to meddle; it was his job, for Presence sake.

Rimble licked his lips and whispered in a singsong manner, "Trickster's my name and change is my game. Trickster's my name and change is my game. Trickster's my name—"

Jinndaven interrupted his brother sharply. "Cut that out, Rimble. This is the Panthe'kinarok, when everything we say translates—"

"Yup," snapped Rimble, his pied eyes flashing with fury. "Trickster's my name and change is my game. Trickster's—"

Finally hearing Rimble's words, Mattermat jumped to his feet. "Shut up! You just shut up, Trickster! Don't you dare do one more thing to one more world! I tell you, I won't have it! I won't!"

Now Mattermat appealed to the Greatkin whom the rest of the family lovingly referred to as Eldest. Her real name was Themyth. She was the Greatkin of Civilization. No Panthe'kinarok could begin without her opening libation to the Presence. Her word was final in all disputes. Eldest, who had been Rimble's lover recently, was dressed in a brightly colored patchwork quilt, her gray hair tumbling free from its habitual, elegant bun. Under the quilt, Eldest wore loose mix-matched clothing. No one had ever seen Eldest attired in this fashion. It had been the silent conclusion at the table that Rimble's lovemaking had influenced the Greatkin of Civilization. Everyone hoped this influence would pass. It had been a great relief to some that the place cards on the table had been arranged in such a manner that sat Rimble next to Love and Imagination instead of Greatkin Themyth. The seating arrangements had been Themyth's idea. Bedding Rimble was one thing. Sitting next to him for a nine-course dinner was quite another. Making love with Trickster would give all the civilizations in all the known universes a small jolt; anything more extended might cause unwanted anarchy. Mattermat hit the table with his fist. "*Do* something, Eldest!" Fruit rolled out of a silver cornucopia and teetered on the table's edge.

Earthquakes abounded throughout creation.

"Mattie, dear, be *careful*," said Themyth as she deftly caught the fruit before it hit the floor. She replaced the apple and peach gently.

But Mattermat would not be calmed. "I want him stopped! I want him contained! I want him *out* of this council!"

Eldest grabbed the wooden cane that rested against her chair and thwacked it against the wooden floor. The sound resembled that of a very loud and very uncompromising thunderclap. Everyone jumped, including Rimble. Startled for the moment, Trickster broke off his litany for change.

"Now," said Themyth with great dignity, "we'll have no more of *that* at this table. From either of you. Clear?"

Neither Mattermat nor Rimble said anything.

Eldest eyed both brothers coolly. Turning again to Rimble, she studied his rather wild appearance. Rimble had painted his bare torso with yellow and black diagonals during the break between the fourth and fifth courses. He had pulled on fur pants made of the skin of coyotes and hung several gourd rattles from a braided belt. Incongruously, Rimble wore a black bow tie around his neck. Eldest cleared her throat. "Do you promise to leave Mattie's things alone for the rest of dinner?"

As if on cue, Trickster jumped on his chair, let out a bloodcurdling shriek, and yelled, "I don't have to stay here!"

When Jinndaven had recovered from Rimble's shout, he wiped his brow with a lavender handkerchief several times and said, "I knew this was coming. I just knew it. O sweet Presence preserve us—"

Eldest peered at Rimble. "Explain."

Rimble crossed his arms over his painted chest. "Ain't

got nothing *to* explain, Eldest. Nothing to explain at all. You don't want me here? Fine. I'll go elsewhere."

Themyth frowned. "You can't go out of the universe, Rimble—"

Rimble snorted. "I got me the perfect antidote to Mr. Permanence and Resistance over there," he said, inclining his head toward Mattermat. Mattermat's face was scarlet with outrage. Trickster grinned and said, "I think I likes changing matter from the inside the best. It's so irrevocable—"

"Not in *this* universe, you don't!" yelled Mattermat.

"Exactly," said Trickster. "Not in this universe at all."

Greatkin Themyth was truly alarmed now. "Rimble—"

Trickster cut her off rudely. "And you know how I turns the inside inside out, hmm? Myth. That's how I does it. Myth. See, myth molds matter," said Trickster, making a pun on Mattermat's creative function. "Myth decides what matters and what don't."

"That's absurd, Rimble," snapped Mattermat, more fearful than he wanted Rimble to know. "We're the Greatkin. *We're* the ones who give myths meaning. Not the other way around."

Trickster sniggered nastily. "Just told a myth called *Contrarywise*. Told it in a Distant Place. And know what, folks? It's affecting us here."

"Nonsense," retorted Mattermat.

"Just where *is* this Distant Place?" asked Sathmadd. As the Greatkin of Organization, it was her job to know all the place names in the known universes. "A Distant Place" rang no bells whatsoever.

Trickster ignored Sathmadd's question. "Feel another one coming on. Think I'll call it *Trickster's Touch*. Might as well take *all* the credit for all the havoc—seeing as how you folks don't want any. Of course, if everything turns out well, I'll take the credit for that, too."

No one said anything.

Trickster went merrily on. "I wasn't finished with Mnemlith. Started the Jinnaeon with the shock of the New. Anchored it through Zendrak and then finally through Kelandris when she turned in Speakinghast town. But that's not enough. Got to do something with the New once it's there. Otherwise, it turns on *itself*. Especially if something gets to blocking it," he added, looking directly at Mattermat. "So we improvise a little. We take it elsewhere—where it *isn't* blocked."

"Im—im—improvise?" asked Jinndaven. He was so nervous about what he imagined Trickster might be up to that he stuttered.

"Yeah," said Rimble gaily. "Improvise. You folks want peace, so you say. Well, I'll give you peace. My way. And that's the way of Neath." He paused, his voice suddenly menacing. "In Neath, we're not always so nice. In Neath, things go bump in the night."

The residents of Eranossa, principally Mattermat, Sathmadd, and Jinndaven, paled.

The residents of Neath, however, chuckled.

The Greatkin of Death rubbed his dark hands together with undisguised glee. "This should be fun."

Chapter One

UNLIKE HIS LESS flexible brothers and sisters, Greatkin Rimble had long ago embraced multiplicity as part and parcel of his divine being. As a result he alone of all his family was able to exist in more than one reality at a time. So while Greatkin Mattermat, Jinndaven, and Sathmadd criticized Rimble for meddling in the known universes, Rimble defended himself vigorously *and* slipped out the back door of Eranossa. As the argument between the Greatkin raged, Rimble neatly materialized on one of the northernmost islands belonging to the Soaringsea archipelago of the world called Mnemlith. Here Rimble planned to indulge in one of his favorite pastimes, a game called "Messing with Mattie." In order to do it effectively, Rimble would need the help of the most fabulous race ever to walk the world of Mnemlith: the Mythrrim Beasts.

The Mythrrim of Soaringsea were long-lived and large. They resembled an uncomfortable mixture of falcon, hyena, spiked dinosaur, and lion. They had brindle bodies, magnificent wings, horns that ridged their backs, protruding eyes, and a wildly infectious laugh. They were carnivorous and very fond of storytelling. Indeed, the *landdraw* of this particular race had given them the gift of racial memory and mimicry. Possessing seven sets of vocal cords, the Mythrrim could imitate any sound in the universe. They were natural linguists, their native tongue called Oldspeech. It was the Mythrrim who had taught the two-leggeds about the world and about the Presence. It was the Mythrrim who had recited the names of the Greatkin to the cave dwellers at the beginning of time. It was the Mythrrim who had told the

Great Stories, the myths, about each Greatkin and instructed the two-leggeds in their rituals of remembrance for each Greatkin.

Then the Mythrrim had disappeared.

In their place the Mythrrim had left the Mayanabi Nomads, a body of people culled from all the two-legged *landdraws* of Mnemlith and entrusted them with the Great Stories the Mythrrim had once told. It was time, said the Greatkin, for the two-leggeds to grow up. They needed to be able to teach themselves now. The two-leggeds must make their own mistakes and learn from them. The Mythrrim left sorrowing; they had come to love the two-leggeds as much as their own four-legged offspring. The Mythrrim, however, were ever obedient to the wishes of the Greatkin, and so did as they were bid. Centuries passed. In time, only the Mayanabi Nomads remembered that the Mythrrim Beasts had ever existed in physical reality. To most of the peoples of Mnemlith, the Mythrrim Beasts of Soaringsea were the stuff of fantasy.

Rimble appeared on the hillside of the tallest and most willful mountain in all Mnemlith. It was called Mount Gaveralin. Intelligent and dangerous, Gaveralin immediately caused a blizzard to come out of nowhere and buffet Trickster. Rimble, who was still having an argument with the Greatkin of Matter in their ancestral home at Eranossa, scowled at the mountain and said, "I got rights here! I'm a guest of the Mythrrim—"

They know you're coming? I don't seem to recall any orders instructing me to let you pass, Greatkin Rimble.

Trickster scowled, wiping snow off his black hair. His bare upper torso prickled with goose bumps. Swearing at Mattermat—since the mountain was very definitely one of Mattermat's representatives—Rimble changed his costume. Now he wore furs and leather and snug boots. A multicolored woolen hat covered his small ears. Continuing to speak to Gaveralin, Rimble said, "Let me pass or I'll make you a mutant."

A mutant mountain? There's no such thing—

Rimble lost his temper. "I'll blow off your summit!"

The snowstorm stopped instantly. Among other things, the mountains of Soaringsea were volcanic. Rimble could make good his threat.

"Thank you," said Trickster through clenched teeth, and stomped up the trail to a cluster of caves whose tunnels interconnected like the corridors of a labyrinth. Rimble, who had visited here many times before, headed for the opening of the largest cave and turned right, then left, then two rights, then a sharp left until he found himself in a large underground chamber.

You may wonder why Rimble didn't materialize directly into the chamber in the first place. Rimble loved the Mythrrim. He was the father of this particular race. Themyth was its mother. When the Mythrrim had retired to Soaringsea, they wished to prevent the two-leggeds from trailing them there. Gaveralin was their sentry. No one, not even the Greatkin, were allowed to reach the Mythrrim without their knowledge. Thus, by the time Rimble actually arrived at the place where the Mythrrim now gathered, everyone knew he was coming. He was met with a resounding chorus of hellos and wing-flapping. Rimble grinned at their obvious pleasure at seeing Dear Old Dad. Doffing his woolen cap, Trickster said, "I need your help."

The oldest and wisest Mythrrim was named Kindra. She had yellowed teeth and blue feathers that had turned white with age. She inclined her enormous, ugly head toward Rimble. "We're keeping *kinhearth,* Father. Care to join us?"

"Keeping *kinhearth*" was the phrase the Mythrrim used to describe their practice of remembering the Presence, and the Greatkin. In the large chamber, wood blazed in a huge stone fireplace. Flames leapt as high as ten feet. Around this fire, the Mythrrim gathered and told the great myths of the world.

"What're you telling?" asked Trickster.

"The Mythrrim of Origin."

Rimble's expression turned wistful. "That's my favorite."

"I know," said Kindra with a twinkle in her old eyes. "Here. Sit between my paws, and I'll start over from the beginning. We'll cast the spell of Once Upon."

Rimble sighed happily and climbed inside the large, brindle paws of Kindra. The ancient Mythrrim Beast cleared her throat. During the telling of the tale she would re-create every sound effect needed to make the story real through her splendid set of vocal cords. Smiling and exposing her yellow teeth, Kindra spoke with authority.

The Mythrrim of Origin

Once there was a Great Being. It was a radiant intelligence in which all things were contained. This Great Being was alone, for in all the universes there was no other like Itself. It was very lonely. So to amuse Itself, Great Being dreamed.

It dreamed of civilizations that rose and fell with the seasons of the Ages, of worlds and all the peoples who lived on them: the Two-Leggeds, the Four-Leggeds, the Leafy and the Scaled, the Crawlers, the Winged Ones and the Wild Winds of the Five Directions. And each of these was named kin, for each sprang from the longing of their one Great Parent, sprang and fell back into the silence.

There were no witnesses.

There was no one to look upon the dreams of Great Being and say, "Good job, Great Being." Or even, "This one needs a little work."

Troubled and sad, Great Being withdrew into Itself. And dreamed. It dreamed for eons. Finally, the dreams of Great Being became so intelligent that they, too, began to dream. And ask questions. But Great Being could not answer their questions, for speech did not exist. Life was still hidden, asleep in incubation. Reality was a divine potential waiting to be released. It was a closed universal—a secret garden of fertile splendor without entrance or exit.

Finally, the dreams of Great Being became unruly in their captivity. Like fruit too long on the vine, they became a poison that threatened the sanity of Great Being Itself. Daily the dreams clamored to be set free. Daily Great Being attempted to do so and could not. The need of both the Dreamer and the Dreams increased a thousand-fold with each Age. Never before had Great Being been beset by such a dire challenge. It thought long and hard about the problem. Then one day, Great Being had a Great Idea.

The Idea was called the Real World.

The Real World, thought Great Being, would be a clever device through which My dreams might know themselves. *And,* thought Great Being with pleasure and fear, the Real World might be a device through which I could know Myself as well. For are not My dreams part of Myself? This Idea pleased Great Being very much. It began to feel a little less lonely. But even so, Great Being still lacked the means to make Its dreams real. The desire to make them manifest was there, but the knowledge of how to do it was not. The frustration and despair of Great Being continued to grow along with Its love for Its captive dreams. Great Being tried everything It could think of to release Itself from this bind. It knew It needed to make a change, but change did not exist, either. Thus Great Being could do nothing but wait and hope. In unspeakable sympathy, Great Being suffered the agony of Its voiceless dreams.

Still, the pressure increased.

The Many and the One reached a terrible impasse. Since division did not yet exist, either, neither the Many nor the One could see each other. There were no distinctions, no shadows. No plays of light against dark. There was no definition, nor depth perception. All was contained—like a road swallowed by the blinding white of a winter blizzard. Finally, one of Great Being's dreams also had a great idea.

This idea was called individuality.

The wise little dream decided to practice what it had conceived, and so in time, its small voice grew louder than the rest. Great Being was perplexed by the continual chatter of this courageous little nag. Great Being was used to hearing the symphony of the spheres inside Its head—in perfect multi-part harmony, of course. This voice was disrupting the perfect pitch of Great Being. Great Being felt annoyed. It called the noisy dream many names—Disharmony, Disorder, Chaos, and Royal Pain. This did not deter the noisy dream in the least. The noisy dream absorbed all the names and added a few of its own—Murphy, Coyote, the Raggedy Man, Uncle Tompa, and Rimble. In this way, the noisy dream became a creator in its own right. Over time, the noisy dream also developed something more than intelligence—it developed personality. As Great Being didn't have any of Its own, Great Being finally decided to seek out the Noisy Dream of Many Names and see if Personality was a Good Idea or a Bad Idea. As Great Being drew near to the Noisy Dream, It heard this:

"Who am I?"

And again.

And again.

"Who am I?"

Great Being could not answer this question, for Great Being could not see the Noisy Dream. In renewed despair, Great Being turned to go. As it did so, the Noisy Dream began to weep. Its small voice trembled with a choking horror:

"Am I alone, then?" it asked.

The loneliness of the Noisy Dream pierced the pain of Great Being's own cosmic solitude. For a moment, Great Being knew and understood this gabby little dream. Great Being reached toward the sorrowing dream and tried to comfort it. The Noisy Dream felt

Great Being's concern. Wailing loudly, the Noisy Dream said:

"Is there no other like me? Must I listen to myself for all eternity? What cruelty is this?" Sobbing, it added, "Why *me*?"

Personal melodrama was conceived in this moment.

Great Being could not bear to be thought of as cruel by the Noisy Dream, for the simple fact that Great Being knew that It wasn't cruel. Unrealized, perhaps, but not cruel. Great Being decided to Do Something. Great Being concluded that though It might split apart in the process, It *would* find a way to prove Its inherent kindness to this loud, disbelieving little dream. In order to do this, however, Great Being knew that It must make a separation of some kind. It must thrust this Noisy Dream away from Itself so that both might see that the other existed. Great Being wondered if this would hurt. Great Being hesitated. What if the Noisy Dream went into the Real World and forgot that Great Being existed? You see, in a strange way, Great Being had come to value the questions of the Noisy Dream. Secretly, Great Being also valued the daring different- ness of the Noisy Dream. Could it be that Great Being *loved* the deviant little thing? Yes.

In a moment of unparalleled generosity, Great Being fought against Its own loneliness so that It might free the Noisy Dream from Itself. It was important, reasoned Great Being, for the Noisy Dream to know without doubt that its nature was identical to that of Great Being—kind. With great bravery, Great Being again resolved to free Its only companion from the void. To do this, Great Being would need to use Short Division.

Arithmetic was conceived in this moment.

Desire and knowledge united—and still a separation between Dreamer and Dream proved to be an arduous task. As the process began, the clamor of *all* the dreams trapped inside Great Being increased to deafening proportions. The internal push and pull was grueling. Great Being saw that It would have to release *everything* in order to release the one different dream that had wept in loneliness. Great Being sighed at the enormity of the challenge—so much work for just one dream. Great Being supposed the Noisy Dream was worth all this trouble. Love decreed it. Great Being sighed again—making no sound.

Sound, thought Great Being. Perhaps I should make a sound with my sigh? And so It tried to do so. At first, the sigh rattled like dry leaves. Then it became smooth like the groan of a distant wind. Now Great Being's sigh took on the depth and roar of a thundering ocean surf. It sounded like this:

"Whhhhhhhhhooooo."

The universes trembled. Suddenly, the Unmanifest poured into the Real World on the vibration of this divine sigh. Emptiness filled. Life spilled forth with exuberance. Shock waves of sound rippled through Great Being and It released all that was within. This was a bright explosion of Being. For the first time, the universes knew a Great Wildness. Dazed by the variety of form dancing before It, Great Being looked upon all the portions of Itself and loved. A million billion dreams returned that love a thousand-fold, each according to its own temperament.

"There is one of you," said Great Being shyly. "There is one of you who is sadder than the others—"

The Noisy Dream of Many Names cleared its throat. "Well, not exactly—your Presence."

Great Being turned toward the Noisy Dream, regarding it for the first time. The Noisy Dream was a tall, radiant being with an ever-changing face.

"You're not sadder than the rest?"

"Not exactly."

Great Being felt perplexed. "I thought you—"

"Well, I had to make you *think* I was sadder, see—otherwise you were never going to get off your creative duff and Do Something about the state of things."

"Oh." said Great Being. "So I was tricked?"

The radiant being considered the question. After a few moments, it said, "If you wish, you may say that I tricked you. Myself, I prefer to think that I helped you Improoove."

"Improve."

"Yeah. That's my nature, you know. I make Improoovements on your ideas."

Great Being frowned. "Did anyone *ask* you to do this?"

The radiant being became indignant. "Well, somebody had to do something about you. Since it was my idea, it might as well be me who gets the credit."

Great Being nodded. "So you'd like all the credit for all the improvements made in the Real World? Even the evolutionary deviances? And—uh—cosmic experiments?"

The radiant being grinned. "Especially those, your Presence. I feel I'd understand that sort of thing, see."

Great Being smiled slyly. "And I suppose I won't need to name you, either. I suppose that being such a creative type you've picked your own?"

"Rimble. Greatkin Rimble—at your service. My friends call me Murphy, though. Or rather, they will. In time. When You invent it."

Great Being regarded Rimble with renewed consternation. "There's more of you?"

Rimble rolled his pied eyes. "Really, your Presence—you've simply *got* to stop thinking about things in such isolation. Of course, there are more of my kind. I have twenty-six squabbling brothers and sisters. All of whom want names from *You*. There. Does that make You happy?"

Great Being nodded, Its sly mood returning. "I'm

glad I'm needed for something, Rimble. Otherwise, I would get very lonely. And sad. Very, very sad."

Rimble stared at Great Being. "You would?"

"Oh, yes."

Trickster though he was, Rimble was not a cruel soul. How could he be? He, like all of creation, had sprung from the kindness of Great Being. So Rimble felt a pang of compassion for Great Being—the first in manifest reality. He eyed Great Being carefully out of the corner of his yellow eye, and said, "Well, maybe me and the rest of the family could keep You company or something. Would that help?"

"That would help a great deal," said Great Being, Its moroseness lifting. "So I can always count on you to help me?"

"Uh—"

"You *don't* want me to be sad. . . ."

"Well—no, your Presence."

"Then it's decided."

"What is?" asked Rimble, who was getting the feeling that Great Being had just duped him.

"You and your twenty-six squabbling brothers and sisters will be my helpers. For all time—"

"*For all time!*" Rimble began dancing a hopping jig of fury. "I never said anything about *all time!*"

"Didn't you?"

Rimble was so stupefied by the question that he didn't answer Great Being.

Great Being smiled broadly. "Do you know what Rimble means?"

Rimble spluttered. "I made it *up!*"

"Then let me give the name meaning. It's my nature, you know, to give meaning." Great Being spoke in perfect mimicry of Rimble's earlier pronouncement about "Improvements."

Rimble paced. Then he said, "Okay. You're on.

You give my name meaning." He paused. "So what's it mean?"

Great Being began to laugh. The boom of Its humor resounded in every corner of the known and unknown universes. Rimble bit his lower lip and asked: "You going to tell me who I am, or not?"

"What, and spoil all the fun of you finding out?" scoffed Great Being. Then in a moment of unexpected seriousness, Great Being added, "I suspect, Rimble, that when all is said and done, you'll know more about yourself than anyone else. And that's a good thing, Rimble. Self-knowledge is power of the right kind." Great Being paused. "Should *I* call you Murphy?"

Rimble put his hands on his hips. "Guess that depends on whether You're my friend or not. Well, when *I* decide, I'll get back to You on it. Meanwhile, I'm Rimble."

"The one who will know something of himself," said the Presence softly.

When Kindra had finished speaking, Rimble sighed happily. Looking upward at the overhang of her canine jowl, Rimble said, "You know, it took me the *longest* time to figure out that the Presence meant just what It said. About the meaning of my name."

Kindra waited for him to continue.

Rimble laughed softly. "I'm so full of tricks myself, I thought the Presence was giving more of the same. I thought I'd have to wait centuries before Great Being would tell me what Rimble meant. And there Great Being had gone and told me in the first place. Rimble means 'the one who knows something of himself.' " Rimble sighed. "Not that anyone in Eranossa thinks so."

"How can we be of service to you?" asked Kindra graciously.

Rimble stood up. He walked to the center of the Myth-rrim ring. In proportion to their great size, Rimble resembled a child's toy. As large as his offspring were, Rimble felt no fear of them. The Mythrrim were a compassionate, intelligent, and good-natured race. It was to these three qualities that Rimble now spoke.

"Things are bad for me at Eranossa right now. See, I've got this charge from the Presence to go broaden the perspective of the known and unknown universes. Basic panoramic mutation, you understand. Happens every hundred millennia or so when the Presence gets bored. Anyway, as usual, Great Being has come to me to do the job." Rimble paused, pulling on his black goatee. "Mattermat's blocking me on every level. So are most of the ninnies in Eranossa—Themyth excepted. I'm going to need to go through Neath to get the job done."

The Mythrrim made howls and squawks of dismay.

"That's the hard way," said Kindra. "Are you sure there's no other?"

Greatkin Rimble shrugged. "Not unless you can think of one."

Kindra cocked her head to the side. Then, speaking in Oldspeech, she conferred with the rest of her family. Tails wagged, wings fluttered. Rimble waited patiently for the Mythrrim to reach a consensus. Since the median age of a Mythrrim Beast was three thousand years, the creatures perceived time in a slower—almost geologic—manner than normal mortals. The family council took three days to reach its decision. At the end of that period, Kindra approached Rimble. The little Greatkin was fast asleep in a nearby cave. The ancient Mythrrim woke the snoring Greatkin gently with her canine nose. "We're ready to resume conversation with you," she said.

Rimble yawned and sat up. "I'm listening."

Kindra hesitated. "You have a great fear, yes? Fear for the future?"

"Yeah," said Trickster. "Great Being says 'change or be changed.' And that means everyone, see. Even the Greatkin. You *know* how Mattermat is about change. It's not his nature. It's mine."

"And if Mattermat doesn't surrender, all of creation will suffer?"

"That's about the size of it," agreed Rimble with a despondent sigh.

Kindra grinned, exposing long teeth, yellowed with age. "How about a jolt of the fantastic. Get Jinndaven to help you—"

"Easier said than done. I've pissed him off recently."

"Nonsense. Jinndaven loves you. What's more he needs you. You're the only Greatkin who'll listen to his wild ideas. The tame ones are fine for everyone else. But he's got nowhere to go with his wild ones—except to you, Father." Kindra purred briefly. "Anyway, we'll do this thing backward."

"Sounds promising," said Trickster. He loved doing things backward.

"We thought you'd like it." Kindra chuckled. "We'll also do the unexpected. We'll go through the mortals. We'll make the change in them first. When they change, it will affect the Greatkin at Eranossa and Neath. Myth does that. It reaches out in *all* directions. Has its impact on Greatkin and mortal alike."

Rimble pursed his lips. Then he said, "Mattie won't expect this. In fact, I don't even think he believes the mortals have any effect on Eranossa at all. Divine Will only goes one way."

"That is his great error," said Kindra, her expression sage.

Trickster started to pace. "And of course the unknown universes interpenetrate the known universes. I likes it, I does. I likes it a *lot*." Trickster looked wistfully at Kindra. "They do nothing but criticize me in Eranossa. I'd dearly love to put them in their highfaluted places. Neath style."

Kindra nodded. "Myths aren't short on blood and horror. We'll tell the tale here. You give us the main players, and we'll embellish. As it's told in Soaringsea, the tale will gather momentum. The people involved will feel the pull of the myth and begin to act on it. Myth and mortal will mold each other. One request, though."

"Anything."

"We want a part."

"You have a part," said Trickster. "You're talking right now—"

"Yes, but this is a *bit* part," countered Kindra and several of the other Mythrrim. "We want to make an appearance in mortal time and space. We've grown curious during our years of retreat. We want to see the progress of the two-leggeds on the mainland. After all, we were their teachers."

"Progress?" said Trickster dubiously. "That's a kind word for it."

"Nevertheless, we want to visit the mainland, Father."

Trickster considered this possibility. "Well, this *is* a tricksterish tale. The unexpected is the norm. Why not? The more havoc the better. You can visit Speakinghast, the bastion of tidiness, logic, and realism. Ugh," added Rimble, rolling his eyes with distaste.

Kindra flapped her wings with annoyance. "We don't wish to create *havoc,* Father. We're creatures of peace—"

"Hey, now, wait a minute. *Peace* isn't my thing at *all*. There's a Greatkin for that and it ain't me. If it's peace you want, go see—"

Kindra interrupted Trickster crisply. "The end of a quantum leap is a new stability, Father. That's a kind of peace. We want a share in it."

Rimble grumbled and swore under his breath.

Kindra began to laugh. "Change or be changed, Father."

Trickster stiffened.

The Mythrrim roared—literally—with guffaws and giggles. The island shook with the sound of their voices. Trickster put his hands over his ears and wondered if he should dematerialize until the Mythrrim subsided. Finally Kindra stopped rolling about on the ground.

Still chuckling, Kindra sat up and said, "Rimble-Rimble on you, Father."

The laughter started all over again.

Chapter Two

By HER OWN admission, Elder Hennin of Suxonli Village
was a world-class villain, and she liked herself this way.
Tammirring-born, she had inherited all of the psychic gifts
of her native *landdraw:* prophecy, telepathy, and visualization. The good she could have made of these gifts was
inestimable. For her own reasons, however, Hennin had
distorted these gifts and bent them to her personal will. A
renegade Mayanabi Nomad of considerable rank, Hennin
possessed the training to twist anything to her advantage.
Interested in enhancing her own spiritual power base in
Suxonli, Hennin had done the unthinkable. She had revised
the original Mythrrim tales about Trickster told by the
Mythrrim Beasts themselves in centuries gone by. The
villagers were an uneducated group for the most part, and
Hennin had dazzled them with her brilliance and persuasive
logic. In time, she had set herself up as an expert on the
rituals of Greatkin Rimble, drawing others like Cobeth into
her webs of intrigue and deceit. Cobeth was dead now due
to an unfortunate accident at a Trickster's Hallows held last
year in Speakinghast. Hennin missed his company, not
because she had liked him, but because he had done her
bidding with eagerness. Cobeth had been her long arm, her
menace at a distance. Now she had no one to carry out
her schemes—until tonight.

Tonight, she had practiced the art of visualization with
such mastery that she had not only bent the *landdraw* of
Suxonli to her will, but she had created a physical form for
the *draw* to use. It was tall, gray, shuffling, and intelligent.
She could never have brought the *draw* under her control if

Greatkin Zendrak had not cursed it sixteen years ago. Fortunately for Hennin's purposes, Zendrak's curse had packed tremendous power—after all, he *was* a Greatkin.

Cursed, the *landdraw* had responded to Zendrak's rage like plants exposed to the conflagration of napalm. The *draw* had screamed, withered, and become hideous. No children born after this time had survived. As it stood now, Suxonli Village had no future. Hennin decided to change this—not out of the goodness of her heart, of course. She had no compassion for the barren women of the village or the mutant things that were born and died within minutes of taking their first breaths. All Hennin wanted was power. Personal power. Control of the *landdraw* assured her an unlimited amount. But what *was landdraw*?

Landdraw was intelligent. In any birth, three factors determined the genetic and psychological inheritance of the child: mother, father, and *draw*. Once a child was conceived, the pregnant mother could not cross from one country or *draw* into another. To do so would abort the child. Each *landdraw* left a specific psychic imprint of talents on the newborn as well as any number of physical and emotional characteristics that faithfully reflected the region in which the child had been conceived. Earthquake-prone Jinnjirri gave birth to a race of people who enjoyed "breaking new ground." Most of them grew up to be artists, iconoclasts, and political dissidents. The hair and gender of this passionate people shifted with their moods like storms and sunshine playing hide-and-seek across the Jinnjirri Central Plains.

In contrast to the freewheeling Jinnjirri, the Saämbolin-born were as emotionally contained as the lakes that dotted Saämbolin's tidy landscape. Speakinghast, the capital of Saämbolin, was clean, orderly, and organized. This city boasted most of Mnemlith's lawmakers, administrators, and educators among its number.

Predictably Sathmadd, the Greatkin of Mathematics, Organization, and Red Tape, was the patron of this fair city.

In the southwest the desert country of Asilliwir produced a people of nomadic temperament. Composed mostly of rolling sand and treeless islands, the *draw* of Asilliwir fashioned a people who lusted for all the things this arid land could not sustain. Over the centuries, the Asilliwir had become the natural traders of Mnemlith, their prices high and their goods exotic. Although this race engaged primarily in commerce and business, its exchange included not only money but news. The Asilliwir caravan wagons covered thousands of miles every year; in short, the Asilliwir kept all of Mnemlith informed about the issues (and gossip) of the day.

To the west lay Piedmerri. This land race echoed the fertile, protected valleys found in this country. Here was a people who were round-faced and blessed with an abundant ability to conceive and foster children everywhere, their schools famous for putting the needs of the children first. Generally cheerful and large-of-lap, the Pieds were a gentle people.

In the southwest stood the sea-loving Dunnsung-born. This race was a close cousin to the artistic Jinnjirri. The Dunnsung were gifted with beautiful voices that slid up and down the scale with ease and power. Theirs was a musical talent that could make even the most callous weep. Dunnsung mothers often gave birth in the shallow waters of the sea which surrounded the Dunnsung peninsula, the rhythm of the waves imprinted on the psyches of this fair-haired people from the first moment of life.

And finally to the far north lay Tammirring. Cold, remote, and mountainous, the Tammirring *draw* impressed its people with a love of secrets. A race of extreme psychic sensitivity, the Tammirring-born usually wore veils to protect themselves. This *draw* produced seers and mystics, and Elder Hennin was no exception. Native ability paired with an accelerated Mayanabi training from her youth now made Elder Hennin a formidable adversary.

Currently, like Rimble, Elder Hennin was conducting an

experiment; she was meddling with nature; specifically, the venom of the holovespa wasp. Unlike Rimble, however, Elder Hennin didn't care one whit if this experiment was remotely in line with the wishes of the Presence. And this was the great difference between Hennin and Trickster. Unfortunately, Hennin's understanding and interpretation of Rimble's activities among the Greatkin sadly missed the bigger picture. For Hennin, Rimble was an excuse to do whatever she pleased to whomever she pleased without guilt or conscience. Since Hennin had been raised in Suxonli Village, the place most sacred to Trickster in all Mnemlith, Hennin felt she had an inside and therefore more correct view of Trickster's real nature. After all, the Mythrrim had given Suxonli the honor of enacting Trickster's ritual of remembrance each fall: Rimble's Revel. Secure in her "knowledge," Elder Hennin believed herself to be a kind of mediumistic mouthpiece for Rimble. No one had challenged this until Trickster's daughter came along and spoiled the charade. Before Kelandris could really speak, however, Hennin silenced her. And for the last sixteen years Kelandris had remained silent—lost in the miasma of her own craziness. With the help of Trickster's son and an argumentative group of seven other Contraries, Kelandris had regained her sanity in the last year. Hennin had recently discovered this and intended to destroy Kelandris for once and for all. A toxic dose of drugs and a severe beating had not killed the woman sixteen years ago. But Akindo would. Hennin smiled. Yes, Akindo most certainly would. Akindo would be her long arm of menace now. It would do her bidding; it would carry a hive of deadly poison on its back to Kelandris. And that was all to the good, she thought as she fed a poisonous pollen to a hive of agitated holovespa wasps. As far as Hennin was concerned, there could be only *one* wasp queen from Suxonli Village.

Hennin.

And while she was at it, she thought to herself with pleasure, she might as well kill off the idiots who lived at that house in Speakinghast. As she saw it, three months ago the Kaleidicopians had indirectly caused the death of her favorite student: Cobeth of Jaiz. So she had a score to settle with them, and with their ring leader, Zendrak. He had once been her Mayanabi teacher. When Hennin refused to wash his dishes one day—informing him that she was beyond "all that"—he kicked her out of his house and told her to return when she had lost some of her arrogance. Hennin liked her arrogance and so had never lost it. Nor did she ever return to Zendrak's tutelage. All in all, Hennin felt terribly justified in harming these people. And now she finally had the perfect means. Akindo. Akindo was the name she had given to the ambulatory *draw* of Suxonli, the thing that shuffled, the thing she now controlled. No one but Hennin herself was immune to Akindo. Hennin smiled, imagining herself to be acting on behalf of Greatkin Rimble himself.

Funny thing about it—she was.

Chapter Three

IT WAS WINTER in Mnemlith. A small inn near the border of Jinnjirri and Saämbolin stood banked in two-foot snow drifts, icicles from last week's momentary thaw hanging off the roof like crystal spikes, the setting sun shining golden through them as it disappeared over the distant mountains. A Jinnjirri-born woman trudged through the freshly fallen snow, her destination the small woodshed behind the inn. Her name was Aunt.

A friend of the innkeeper's, Aunt had just offered to bring in a new load of dry wood for the fireplace in the eating hall. She was bundled from top to bottom in brightly dyed wools and fuzzy boots. Her Jinnjirri hair escaped the confines of her stocking cap, turning a cheery shade of yellow as she whistled a happy tune. Her yellow hair telegraphed her good mood to two stableboys who were busily grooming a couple of horses belonging to guests of the inn. They were Jinnjirri-born like herself, and grinned as she passed them. It would be good, thought Aunt to herself, to be in Jinnjirri shortly. She had spent the last three months in the bustling but stuffy Saämbolin city named Speakinghast. She longed for her Jinnjirri home in the northwest. Nothing *moved* in Saämbolin—not the ground or the opinions of its people.

Aunt sighed opening the door to the woodshed. As she did so a cold blast of air, seemingly from the inside of the squat building, dislodged her hat and spun it against the nearby wall of the stable. Frowning, Aunt went to pick up her hat. The horses she had just passed shied and threw their heads nervously. The Jinnjirri stableboys tried to calm them. They met with remarkably little success. With each passing moment, the agitation of the horses increased. Hearing the frantic whinnies of the horses and the surprised shouts of the boys, Aunt ran back to the stable. When she arrived there, one of the horses threw himself against the rope shank that held him, and broke it. Suddenly free, the bay horse bolted. His stablemate screamed after him, plaintively. Aunt reached up to calm the mare. Snorting the mare reared in fear against her. Shocked, Aunt jumped out of the way. Never in her life had she had an animal respond with fear toward her. Before Aunt could think about this further, the mare also ripped free from the shank that bound her. Like the bay gelding she ducked out of the stable and galloped away across the adjacent snow-covered pasture. None of the three Jinnjirri said anything. They were all speechless. After a while, Aunt grunted and returned to the woodshed.

As she slipped through the half-open door, she was stung instantly on the exposed part of her neck by one of Elder Hennin's holovespa wasps. Aunt flicked it away angrily, saying, "Never heard of such a thing this time of year. Wasps die in fall," she added, rubbing the place where the wasp had deposited her venom. The reaction to the poison would take a few minutes to set in. Unaware that she had less than a quarter hour left to live, Aunt gathered wood for the inn.

As she piled logs in her strong arms, she puzzled over the strange behavior of the horses. "Like they were terribly afraid of something. Me possibly," she noted. Aunt sighed. Nothing in nature had acted as it should for the past year. Autumn had been unseasonably warm and winter had been unusually heavy with snowfall. The way things were going, Aunt wondered if monsoons would replace thunderstorms come summer. But, she reminded herself, this was Jinnaeon, when *nothing* would behave predictably. This was Trickster's glory, the transition between two ages when the foundations of civilization would shake and perhaps tumble to the ground. All that was false would be exposed and all that was true would remain standing. Such was the action of Greatkin Rimble. He was the tester of the Real, and this was his time. Touching the sting on her neck again, Aunt smiled ruefully, thinking about how the constellation known as the Wasp was ascendant in the northern sky now. Had been since fall. Aunt shrugged, picking up some stray kindling. So why should she be the least surprised that a holovespa had managed to survive winter? The Wasp was one of Rimble's other names. Old Yellow Jacket, they called him in Suxonli. Aunt winced. Suxonli. What a disaster.

Aunt was a master herbalist and healer. She was also a member of the spiritual confraternity known as the Order of the Mayanabi Nomads. Her membership in this somewhat secret society gave her access to a world view uniquely different from that held by most of the *landdraws* of Mnemlith. Whereas the villagers of Suxonli blamed Kelandris, Trickster's daughter, for the tragedy of that night, Aunt blamed the ignorance of the villagers themselves.

Aware that two-legged belief and interest in the Greatkin was on the wane, sixteen years ago Trickster devised the means to shock the very geological foundation of Mnemlith into wakefulness and remembrance. This infusion of the New had been a prophesied event. His own daughter, Kelandris, was to have acted as a kind of two-legged ground wire for the geo-electric current that would pour through her body during the turning dance celebrated in Rimble's honor at Trickster's Hallows in Suxonli every autumn. But raised in ignorance like the members of her adopted village, neither Kelandris nor the villagers had known she *was* Rimble's daughter.

That fateful night power had risen in her. Power had poured through her. Power had struck the *draw* and spun out of control. Power had then killed the eight people who had joined her in the turning ceremony. Including Kelandris, this small group was Rimble's original ennead, his Nine. Eight died that night. Only Kelandris survived the turn.

Everyone wanted to know how she had raised such power in the first place. In all the years of dancing for Rimble, nothing like this had ever happened. Then the village discovered Kelandris was menstruating for the first time that night. This was a village taboo. Although no one (except Hennin) knew why, no Wasp Queen was allowed to dance on the eve of her first blood. Perceiving that sixteen-year-old Kelandris had willfully broken this law, the villagers were outraged. Elder Hennin, who had never liked Kelandris since the moment the child had been brought into the community as a homeless infant, decided the girl must be made into an example. The village indulged in a mock trial—or so it seemed to Kelandris—and pronounced her without kin: *akindo*. She must be punished severely, said all of the elders. She must face the Ritual of Akindo. So Kelandris was beaten and force-fed a toxic dose of holovespa venom. Either of these two tortures would have killed a normal person. However, Kelandris was not a normal person. She was a Greatkin. Furthermore, she was the daughter of the Patron of the Impossible, the Unexpected, and the Deviant. So she did not die. Carried by Zendrak her lover-brother, out of Tammirring into nearby Piedmerri, Kelandris of Suxonli was nursed back to physical health by none other than Aunt herself—at Zendrak's request. The emotional healing of Kelandris was still continuing, however. No one knew how long that would take, thought Aunt, again touching the slightly swollen sting on her neck.

She swallowed and frowned. The part Aunt hated most about the whole Suxonli thing was the fact that Suxonli refused to this day to be held accountable for their part in the tragedy. Kelandris had been *prophesied,* for Presence sake. The village elders should have trained her as a mystic. But did they? No. Why? Because the only person in the village with knowledge of this kind had perceived Kelandris as her spiritual rival. Aunt chuckled sourly. Hennin's assessment was truly laughable. Kelandris was so far out of and *above* Hennin's spiritual station, it made one giddy to think about it. Kelandris wasn't a Mayanabi; she was an incarnate Greatkin like her brother, Zendrak. The world had not seen such ones as these for centuries. No, there was no comparison. None.

Aunt swallowed again, noticing that she was having a little trouble doing so. Well, she *had* been stung on the neck; some swelling was to be expected. Aunt carried the wood out of the shed and started back toward the inn. Aunt continued to reflect on Kelandris. Despite Kel's best efforts to make Aunt hate her during the time that Kelandris healed in Piedmerri, Aunt had grown to love the troubled woman and even now wished her well. Aunt weighed what had happened in Suxonli from yet another perspective, and considered the following carefully:

Being a Greatkin, even untrained and ignorant as she had been, Kelandris would naturally have attempted to make the two-leggeds of Mnemlith become aware of their distant but very real relationship to the Greatkin. Greatkin were great kin—not gods and goddesses. And from the Greatkin point of view, two-leggeds were Greatkin in training. In time, the Greatkin expected the entire race of two-leggeds to take their place on the evolutionary line along with their "older" brothers and sisters. So even at sixteen Kelandris would have felt the impulse to help the people of Suxonli remember their divine inheritance. Aunt pursed her lips, the logs in her arms feeling heavier. What if the tragedy in Suxonli had been something more than simply a situation that pitted village law against cosmic law? What if Kelandris had unwittingly but very naturally taken on the ignorance and cruelty of the villagers—brought it out into the open by her *heinous* actions—and tried to absorb it, thus making the emotional burden of this twisted village lighter? It was a possibility that no one had ever looked at, thought Aunt. If this were true, no wonder it was taking Kelandris so long to heal. Thanks to Hennin's influence, for years now Suxonli had been a hotbed of decadence and amorality. Aunt winced. Trickster often duped those he loved best. Was it possible that Kelandris had been his dupe *and* Greatkin self-sacrifice? Was this why he had not told Zendrak of the trial and Ritual of Akindo until it was too late? Because Rimble had wanted Kelandris to help Suxonli? Possible, concluded Aunt. And not very nice if you view it from the two-legged perspective.

Aunt stumbled in the snow.

Falling to her knees, Aunt suddenly realized she was feeling very light-headed. Her pulse was also racing and her throat felt thick. Her healer's senses alert now, she dropped the logs where she sat and staggered through the drifts toward the inn. Pushing open the back door that led into the kitchen, she knocked a serving lad out of the way as she ran into the pantry. Pulling jars of herbs off of the shelf, she ordered the head cook to make her a tea comprised of two parts stingtrap and one part five-alive. The first was an antidote to severely allergic wasp and bee reactions and the second was a heart stimulant. Water already boiled on the wood stove, so Aunt felt confident she would be able to stop the wasp poison from doing her lethal harm. She put the herb mixture to her lips and drank it. Minutes later, she realized her body was going into shock. Opening her trained Mayanabi senses, she slumped against the wall. Then Aunt sent her closest friend a last message.

Protect Kelandris. Protect the Nine. Protect Yafatah.

Outside in the snow near the barn, something dressed in gray shuffled and drooled. A mouth opened on its smooth face, yellow teeth glistening. It smiled. The experiment had been successful. The victim was dead, it said telepathically to Elder Hennin.

What draw?

Jinnjirri. Selection was random.

Fine. Go on to Speakinghast. Tell me when you have killed Rimble's Nine.

As you wish, replied Akindo.

Chapter Four

FASILLA RECEIVED AUNT'S dying message while bartering for a bolt of blue silk at a Jinnjirri shop near the southwest corner of Jinnjirri. The shop stood less than fifty miles from where Aunt lay dead in the kitchen at the Saämbolin inn. Fasilla, who was Asilliwir-born and a natural haggler, stopped bartering midsentence, her thirty-six-year-old face paling. She was not used to hearing voices inside her head; she was not a Tammirring or a Mayanabi Nomad. Licking her lips nervously, Fasilla bought the silk for its original price and hurriedly left the Jinnjirri shop, the bolt under her arm.

Fasilla was on a buying trip for several members of the Kaleidicopia Boarding House in Speakinghast. She had accompanied Aunt as far as the Saämbolin border and left the Jinnjirri Mayanabi there to spend time with Aunt's other Mayanabi cronies. Fasilla, who had a healthy dislike of religious types, had declined Aunt's invitation to stay the night at the inn. Fasilla could tolerate Aunt's involvement in the Order of the Mayanabi Nomads, but only because they went back a long way. Aunt and Fasilla had attended herbalist school in Piedmerri some twenty years ago and remained fast friends ever since. Fasilla had a daughter—her only child—whose name was Yafatah. She had left the girl in Speakinghast under the care of Barlimo, the Jinnjirri architect that ran the Kaleidicopia Boarding House.

Dropping the bolt of blue material into the back of her wagon, Fasilla reached in her pocket and pulled out her daughter's last letter to her. Her hands shook as she unfolded the letter. Had she missed something? What kind of danger were Yafatah and the others in? Swallowing, Fasilla read:

Dearest Ma,

'Tis still snowing here in the city. Has been off and on ever since you left two weeks ago, so we now have three-foot drifts outside the "K." Being a northern Tammi myself, of course I love it. I doon't think the rest of the Kaleidicopians share me joy, though. I think I've shoveled more snow than anybody else here! Well, except maybe Mab. She always does her chores and a bit of everybody else's, too. But I doon't need to tell *you* that. You've been living here same as me these past three months. So I should give you all the most recent news. (*Gossip,* says Timmer, who do be reading this letter over me very shoulder. No privacy anywhere in this hooligan house.)

Anyway, as I was saying, the news be this: Janusin has started a new sculpture in the back studio and he willna' let a single soul see it 'til it do be done. Barlimo says the Jinn *draw* get like that about their art sometimes. Says nobody should take it personally. Janusin just wants us to keep our criticisms and opinions to ourselves 'til he do be satisfied with it. Po says—well, who cares what Po says? You guessed it, Ma. That rotten rascal hasna' done one dish since you do be gone. Everybody keeps telling Zendrak to *do* something about Podiddley, but Zendrak just smiles that mystery smile of his and lets the bum get away with it. I think Kelandris do be ready to punch Po out. *I* wouldna' wish such a fate. Kel be a Greatkin and powerful tall, as you know. That Po, though. Stinky.

Mab do be pretty good these days. Those bad dreams about Cobeth have stopped and she doesna' cry every time somebody says something about drugs. Po though—he was baiting Mab for a while. I swear he talked about the drugs in the street just to make Mab bawl her eyes out in the downstairs bathroom. Zendrak—*he* says Po was helping Mab get over the thing with Cobeth. Making her less sensitive or something. I *guess*. Actually, Zendrak says I would like Po if I'd just give him a chance to be something other than what he looks like—which is stinky. Sometimes, I think Zendrak sees the good in people too much. I mean, Zendrak says Po do be a *teacher* for me. *I* say no, no, no.

About Zendrak and Kelandris? Well, Tree says they do be starting to squabble again at night. Something about sex. Tree says he canna' imagine the act with either of them two. Tree says the Jinn like their sheet-sharing playful, and them two Greatkin are anything *but* these days. Po says Zendrak told him the GK are arguing at their dinner thing at Eranossa and so naturally Kel and Zendrak are feeling the bad times, both of them being GK themselves. But who *cares* what Po thinks!

Now that I've mentioned Tree, let me consider what to tell you about him. He do be working over at the university now. Professor Rowenaster got him the job. Pays to have friends on the Hill. Mostly, Tree says he hates it. Says them Saämbolin are so *nasty* to the Jinnjirri that he feels like starting a student protest. He may, too. I doon't think he's had green hair in three days. Just a furious Jinnjirri red. As usual, Tree blames all the trouble on Guildmaster Gadorian. Says if he didna' love the theater and his pyro stuff so much, he'd quit. But Tree does love it, so he keeps bringing home the silivrain and coppers to Barl.

Speaking of the rent, I paid ours to Barlimo last night. She acted fierce pleased. Said the Housing Commission do be still sniffing around—looking for a way to close the "K." Having enough coppers and silies to keep things up to code helps, she said. Of course, Zendrak bails her out when it gets really bad.

It *is* his place, after all, and so I suppose he wants to keep it going. He's mostly Zendrak these days, by the way. Hardly ever old Doogat. It's okay by me, Zendrak being just Zendrak. Gets confusing otherwise. And so like Trickster. Oh, yes—the brindle dog has disappeared again. Mab still willna' believe the dog was Greatkin Rimble. Everybody else do be convinced, however. Especially Timmer. Excuse the language, but Timmer says every time she muttered the word "shit" under her breath, the dog would shit. When she said "fuck," the dog would start humping her leg. Nobody misses the dog except me. Pi kept me company in my room after you left. And he was always nice.

Timmertandi has been playing music at a couple of *Jinn* cafes! She says they do be more lively than her native Dunnsung ones. Tree and Janusin say playing for the Jinnjirri will revolutionize her music. Barlimo says maybe—maybe not. In any event, Timmer seems quite happy playing for the Shifttime Tavern on Nerjii Street.

Let's see. Who did I leave out? The professor. Well, he do be teaching as usual over at Speakinghast University, flunking half the class. That Rowenaster do be such a tough teacher. But what a nice old man, really. I think I like him best of all the ruffians at this house. He do be so regular, you know. Him and his "afternoon cookie" at teatime every day. And he do be so cheery. I'd like to be that cheery when I get that old. But being just sixteen, I guess I have some time yet before that happens.

And about me? I do be mostly fine. I miss the dog, Pi, like I said. Also miss you and Aunt. Everybody was sorry to see Aunt go. Especially Barlimo. Them both being Jinn, they were acting almost like sisters by the time Aunt said she had to get back to her student, Burni. And her hollyhocks. For Presence sake, we

canna' forget the hollyhocks even in winter! Right
now, I do be reading some books of the professor's.
Easy stuff about the Greatkin. It do be nice to learn
about them. They must have been a wonderful race.
Wish I could've met them. Well, I guess I shouldna'
say *that*. I mean, I do be living with two of that
race—Kelandris and Zendrak. But in truth, Ma, them
two doon't act like the GK in the professor's history
books. The GK in the books do be sweet and loving
and almost perfect. Kelandris and Zendrak? They do
be always bickering about something or running off
and never saying when they'll be coming home. No,
they doon't act like Greatkin at all. Besides, Kel's
socks smell.

Hope you find all the goodies everybody asked for
from Jinnjirri. If you do be still with Aunt, give her me
love. See you in a few weeks.

Love and merry meet!
Ya

Fasilla folded the letter from her daughter again and
slipped it back into her tunic pocket. She bit her lower lip
anxiously. Nothing in Yafatah's letter seemed amiss. Then
why had Aunt sent her such a desperate message? Protect
Yafatah and the others? From what? Surely Barlimo was
capable of handling any adolescent crisis that might de-
velop. And as the child said, she was living with two
Greatkin. That ought to count for something. Still, if
Zendrak said the Greatkin were fighting at Eranossa, it was
possible that neither Zendrak nor Kelandris would be able to
keep the peace in Speakinghast. Fasilla ran her fingers
through her short brown hair. She had barely begun to do
the shopping she needed to do in Jinnjirri. Should she return
to Speakinghast? Maybe a visit with Aunt was in order.
Fasilla squinted at the early afternoon sun. If she rode a fast
horse, she might still catch Aunt at the Saämbolin inn by
nightfall. Maybe that would be best, she decided. Go and

see Aunt. Find out why she had sent such a message.
Asilliwir-born, Fasilla did not possess the Mayanabi ability
to check on a person's welfare long-distance. Still, Fasilla
had sound mothering instincts. At this particular moment,
she felt no fear in her heart for her daughter's safety. And
Fasilla was a natural worrier. Frowning, Fasilla unhooked
one of her roans from the harness. She would ride to the
Saämbolin border in haste. Something wasn't right.

Indeed it wasn't.

Chapter Five

TODAY WAS THE second month in the winter school term in
Speakinghast. Professor Rowenaster wore the academic
finery to suit the icy weather outside. Clad in yellow velvet,
white fur, and gold trim, he cut a regal figure. The
seventy-one-year-old educator walked in a stately manner
toward the podium of his lecture hall. As always, he was
teaching the first-year students. His Greatkin Survey course
was a requirement at Speakinghast University; it was also so
celebrated that many of Rowen's students came back to visit
it, adding their comments to classroom discussion. The
professor encouraged this. Teaching this course was the
love of his life, and if students felt they had missed
something the first time around—entirely possible, as
Rowenaster covered vast amounts of difficult material in
each short term—they were welcome to return and refresh
their memories. There was one danger in this, though. If no
one in his current enrollment knew the answer to a question,
Rowenaster would call on the old-timers. Guildmaster
Gadorian had been Rowen's student some twenty years ago;
he now entered the lecture hall.

Rowenaster turned to the Saämbolin guildmaster, who
had just taken a back-row seat. The guildmaster was a
personal friend of Rowen's and had it in mind to ask
Rowenaster out to lunch when class was over. Unfortunately for Guildmaster Gadorian, no one knew the answer
to the next question. Gadorian saw Rowen look in his
direction and froze.

"Perhaps you'd like to tell the class your recollection of
what a Greatkin is?"

Gadorian's face went scarlet. "Presence alive, Rowen!" he protested. "You can't be serious. I took this class years ago. I don't remember what a Greatkin is." He shrugged. "The stuff of folktales."

The class tittered with amusement. Guildmaster Gadorian was a large man of three hundred pounds and a formidable politician. He wielded power easily, as did most Saämbolin. It was hard to imagine him as forgetful. Gadorian scowled at the eighteen-year-old faces in the room. He drew himself up in his chair, his blue robe rustling as he did so.

"Well?" asked Rowen. "I'm waiting."

Gadorian stared at Rowenaster. Then he burst into laughter. "That's *exactly* what you used to say to me in class. And I never knew the answer."

Rowenaster grinned. "He was a terrible student," he said to the students surrounding him. "Never studied. Personally, I think he was eyeing the girls." Rowen chuckled. "Maybe he still is," added the professor raising a single gray eyebrow.

The Saämbolin girls in the room looked aghast; Gadorian was very married, and everyone in Speakinghast knew it.

Seeing the mischievous smile on Rowenaster's old face, Gadorian settled back in his chair, certain that Rowenaster would leave him alone now. But this was not to be. Rowenaster's special area of emphasis was Greatkin Rimble. After years of studying Trickster, a year of living with Rimble's own children—Kelandris and Zendrak—and having participated in a turning ceremony last year during a party his housemates threw for Trickster's Hallows, Rowenaster had become a little tricky himself.

"Give it your best shot," said Rowen, coming over to stand next to Gadorian's chair.

The Guildmaster blinked. "Now, don't take this too far," he muttered in a low voice to the professor. "I don't know what a Greatkin is, and furthermore I don't *care* what a Greatkin is."

"Well, you should," said Rowen coolly.

"My business is with this city. It's alive. The Greatkin are part of a dead religion. They're finished. And they've nothing to do with me."

"Ah, the modern mind," said Rowenaster, his voice slightly sarcastic. Turning to the class, he asked, "Let's see a show of hands. How many of you think the Greatkin ever existed?"

Everyone's hand shot into the air, including Rowen's and Gadorian's.

"Okay," continued the professor. "How many of you think there are Greatkin alive now?"

Only Rowenaster raised his hand.

"Worse than last year," said Rowen. "But hardly surprising. This is the Jinnaeon: the *shifttime* of the world when no one can tell the difference between what is seemingly urgent—election results and grades—and what is unquestionably most important. The Greatkin being the latter," he added with a sigh.

"Professor?" asked a Saämbolin girl in the front row. "May I ask *you* a question now? Actually, a bunch of us were discussing this before class began. We're all dying to know, see?"

Rowenaster smiled, regarding the girl steadily over the top of his silver bifocals. The professor was still a handsome man, his hair gray, his skin dark brown, his posture absolutely perfect. His beard was neat, as were his fingernails. Like most Saämbolin, Rowenaster was a fastidious dresser. He crossed his arms over his chest, stroking his beard with his right hand. "Ask," he said.

"What is it *like* living at the Kaleidicopia? I mean, what's it like living with all the *landdraws* of Mnemlith at once?"

Rowenaster looked at the ceiling for a few moments. The girl *would* have to ask a question like this with Gadorian sitting in the room. Out of the corner of his eye, the professor saw Gadorian sit forward in his chair to listen to his reply. Rowen pursed his lips. He would have to be very careful how he answered the girl. There were Jinnjirri present and Gadorian's *draw* antipathy toward the Jinn was well documented. Rowen smiled and said, "It's emotional, surprising—*always* interesting. Educational."

The Saämbolin girl nodded. "Must be fun."

"It often is," agreed the professor, trying to forget the row he had witnessed between Janusin and Po this morning over Po's dirty laundry, which was presently escaping the confines of Po's room on the first floor and spreading into the front hallway.

"Okay," said Gadorian pleasantly. "My turn."

Professor Rowenaster braced himself internally. He knew Gadorian was looking harder than ever for the means to shut down the Kaleidicopia. And why not? Cobeth—one of Saämbolin's most notorious Jinnjirri actors, religious fanatics, and drug addicts—had overdosed at the Kaleidicopia last fall. Gadorian represented the conservative constituency of Speakinghast. He disliked anything and anyone who introduced disorder into his tidy municipality. Out of deference to his friend Rowenaster, Gadorian had tolerated the presence of the Kaleidicopia in the Jinnjirri Quarter of the city just barely. For years, the guildmaster had been trying to convince Rowen to move into a more respectable section of town. The professor had always steadfastly refused to entertain the notion of leaving the Kaleidicopia Boarding House. Although Rowenaster had explained his reasons for wishing to stay right where he was on countless occasions, the guildmaster never seemed to accept those reasons—much less understand them. Now that the Kaleidicopia had been linked to Cobeth's name, Rowen was certain it was a matter of time before the guildmaster discovered that Cobeth had actually been a five-year resident of the "K." When that tidbit got out, the "K" would close for sure. In the guildmaster's mind, Cobeth represented everything Gadorian was trying to eradicate from Speakinghast. If for one moment Gadorian thought that the residents of the Kaleidicopia had supported or even engaged in Cobeth's decadence—well, best not to think about it,

Rowenaster told himself. Smiling pleasantly at the guild-master, Professor Rowenaster said, "Ask away, Gad. We've no secrets here in this classroom."

Gadorian leaned back in his chair, his expression self-satisfied. Pointing to the Jinnjirri in Rowen's classroom, Gadorian asked, "How can a nice, tenured professor like yourself live with shifts?"

There was dead silence.

The Jinnjirri present had been sitting with their hair exposed—"unhatted" as it was called in Mnemlith. Now every Jinnjirri head in the room turned an outraged red. Out of respect to Rowenaster, not to Gadorian, who outranked the professor by a great deal, the Jinn in Rowen's class had remained seated when Gadorian entered the room. Now they got to their feet. Giving Rowen furious scowls, the Jinnjirri students walked out, their hair fluctuating scarlet and black. Rowenaster watched them go, his expression stunned. He whirled on the guildmaster.

"How could you do that, Gad? This is *my* classroom. This is a safe place for them to come. I don't allow that kind of bigotry here. Damn you!" he added, his eyes blazing with indignation.

"I think the question was quite fair," said Gadorian. The guildmaster paused, listening to the city bells as they tolled the noon hour. Class was over. "You interested in lunch?" he asked as the remaining students filed out quickly, all of them thankful to be escaping the bad feeling in Rowen's classroom.

Rowenaster glared at Gadorian. "You interested in the Jinnjirri?"

Gadorian chuckled. "Only in election years."

"Then I'm not interested in lunch. Furthermore, we've been through this over and over. Now, get this once and for all: I like living at the Kaleidicopia!"

Gadorian raised an eyebrow. He got to his feet slowly. "Look, Rowen—it was an honest question. To a chauvin-istic Saäm like me, the way you live looks pretty strange.

And anyway, you don't need shifts in your class. What good is a classical education going to do any of them? They'll just waste the space. Better the seat should be taken by someone with a future."

"The Greatkin Survey course is for everyone," said Rowenaster icily. "The Greatkin created all the *draws*, including the Jinnjirri."

Gadorian snorted, his expression amused. "Surely you don't believe that. Not really."

Rowenaster refused to comment. Without a word, he turned away from Guildmaster Gadorian. Rowen walked up the stairs leading out of the lecture hall and slammed the door behind him.

Gadorian shook his head. "Shit if he isn't starting to act like a shift. Passion for passion's sake." He grunted. "Well, I hate surprises. Especially among my own *draw*."

While Rowenaster walked angrily toward the Jinnjirri Quarter of Speakinghast, intent upon grabbing a quick bite of lunch at home, trickstcrish trouble was afoot at the "K." The Kaleidicopia Boarding House, or the "K" as it was affectionately called by the nine people who lived there, was an *almost* legal establishment located deep in the bohemian, renegade section of the city: the Jinnjirri Quarter. As Guildmaster Gadorian had just pointed out, living in such a place was an odd choice for a tenured, fastidious, Saämbolin professor of independent means. Usually students populated this low-rent, flamboyant district—the majority of them Jinnjirri. Like the rest of his housemates, Rowenaster resided at the "K" for reasons that few in Speakinghast would understand. Rowenaster was one of a select circle of nine Contraries, one of Greatkin Rimble's Own. This did not mean that he was biologically related to Trickster, only that he had proved to have a "certain capacity." Rowen was not exactly sure just what this "certain capacity" was. He suspected it might have to do with a kind of flexibility of mind and contrariness of spirit.

For some reason both of these qualities had endeared him to Greatkin Rimble—so said Kelandris.

"Whatever *that* means," muttered the professor under his breath as he walked up the stairs leading to the fuchsia-colored front door to the Kaleidicopia Boarding House. It was a *loud* shade of pink, one well suited to the Jinnjirri neighborhood in which the house was located; keeping up with the neighbors was a creative, demanding task in this quarter of town. Rowenaster opened the front door and walked in.

The sound of bedlam met his ears.

Rowenaster sighed, looking toward the large spiral staircase that led to the upper two floors of the house. Bedlam was a normal occurrence at the "K." Even so, thought the professor, someone screaming in terror on the second floor was a *little* out of the ordinary. He decided to investigate. Apparently three other members of the Kaleidicopia decided to do the same thing. Zendrak, dressed in green as usual, tore up the stairs. Podiddley, an Asilliwir pickpocket, and Kelandris, dressed in yellow, followed Zendrak swiftly. Rowenaster took the stairs at a slower pace. When the elderly man reached the second floor, he heard frantic crying coming out of Yafatah's room. Yafatah was black-haired like all of her *draw* and possessed a compelling voice that was both husky and pure. At the moment, however, her voice was cracking with fear and whimpers. Frowning, Rowenaster entered her room. He was met with the unexpected sight of Zendrak pulling stinging wasps out of Yafatah's long dark hair.

It seemed that the sixteen-year-old had been washing the outside windowpanes of her second-storey bedroom when she accidentally jostled a nest of yellow jackets under the eave of the house. Yafatah had nearly fallen off the roof when the wasps swarmed her. She had stumbled back through the open, circular window of her room and shut it as best she could, crushing a few of the marauding insects on the windowsill as she did so. Now she struggled against

Zendrak's patient ministrations. Catching sight of several wasps lighting on Zendrak's shoulder, Yafatah cried, "Zendrak—watch out! You'll get stung, too!"

The man in green chuckled. "One of Rimble's best known names is Old Yellow Jacket. I am his son. These angry little beasties won't harm me. At least, they *better* not," he added, picking a wasp up by the waist and eyeing it carefully. The worker-wasp buzzed at him. Zendrak made an answering reply, his eyes amused.

Podiddley craned his neck forward. "What did the wasp say?"

Zendrak smiled. "Seems she dislikes getting caught in Yafatah's hair as much as Yafatah dislikes being stung."

Yafatah swore. "It doon't be fair! I must have thirty stings. And I didna' do *anything* to them beasties."

Zendrak opened the window and let the captive wasps fly free. The rest of the swarm who still remained outside the house did not enter Yafatah's yellow bedroom. Rowenaster thought this was odd.

"Why aren't they coming in?" he asked.

"Because he told them not to," said Kelandris in a monotone. Nearly equal in height to her brother, Zendrak, Kelandris cut a formidable figure at six-feet-four. Born in the land of Tammirring, she usually wore a veil to hide her face and feelings. Inside the Kaleidicopia, however, she tended to leave the veil in her bedroom on the third floor.

Rowenaster sighed. Day after day at the university, he tried to teach people the names of the Greatkin, a process that most students vigorously resisted. To the modern mind, the Greatkin were the personages of myth and were therefore unimportant. To Rowenaster, who happened to live with Greatkin, they were a bold, disconcerting reality. The professor had long ago concluded that what scholars wrote in the history books and thought about the Greatkin was mostly romantic doggerel. Pulp at worst and speculation at best. Clearly, the academics had never had firsthand experience with a Greatkin. Scholars thought the Greatkin were gentle beings of endless compassion. Rowenaster shook his head. On more than one occasion, he had seen Zendrak box both of Po's ears. And Kelandris? Well, she was mostly like ice.

As if to prove Rowen's point, Kelandris continued speaking to Yafatah, her voice without inflection, her green eyes distant. "In Suxonli they say wasps are the messengers of Rimble." She chuckled derisively. "His holy messengers. If they sting you, we say you've been kissed by the Power of the Fertile Dark. You'll never be the same afterward, of course."

"Thanks!" snapped Yafatah, who was beginning to feel ill with the poison of her many stings. "You do be real comforting there, Kel. Just a joy to be around. Why doon't you take your sarcasm and bad times to *your* room, huh? I doon't remember inviting you in."

"Suit yourself," said Kelandris stiffly, and left.

Zendrak inclined his head toward Yafatah. "I think you hurt her feelings."

"Impossible," retorted the young girl sullenly. "That bitch hasna' got any. And doon't you lecture me on my mouth."

"I wouldn't dream of it, Ya," said Zendrak mildly.

Rowenaster interrupted at this point. "Well, *I* think you should show a little respect there, Yafatah. After all, Kelandris is a Greatkin."

Yafatah pulled away from Zendrak's hands, her face slightly puffy, her expression furious. "Yeah? Then why doesna' she act like one?"

Zendrak pulled Yafatah's head toward him again. "And how should a Greatkin act?" he asked.

"Like this," she replied. "Like what you're doing. You know, helpful."

Podiddley burst into peals of laughter.

Po, who was a street-wise criminal by profession, was also a Mayanabi Nomad. For the past twelve years he had been a member of this heretical spiritual order, and for the same period of time, Zendrak had been his spiritual guide. In addition to being Trickster's son, Zendrak was also the ranking Mayanabi in all Mnemlith. This was understandable. Zendrak was over five hundred years old. Five centuries was ample time to perfect one's spirit. The combination of Zendrak's Tricksterish blood and his long years of training as a Mayanabi master made him a tough, inventive teacher. It also made him unorthodox. Podiddley was laughing now because he thought Zendrak was rarely helpful in the usual sense of the word. Everyone in the room, including Zendrak, knew Po's feelings on the subject.

Zendrak glanced at Po. "Go fetch some stingtrap from Barlimo's herb pantry. Mix it into a paste with boiling water and bring it to me. Quickly."

Po, who was feeling lazy, began to argue.

"Just do it."

Po scowled.

Rowenaster smiled, impressed. Zendrak could turn anything into a teaching situation, he thought with admiration. Rowen watched Po stride out of the room angrily. Now Yafatah spoke. "Did you say stingtrap?" she asked Zendrak.

"I did."

Yafatah groaned. "That'll turn my scalp green. I doon't want my scalp to turn green."

"Do you want to survive all these stings? Or would you prefer to die tonight?" he asked amiably.

Yafatah stared at the Greatkin. "*Die?*"

Zendrak nodded. "Thirty stings of this particular wasp can kill. It's a southern variety. Just arrived." He winked. "Rimble-Rimble."

"Just arrived?" asked Rowenaster, feeling puzzled.

"Yes," said Zendrak, his black eyes suddenly reflective like mirrors. "These are the heralds of the Jinnaeon. They are the new breed. Trickster calls them univer'silsila.

According to dear old Dad, there's something special about these wasps—that *we* get to discover, of course."

"Of course," said Yafatah without enthusiasm.

"You want life too easy, Ya. You want all the answers immediately. You want adults to behave predictably. And Greatkin to be perfect."

"What's that supposed to mean?"

Before Zendrak could answer, Po returned with the steaming stingtrap. Yafatah grimaced at the smell and sight of the foul herb. She shut her eyes, clearly feeling unwell. When she opened them again, Zendrak asked, "Trust me?"

"Sometimes."

"So trust me now, and I'll make you all better," said Trickster's son.

Yafatah regarded him warily. "Yeah, Rimble-Rimble. Trusting you could make me an idiot in three counties."

"Maybe," replied Zendrak, dipping his hands into the paste, his dark eyes amused. "You seem to forget one thing."

"What's that?"

"Rimble's my father, yes. But Themyth's my mother. And she's the Patron of Civilization. This means that I can be constructive. As you say—helpful on occasion."

Rowenaster thought this was funny and began to laugh. He subsided when Zendrak glared at him.

Yafatah eyed the green mess in Zendrak's hands. "I hope this is one of those occasions," she grumbled.

Rowenaster braced himself for the yells he knew were coming. Stingtrap was a powerful antiseptic as well as a tried-and-true remedy for wasp venom. Rowen's mother had dressed a cut with it once when he was a small child; all Rowen could remember of the episode was that the stingtrap hurt worse than the cut. He winced. Such were the ways of some types of healing.

Chapter Six

FASILLA REACHED THE Saämbolin town of Window by dusk. She and her roan mare passed through the Jinnjirri *landdraw* border without mishap, receiving little more than a feeling of slight disorientation. Window was aptly named, thought Fasilla, reining her mare to a walk as she approached the town limits. Window was just that—a Saämbolin trading city that looked out across rolling, verdant Jinnjirri. Asilli-wir caravans made regular stops in Window, *landdraws* from every country in Mnemlith enjoying the laxness of the border rules thanks to the nearby Jinn influence. Border towns in Mnemlith were often like this. Where two or more *draws* met, customs and strict identities blurred. Anything could happen in a border town, and often did. Still, the prevailing *draw* of the land directly under the town would hold the strongest influence. Window rested on glacial territory, the oldness of the earth informing its people with a sense of history and pride in tradition. Therefore, it was not surprising to Fasilla that the keepers of spiritual tradition in Mnemlith, the Order of the Mayanabi Nomads, frequented Window.

Fasilla eyed the Saämbolin inn straight ahead of her with distaste. Aunt said the place was a notorious meeting place for Mayanabi. In earlier, less tolerant days, this particular inn had protected the Mayanabi, too. Fasilla dismounted from her roan. Hobbling the mare, she turned toward the Inn of the Guest. In Mayanabi theology, the Presence was often referred to as the Guest. Fasilla hesitated, her stomach turning in fear. Fasilla didn't fear the Mayanabi as much as she feared the fact that the order was an ancient, secret society. Although she had never met a Mayanabi she hadn't eventually liked—with the two single exceptions of Podiddley and a pied-eyed crone named Old Jamilla—Fasilla wished to keep her affairs in the daylight. Dealings with people who met in underground rooms and behind closed doors could only end badly, she thought. If she had been a praying sort of person, Fasilla would have chosen one of the denizens of Eranossa as her patron Greatkin. The Mayanabi had too much of Neath about them to make Fasilla feel safe. Fasilla walked to the front door of the Inn of the Guest and knocked tentatively.

When no one answered, Fasilla felt a mixture of relief and irritation. If the message from Aunt had been about anything other than Fasilla's beloved child, the Asilliwir herbalist would have left Window without a further attempt to make her presence known. Biting her lower lip, Fasilla knocked a second time. Still no one answered.

"What kind of inn do this be?" she muttered under her breath. Fasilla stepped back from the oak door and scanned the upper dormer windows. Fasilla frowned. Every window curtain was drawn shut. Odd, she thought. Putting her hands on her hips, Fasilla decided to just make a nuisance of herself until someone came out to shut her up. Cupping her hands to her lips, Fasilla yelled, "Aunt? Aunt, where are you? It do be your friend, Fasilla!"

At the mention of the word "friend," the front door of the Inn of the Guest opened. Fasilla peered into the darkness of the building. Glancing over her shoulder at the last soft light from the setting sun behind her, Fasilla hesitated, chills creeping across the back of her neck.

"If this werena' for me Yafatah, I wouldna' do this thing," she grumbled, and walked into the Mayanabi stronghold.

Fasilla was met inside by a tall man with a beard and quiet brown eyes named Himayat. He was about forty-five, his temples graying. He wore a pair of brown glasses perched on his large nose. He smiled at Fasilla and welcomed her in her native tongue. From his physical appearance, she judged Himayat to be Asilliwir-born like herself.

Relieved, Fasilla said, "Well, I do be pleased to meet you, Mr. Himayat. I was fierce scared that—well, never you mind 'Tis me own fears."

Himayat chuckled, his brown eyes forgiving. "Be of good cheer. You're among Friends," added the Mayanabi, putting ever so slight an emphasis on "Friends."

Fasilla took a deep breath. "Well, *that* be good news." She smiled raggedly. "I be looking for the Jinnjirri named Aunt. Do you know where I may find her?"

Himayat's face sobered. He reached for Fasilla's hands. She gave them to him without knowing why she did so. Himayat's eyes grew wet with tears. "I am sorry." He paused. "Aunt died early this afternoon."

Fasilla's face paled. "Died?" she said in a disbelieving voice. Tears sprang to her own eyes now and slipped down her cheeks. "Aunt is *dead*?" Sobs rose from deep inside her. Aunt had been Fasilla's closest and oldest friend. They had shared everything together. Fasilla's knees gave way and she slumped to the floor. Himayat put his arms around her and held her as she wept. After a few minutes, Fasilla coughed back her tears and said, "I came because Aunt told me something in me mind. Something important. It must've been just before she died," added Fasilla, her voice trailing off into a numb silence. Her mind felt empty with shock.

"We will speak of it, Fasilla. But perhaps not right now? Maybe you would join us for a bite of supper. You may bathe first if you so desire. Our house is yours," he added, opening his arms to include the entirety of the Inn of the Guest.

"But why?" asked Fasilla, her expression bewildered. "I doon't even know you."

"You are Aunt's friend. That makes you our Friend."

Fasilla swallowed. Hospitality as generous as this wasn't known to Fasilla outside her own Asilliwir clan. She closed her eyes, feeling suddenly overwhelmed. Without introduction, she asked Himayat how Aunt had died.

Himayat replied calmly, "Aunt was stung by a holovespa wasp. She had a lethal reaction to it. It happens sometimes. Even with people who have no previous history of allergies."

Fasilla pressed her lips together. *Not* to Aunt, she thought stubbornly. Fasilla didn't know how she knew, but she was absolutely certain that Aunt had not died from a toxic reaction to a wasp. Something in the urgency of Aunt's last message made Fasilla feel suspicious—and angry. But why? she asked herself. I have noo reason to think this Himayat a liar. Then she thought, Maybe he didna' know Aunt as well as me. Fasilla nodded quietly to herself. Taking a deep breath, she got to her feet and asked where she could bathe. She would talk to these Mayanabi. She would find out everything they knew and didn't know about Aunt's death. Then maybe she would know why Aunt thought Yafatah was in danger.

As it turned out, dinner was a preparation for Aunt's burial ceremony—Mayanabi style. The meal was celebrated in the same spirit as a wedding feast. Those cooking for it referred to the Presence as the Beloved and to Aunt as the lover who was now returning to the Beloved's house. This was a strange concept to Fasilla, but she held her tongue as she helped decorate cakes and other pastries.

As evening wore on, out-of-town Mayanabi began to arrive in Window by the droves. It seemed that Aunt had been very well known and well loved by several generations of Mayanabi. Incredible, thought Fasilla, when one remembered Aunt was thirty-six years old at the time of her death.

Special Dunnsung-born musicians gathered in the cozy eating hall of the Inn of the Guest. As they set up their lotaris and drums, Fasilla overheard the following conversation.

"I came by way of the Feyborne, how about you?"

"I'm wintering in Dunnsung. So I rode in from the south. Weather's chill on the peninsula. More chill than I've ever remembered it, Shruddi. Here, let me help you with that case."

"Thanks," said the first musician, pulling out a ceramic drum with a floral design stained on the leather drumhead. "It was so weird," she added.

"What was?"

"What I saw—I mean, what I *didn't* see on the cliffs."

"You're not making any sense. Start over."

"You know the flower the winterbloom?"

"Sure. They bloom in the dead of winter." He grinned. "When no flower in its right mind would do so."

"That's right. That's their magic. Their message. Winterbloom flower when nothing else can. And this is their season. Winter." Shruddi paused, her voice slightly tense. "There wasn't a single winterbloom to be seen in the Feyborne."

The lotari player shrugged. "There's been an awful lot of snow, Shruddi. Maybe the blooms were buried."

She nodded. "That's what I thought. So I got off my horse and dug into the snow. I found the winterbloom. They were dead."

The lotari player, who was also a Mayanabi Nomad, stiffened. "Dead?" He whistled low under his breath. "What kind of sign is *that*?"

"I don't know," said Shruddi anxiously. "But I think we better have a council and discuss it. Nature doesn't act like this. Even during a Jinnaeon, it doesn't act like this. I'm worried."

Fasilla stopped arranging the dried winter flowers on the table in front of her. She straightened. Now she was more than certain Aunt's death wasn't an accident. She could feel it in her *draw* and in the uneasy voices of the musicians.

A few minutes later, Himayat called all the Mayanabi together. He indicated that Fasilla could sit in their circle. The food rested on tables behind the circle near a roaring fire. Fasilla sat in a kneeling position next to Himayat. Himayat took her left hand and the Dunnsung musician named Shruddi took her right. They closed their eyes. Fasilla kept hers open, feeling sad and out of place in this strange group. The Mayanabi began an invocation:

> "O Thou, Beloved Guest,
> Be Thou welcome in our midst.
> Enter every wounded heart,
> Lighten every earthly burden,
> For ours is not a caravan of sorrow
> But an abode of joy
> Where all meet at one table
> And give Thee thanks."

When the invocation was finished, the Mayanabi Nomads sat in silence for a few moments, their bodies still, their breathing regular. Fasilla felt a deep sense of peace emanating from all those seated around her. Fresh tears sprang to her eyes. This was the same peace she had always felt around Aunt. She shut her eyes tightly, trying to keep back the pain of her loss in Aunt as a friend. Since the others held her hands, Fasilla could not wipe her face. Her tears streamed freely down her cheeks.

Himayat opened his eyes. Seeing Fasilla's distress, he motioned for one of the Mayanabi near Fasilla to hand her a handkerchief. Feeling someone touch her arm, Fasilla opened her eyes, her expression startled. Seeing the handkerchief, she took it gratefully and blew her nose. As she did so, several Mayanabi left the room. Fasilla noted that all of them were wearing white. When this group of six returned, they carried Aunt's body with them. Fasilla stiffened. She had not expected to see such disfiguration in Aunt's face from the swelling caused by the wasp venom. Fasilla blinked, mildly horrified.

At that moment, Himayat leaned toward her and asked, "Would you like to take part in this?" He offered a slip of white paper with words written on it. Fasilla accepted the paper weakly, her face pale. "I'll tell you when to speak," he whispered.

Fasilla nodded, feeling too shocked by the day's events to say anything.

Himayat got to his feet slowly. He was dressed in a long robe of black. He wore a red belt around his middle. It ended in tassels and tiny bells that tinkled gently like lilting wind chimes as he moved. Bowing to his own people and to Fasilla, Himayat began the burial service saying:

"Mourn not o'er the death of the beloved, call not back the traveler who is on her journey toward her goal; for ye know not what she seeketh! Ye are on the earth, but now she is in heaven.

"By weeping for the dead, ye will make sad the soul who cannot return to earth; by wishing to communicate with her, ye do but distress her. She is happy in the place at which she has arrived; by wanting to go to her ye do not help her; your life's purpose still keepeth you on earth. No creature that hath ever been born belonged in reality to any other; every soul is the beloved of the Presence. Doth the Presence not love as we two-leggeds cannot? Death, therefore, doth unite man and woman with the Presence. For to whom doth the soul in truth belong, to the Presence in the end is its return, sooner or later.

"Verily, death is a veil behind which is hidden life that is beyond comprehension of the man or woman on earth. If ye knew the freedom of that world and how the sad hearts are unburdened of their load; if ye knew how the sick are cured, how the wounded are healed, and what freedom the soul experiences as it goes further from this earthly life of limitations, ye would no more mourn those who have passed, but pray for their happiness in their further journey and for the peace of their souls."

After Himayat finished speaking, a man of Piedmerri *draw* handed him a golden censer. Himayat lit the cones of woody incense inside. As the pungent smoke spilled into the eating hall, Himayat circled the body of Aunt, going from left to right. He did not swing the censer but carried it motionless in his cupped hands. The smoke followed his movements, swirling into filmy ribbons of gray behind him. Himayat handed the censer back to the Piedmerri. Then he knelt beside Aunt's shrouded form and said his people's Prayer for the Dead:

"O Thou, the Cause and Effect of the whole Universe, the Source whence we have come and the Goal toward which all are bound. Receive this soul who is coming to Thee into Thy parental arms. May Thy forgiving glance heal her heart. Lift her from the denseness of the earth, surround her with the light of Thine own Spirit. Raise her up to Heaven, which is her true dwelling place. We pray Thee, grant her the blessing of Thy most exalted Presence. May her life upon earth become as a dream to her waking soul, and let her thirsting eyes behold the glorious vision of Thy Sunshine."

Himayat finished speaking and nodded to Fasilla. She remained seated. Her hands shook as she smoothed out the paper and cleared her throat. Her voice hoarse with emotion and nervousness, Fasilla read the following:

"Heal Aunt's spirit, O Sovereign One, from all the wounds that her heart has suffered through this life of limitation upon the earth. Purify her heart with Thy Divine Light and send upon her spirit Thy Mercy, Thy Compassion, and Thy Peace."

"So be it," said Himayat. Taking a deep breath, he smiled at Fasilla and the rest of the people sitting in the circle. "Lest this moment become dour, I invite you to dance in celebration. Please stand."

Himayat remained in the center of the circle near Aunt's body. He opened his arms wide as if to take in the entire circle of people and the universe, too. "It is customary among my people," he said to Fasilla, "to think of death as a wedding."

Fasilla shrugged, trying to get into the spirit of it, and having difficulty.

Himayat smiled broadly. "Aunt is dead, but only her body is thus. Her soul is united with the Presence. And to this, we will drink tonight. We will toast Aunt's good fortune. She is the lover returning to the Beloved. But do not think that by our emphasis on joy at this time that we despise the earthly existence. Do not think we eagerly wait to leave here. This earthly life is a good one. And for the opportunity of living it, we give thanks. But we also know that when we are called back to the Presence, we should not complain. Indeed we should leave with happiness in our hearts. Ours is not a caravan of despair or tragedy. Ours is a caravan of knowledge." Himayat nodded at a middle-aged Mayanabi. She was dressed in rough woolens and had very few teeth. Her eyes were strange. One was yellow and one was black. Her step was spry. She entered the circle, carrying a ceramic drum. Himayat gave her a rhythm and she began to set the pace of the dance. As she played, Himayat said, "This is a dance of the Universal. This is a dance for all *landdraws*. And for all times. The concentration is light. See the light in the eyes and countenance of the person on either side of you. Now bow."

The dance moved slowly to the right. Fasilla had no trouble learning the simple steps to the dance. The chanting and breath control were a little more demanding. Unexpectedly, she felt a surge of joy flood her body and face. Her eyes danced with her feet. *This is it,* Fasilla thought. *This is the way it should be. Dances for all draws for all times. A kind of universal ritual that raised everyone above individual differences and distinctions.*

Tears sprang to her eyes once again. She blinked them back, bewildered at the intensity of her own emotion. She glanced at Shruddi, who stood to her right. To her surprise, she saw that Shruddi had her head turned toward her. Was she staring at her? Fasilla didn't know. Fasilla had no time to conclude anything; Himayat started the next dance a moment later.

After an hour of this, everyone's spirits were soaring. Himayat finally called the celebration to a close. After a short prayer, several Asilliwir-born Mayanabi fetched food and drink for all to share. Even though Aunt's shrouded body still lay in the center of the circle, the mood was festive.

Surprised that she could feel hungry with Aunt's body lying in plain view of the table, Fasilla got in line with the Mayanabi. As a Jinnjirri woman handed her a steaming portion of roasted, glazed fowl, Shruddi walked up beside Fasilla and said, "You felt something in our circle, didn't you?"

Fasilla shrugged lamely. "I was giddy with dancing—"

"No, you weren't," said Shruddi evenly. "You danced like an old hand. Who is your Mayanabi master?"

Fasilla stepped backward. "I doon't have one—"

Shruddi stared at Fasilla. "I can feel him near you. Even as we speak. He's one of the great ones, I think."

"Oh," said Fasilla with visible relief. "You mean *Zendrak*. He's just one of my housemates—"

The people nearest Shruddi and Fasilla stopped speaking, their faces astonished. Shruddi seemed to be feeling the same emotion, for she struggled to find words in the ensuing silence. Finally Shruddi said, "*Just* Zendrak? Is *that* what you said?" she added in a shocked squeak.

Fasilla bit her lower lip. She had gotten so used to Zendrak's presence at the Kaleidicopia, she had forgotten that he was *the* ranking Mayanabi master in all Mnemlith.

Not to mention an incarnate Greatkin. Titles like those meant a great deal to the people in this room, Fasilla reminded herself sharply. Trying to muster up some respect for Zendrak, Fasilla said, "I forget who he be sometimes. We had breakfast every morning for the past three months— along with the rest of them misfits at the 'K.' When you see someone pick his teeth with a fork, you don't always remember he be a Mayanabi master."

Himayat entered the conversation now. "And so you see the human side of a First Rank Mayanabi master. How wonderful. And what a challenge."

"I beg your pardon?" said Fasilla, not sure she had understood Himayat correctly.

Himayat chuckled. "Those of us in the room have it easy. We can imagine Master Zendrak being anything and everything. We can create him in our own image. Our own fantasy. But you, Fasilla—you know the reality of the man. You know his bad habits. And his good. You have the opportunity to accept the reality. Not just the fantasy. The legend." He paused. "Do you see my meaning?"

Fasilla took a deep breath. "I suppose. I mean, I suppose it could be like that." She shrugged. "Only, he doon't be very nice sometimes. Sometimes he loses his temper fierce bad."

"So much the better," said Himayat, starting to laugh in earnest now.

"The better for *what*?" asked Fasilla crossly.

Himayat grinned. "Don't you realize he's teaching you when he does that? Don't you realize he's asking you to learn flexibility?"

Fasilla said nothing, her face coloring pink. Flexibility wasn't one of her strong suits.

Chapter Seven

EVER SINCE THE Ritual of Akindo, Kelandris had slept fitfully, her dreams often turning into nightmares. These night terrors were a grim legacy of the trauma Kelandris had experienced in Suxonli. For three nights now, she had cried in her sleep. Private and Tammirring by *draw,* this was a side to her personality that Kelandris let no one but Zendrak see. And it was only in sleep, when her body relaxed, that she showed him the pain she lived with. Their bed was full of secrets.

The man in green gently woke Kelandris again. She gasped for air as she came out of the dream, her forehead damp with a cold sweat, her unveiled eyes nervous and unfocused. Kelandris sat up. Pressing her back against the wall, she hunched against her knees, pulling the blankets around her tightly. Zendrak said nothing, watching. Among other things, Zendrak was a healer. And among other things, Kelandris had been in his care for the past year. Zendrak rarely spoke of this portion of their relationship to Kelandris. Kel knew she needed his help, but she was also proud and would not ask for such help unless she were close to death and certain she could not help herself. Zendrak respected her pride, although admittedly Kel's pride made his healing of her much more difficult. Zendrak continued to watch Kelandris, waiting for her to speak. Finally Kel said, "She's coming for *you* this time."

"Who?"

"Elder Hennin," she said hoarsely.

Zendrak shrugged. "Let her."

"You're not invulnerable," Kelandris snapped, her green eyes angry.

"I never said I was," he replied, and ran his fingers through his dark hair. "Elder Hennin is nothing more than a great nuisance—"

Kelandris said nothing. Hennin had proved herself to be a formidable adversary to her in Suxonli, certainly more than a simple "nuisance." Of course, Kel reasoned in silence, *Zendrak did not have to go through that. I did.* Kelandris sat up in bed, her shoulders hunched with the weight of her memories. Finally she said, "You're a fool, Zendrak, if you think she can't hurt you. You've lived too long. You've forgotten what it's like to hurt. You've forgotten what it's like when every nerve is alive with pain and every emotion is stirred into anguish."

"I've outgrown those things, Kel. At my age, emotions—all of them—lose their edge. They become almost boring."

Kelandris sat bolt upright. "My pain bores you?" She felt outraged, the desires of her heart made insignificant by the dispassionate sweep of his longevity. She glared at him. "You have outlived your dreams, Zendrak. And so mine become, like Hennin, a nuisance to endure—but not indulge?"

Zendrak said nothing for a few moments. "I do not like to see your pain, Kel," he admitted. "In seeing yours, I have to remember my own."

Kelandris swore and got out of bed. She pulled on a black bathrobe, her motions angry. Turning to look at him, she said, "If you're what I am to become, then I refuse it. I refuse to live five hundred years like you. Life is feeling. If you don't feel, you're dead."

Zendrak smiled. Then seeing Kelandris stare at him, he sobered.

"You find me *funny* now?" she cried.

Zendrak shook his head. "No—I just—well, I've waited a long time to hear you give me that lecture."

Kelandris advanced on him. "Don't you play your Mayanabi games on me, mister. I pack a pretty good punch," she said, making a fist with her left hand. Kelandris had proved her mastery of fisticuffs on more than one occasion in Zendrak's presence. Even Podiddley had been at the wrong end of Kel's arm once.

Zendrak eyed Kelandris cautiously. Then he said, "Do you truly believe I have no feelings, Kel?"

She hesitated. Lowering her head slightly, she said, "I don't know."

"Do you want to know?"

"I don't know."

Zendrak shrugged. "I have more than enough passion still left in me, Kelandris. And I have a desire for you that the years have not subdued."

Kel's eyes widened a little bit. She took a step backward. Although she and Zendrak slept next to each other in bed, theirs was a purely platonic relationship at this point. It was all that Kelandris could handle, although she would never have admitted this to anyone—including Zendrak. Now it appeared that Zendrak wanted to change their relationship, perhaps be her lover again, as he had been once in Suxonli, seventeen years ago. Kelandris stiffened involuntarily. She did not know what to do. Her own indecision and vulnerability angered her. Biting her lower lip, she whirled away from Zendrak, announcing over her shoulder, "I'm going to take a shower."

Opening the door to her room, she quickly scanned the hallway to see if she could get to the bathroom without running into anyone else from the Kaleidicopia. At three in the morning, the wide hallway was empty. Kelandris gathered her black bathrobe against her otherwise naked body and ran toward the third-floor bathroom. She ducked inside and shut the door, her heart pounding, her emotions extreme. She leaned against the door, her head bowed and her green eyes closed. Her mind flooded with questions. Would Zendrak still be in their bedroom when she returned?

What would he say to her? What would he expect of her? Kelandris gritted her teeth. She didn't want to think about these kinds of questions. She didn't want to feel these feelings. Despite her brave lecture on the benefits of feeling life deeply, ever since the Ritual of Akindo Kelandris had disciplined herself to feel nothing. It was a survival technique more than anything else. To feel *anything* was to open a veritable box of emotional trouble. Experience had taught her that passion of any kind put you at the mercy of other people. So to remain in control of her life—such as it was—Kelandris had used her formidable will to numb her emotions. She had promised herself she would never feel deeply again about anything. Or anyone. It was a matter of survival.

"Damn you, Zendrak," she swore, tears filling her eyes. "Everything was fine between us and then you just *had* to go and spoil it."

Continuing to swear, Kelandris turned on the water in the shower. She waited for it to warm up. When the room became steamy, Kelandris dropped her black bathrobe. It fell to the floor revealing a muscular but surprisingly feminine body. Her bones were long to support her weight, but they were also delicate. Her belly was slightly rounded, her breasts soft and inviting. She stepped into the shower, letting the hot water beat her senses into forgetfulness. Moments later, she felt a draft. She poked her head out of the shower, her long blue-black hair clinging to her face and neck and breasts. Zendrak stood inside the room, closing the door as she stared at him in astonished indignation.

"I locked that door!"

"And I opened it," he said. He too dropped his bathrobe. Around his neck hung a necklace of black stones. The necklace was made of obsidian, and it had been forged in Soaringsea. Like Kel, his body was muscular; his chest was covered with fine dark hair. Although his body was considerably older than hers, it was a mirror image except that it was harsher and male. Without asking permission, he climbed into the shower with Kelandris. Kel reacted like a cornered animal. She pulled away from him, cowering against the wall. Zendrak ignored her fear of him and his sex and reached for her. Water streaming down his scarred face, he pulled Kelandris toward him and held her in silence. He kept his hands free of the erogenous places, touching her only as a friend might. Trembling, she made fists with her hands but she did not strike him. She could not. In her heart, she knew he meant her no harm. And had never meant her any harm. He had been ensnared by the events in Suxonli as much as she had. And yet, she could not accept this—not entirely. He had made love with her and left her just before the revel began. And when the night turned from a festival into a trial, Zendrak was nowhere to be found. Kelandris had never found a way to forgive him for this. Nor had she ever been able to bring herself to question him about his disappearance that night. She feared he would tell her that he was on Rimble's business. Kelandris could not bear the possibility that Trickster's business might be more important than her sanity—or life. Standing in the shower with him so close now, she felt she must now ask. Clearly he wanted to make love with her. This was an impossibility as long as she felt he had betrayed her.

Kelandris raised her head. Without introduction, she asked, "Why did you leave?"

Understanding the question without need of amplification, Zendrak said, "I left because I was overwhelmed with my own feelings for you. The smell of your blood that night acted wildly on my senses—it was a Tricksterish thing. And a Mythrrim thing. Until that time, I had not known there was anyone like me in all the world. I thought I was alone." He paused, his face contorting with the pain of that statement. "Can you imagine what it is like to walk the world for five hundred years with no hope of ever meeting anyone who would understand what I am? And then there you were—so beautiful, so trusting, so willing to love me.

I was taken unawares, Kel. And it hit me very hard. I know this cannot make sense to you now. But I was used to my loneliness. In one night, you changed all of that forever." He paused, stroking her wet hair with his long fingers. "Rimble-Rimble on me," he said quietly.

"Then why did you come back at all?" she asked bitterly.

Zendrak took a deep breath. "I heard your scream, Kel. Overneath time, on the back of Further, I heard your scream. It shocked me. I fell off my mare—between time and space. If Further hadn't gone after me, I would've been lost in a backwash of time. I ride the lines of coincidence. It is a dangerous business. When I reached you, I was ill myself. It was all I could do to take you across the border into Piedmerri."

There was a long silence between them.

Kelandris turned away from Zendrak, her face to the wall of the steaming shower, her arms over her belly, her fists clenched. Zendrak moved closer to her but did not touch her.

"Talk to me," he whispered fiercely.

"I—I can't," she said, her face twisting in agony.

Zendrak swore, looking at the floor of the shower. Hot water swirled over his toes. He raised his head, his expression wild. "*Speak* to me, Kel. You've kept these things in your heart for seventeen years, my beloved. They have rotted there and made you mad. For Presence sake, speak. Free us both from Suxonli."

Kelandris leaned back against the shower wall, her chin lifted, her eyes closed. She took a ragged breath and said, "I was pregnant."

"I know that," replied Zendrak fiercely. "You lost the child during the Ritual of Akindo. The holovespa dose they gave you changed your genes. The *draw* knew this. So the child was given to Fasilla by the *draw*. She had been raped by Cobeth only an hour or so before the Ritual—conception hadn't taken place. And wouldn't have if the blasted *draw* hadn't intervened. For that I cursed it. I would've rather had

a monster than give that child—born of our love—to someone else."

Kelandris swallowed. "What noble sentiments. That's a
very pretty picture, Zendrak."

Zendrak snorted. "I'd hardly call it that, Kelandris."

"A very pretty picture that you've been telling yourself
for years."

Zendrak stiffened. "I beg your pardon?"

Kelandris regarded him coolly. "You've been lying to
yourself—"

Zendrak stared at Kelandris. "I *never* lie—"

"Yes, you do," she countered, her voice hard. "I am a
Mythrrim now. Thanks to you—and I *do* thank you for it—I
am a Mythrrim who can remember telling *The Turn of
Trickster's Daughter* in the Great Library Maze last fall."

There was a short silence.

"So?" said Zendrak impatiently, his dark eyes hooded.

"So I *know* what happened. Let me quote you the lines:

"Touching her battered body with a lover's care
The King lifted the Queen to the back of his mare,
Riding in silence, they left Tammirring.
Now Zendrak crossed the border shift and wilds,
Listening to the Queen's frantic whimpering—
He realized she would lose their unborn child."

Zendrak's face contorted with fury. "You think I'm a
murderer? I'm telling you, the *draw* intervened! You think
I would willingly take you across the *draw* border and cause
you to abort our own child?"

Kelandris laughed raggedly. "I think that's exactly what
you did. It's funny I never saw it before so clearly. Being
branded as a murderer myself, I guess I never thought to
accuse you of the same crime. I suppose I needed you to be
stainless. It made my own degradation bearable."

Zendrak said nothing. After a few moments, he said,
"I'm getting out."

"Out of the shower? Or out of the conversation?" said Kelandris icily. Then she added, "Some Greatkin you are. We're supposed to be exemplars of truth, you know. Makes the two-leggeds nervous when we aren't."

Zendrak glared at her and climbed out of the shower.

Kelandris sat down in the shower and began to weep quietly, the water beating on her face and knees and drowning out her sobs. Being a Greatkin, Zendrak felt her pain and was brought up short by it. Swearing, he took off the yellow towel he had just wrapped around his torso and climbed back in the shower with Kelandris. He put his arms around her. She reached for him soundlessly.

After a few minutes, Zendrak pulled back and said, "I had no idea you claiming your Mythrrim inheritance would trigger a memory like this one. I thought the Ritual of Akindo had wiped it from your mind. You see, I didn't want you to know, Kelandris. About taking you across the *draw*. I didn't think you would be able to forgive me."

Kelandris raised her face, her expression exhausted. "I'm not sure I ever shall," she said simply.

Zendrak groaned. "How am I to live with that?"

"How am I to live with what you did?"

Zendrak ran his fingers through his wet, black hair slowly. "There *was* a reason for that abortion, Kelandris."

"Right. Rimble made you do it, I suppose?"

Zendrak swallowed. He disengaged himself from Kelandris fully. "No. Rimble didn't *make* me do it. But he pointed out what would happen if I didn't do it."

"And what exactly was that?" asked Kelandris, her voice cruel.

Zendrak put his head in his hands. "When I saw what Hennin had done to you—what the whole village had done to you—I cursed the *draw*—"

"I know that!" interrupted Kelandris impatiently.

"Shut up and *listen!*" he yelled at her, his expression furious.

There was a terrible silence between them.

Zendrak swallowed and continued. "I thought I was cursing the *draw* out of my own sense of outrage at the barbarism and brutality of the Ritual of Akindo. That was only partially true." He paused. "Now, listen carefully, Kelandris. I cursed the *draw* because Elder Hennin directed me to do so."

Kel's eyes widened. She felt as though she might start screaming and never stop. All she said, however, was, "You did what *Hennin* told you to do? You killed our baby because that bitch *told* you to?" Kelandris started weeping wildly. She crawled away from Zendrak, her back pressed against the wall. "How could you?" she whispered. "How could you?"

Zendrak's face looked drained of life. Speaking hoarsely, he replied, "I was Hennin's teacher. Her Mayanabi teacher, Kelandris. She left me twenty years before she put you through the Ritual of Akindo. During that time, she gained in power and mastery. I had no idea she had become that powerful. She had always been a quick study. Extraordinary, really. And terribly ambitious." He paused. Then Zendrak said, "You see, Hennin knew *I* was a Greatkin. She figured it out after she left me. She suspected—when you didn't die after the Ritual of Akindo—that you were one, too. She was—and is—a very good psychic, Kelandris. She knew you were pregnant with Yafatah. She knew that child—born of two full-blooded Greatkin—would be a spiritual giant. One that would rival her. So she wanted that possibility killed. That future destroyed. The cursing of an entire *draw* was a small price to pay in Hennin's mind. So I cursed it. And mutated it. Think, Kel. Think what this means. A mutant *Greatkin*? Born out of my rage and your despair? Such a child would be a monster. Rimble begged me to put a stop to your pregnancy. So did Themyth. Thus the incoming soul—which had a right to live—was given to Fasilla."

"But Fasilla was on Tammi soil, same as me!" cried Kelandris. "She drew from Tammirring, same as me. That's the law. Where you conceive determines the *draw*. Her child would be a mutant, too, and Yafatah is not!"

"But Fasilla was *not* on Tammi soil! She had wandered far from the revel site. So had Cobeth. They were both on drugs. They had no idea where they were. Well, they were in the Feyborne mountains, *in* the border between Tammir-ring and Piedmerri. You know how borders are. Anything can happen in the borders. Well, anything did. When I took you across the Piedmerri border, Piedmerri took pity on us. Piedmerri *landdraw* protects children. So it did just that. It took our child from you and gave it to Fasilla, who had not yet conceived. The *draw* of Piedmerri allowed Yafatah to keep her Tammi bearings but protected her against my stupidity. My curse. Piedmerri protected Ya all the way through the pregnancy. It was a miracle, really. A bit of grace that I certainly didn't deserve. In short, the *draw* of Piedmerri took the brunt of my curse—and turned it away from Yafatah. Yafatah, true to Trickster's influence, is the impossible possibility. She is a cross between two *draws*. She has the warmth and sociability of a Pied and the body of a Tammi."

"Why didn't you tell me?" Kelandris said accusingly. "Why didn't you confess what you had done before now?"

"Partly pride. And partly to protect you."

"*Pride?*"

Zendrak glared at Kelandris. "How do you think I felt—*feel*—knowing that Eldèr Hennin had gotten inside my brain—me, a Greatkin—and given me orders that *I followed out*? Orders that nearly scuttled everything Rimble had been working toward for at least five centuries? Well, I will tell you how I felt. Like an idiot. And an unwitting traitor. On top of everything else—losing you and the baby—knowing that I had been duped by Hennin scarred my mind. As she no doubt hoped it would." He paused. "Since I'm speaking my heart with you right now, I might as well say this, too: I didn't tell you why I took you into

Piedmerri because I thought you'd lose confidence in me—"

"I have!"

"That you might never regain—"

"I won't!"

"Since Hennin directed me to curse the *draw* in the first place," he mumbled, his voice trailing off painfully. Zendrak took a deep breath. "Like you said, I'm not much of a Greatkin, am I?"

"You certainly aren't!" cried Kelandris, getting to her feet. She climbed out of the shower. Without another word to Zendrak, she hurriedly dried herself and pulled on her bathrobe. She opened the door to the bathroom and left. The door slammed after her. Zendrak did not follow. He was too devastated by her reaction to be able to do anything else except sit in the hot shower and try to keep from putting his fist through the wall. A few minutes later, someone banged loudly on the door.

It was Janusin.

"I don't know what you two Greatkin were doing in there—fighting or fucking—but whatever it is, knock it off!"

Zendrak rolled his eyes and stepped out of the shower. Janusin lived on the third floor in a room to the right of Zendrak and Kel's. He was a man of forty years and much accomplishment; he was one of Speakinghast's only working Jinnjirri sculptors. Although Janusin was normally a polite soul—as Jinn went—at three-thirty in the morning he was apt to be blunt of speech.

"Hello in there? Did you hear me, Zendrak?"

Swearing, Zendrak yelled through the closed door, "What's the problem?"

"You and Kelandris have started a fire out here in the hallway. It's the second—nope—Barlimo says it's the third fire this week. She also says she would appreciate it greatly if you would *not* burn the house down. She spent a lot of long hours building and designing the 'K'—according to *your* requirements."

"Is the fire out?"

"Yes," cried a chorus of voices.

Chapter Eight

BY THE TIME Zendrak got dried off and dressed enough to come out of the bathroom, a small crowd of annoyed Kaleidicopians had gathered in the third-floor hallway. Present were the three Jinnjirri: Janusin, Barlimo, and Tree. These three shared the top floor of the "K" with the two Greatkin. It had been decided at a house meeting some months ago that only the Jinnjirri-born would be able to deal with the intensity of emotion that Zendrak and Kelandris generated between them. Tree, who was the last of the three to join the group, yawned and rubbed his eyes groggily. His autumn-colored bathrobe rustled as he shuffled toward Janusin and Barlimo. Tree was not a tree; however, he *was* a talented makeup artist who very much resembled a two-legged tree—complete with twiggy fingers and skin the texture of redwood bark. He was twenty-two, marginally employed, and generally good-natured. Sniffing the smoky air, he inquired, "Are we on fire again?"

Janusin pointed to a charred pile of empty boxes stacked in the hall.

Barlimo, the Jinnjirri who had designed and built the Kaleidicopia, added, "Like Jan said, that makes the third time this week. You and Kelandris better make up or make love before you burn us down. Understood?"

Zendrak nodded, too sad about what had passed between himself and Kelandris to say anything conversational.

Barlimo waved smoke out of her face. "Good. Now that we've got that settled, anybody want cocoa? I'm sure the kitchen embers are still hot from dinner."

Even Janusin's mood brightened at this thought. "I was

freezing in my room," he admitted, nodding. "This fall is so cold compared to last year's. Especially now that Cobeth's gone," he added lamely, knowing that none of his housemates, particularly Kelandris, missed Cobeth in the least. The sculptor sighed. It was hard being a minority of one. Despite all of Cobeth's misdeeds and infidelities, Janusin still kept a tender place in his heart for Cobeth. They had been lovers for five years.

"Give it a rest, will you?" said Tree sourly. "Cobeth was a dangerous man, and you know it, Janusin. And what's more, he didn't love you. I doubt he ever did—"

"Tree! Janusin!" snapped Barlimo. "Both of you stop it. It's three in the morning and no time for disputes."

Changing his mood instantly with true Jinnjirri speed, his hair turning from red to green, Tree put his hands in front of him and pretended to be sleep-walking. "Cocoa," he moaned. "Cooocoa."

Zendrak and Barlimo laughed. Janusin ignored Tree's antics, but said nothing more about Cobeth. Everyone trouped downstairs. When they reached the first-floor landing, they were met with the scent of cocoa already simmering. It seemed that Podiddley had just put a pot of milk and chocolate on the fire. Seeing the third-floor group enter the kitchen, Po glowered at the Jinnjirri and their changeable hair, saying, "Now the party *will* be spoiled. Look at Barlimo's hair. Already a disapproving red. And—yes—there goes Janusin's. Well, Tree? Are you turning red, too? No? Just garbage green?"

Tree ignored Po's jibes. "All we need now are Timmer and Rowen, and we'll have most of the whole house up at this silly hour."

"Preposterous hour would describe it better, Tree," said seventy-year-old Professor Rowenaster as he walked slowly into the kitchen, a scarlet kerchief on his head matched by a flannel nightgown of the same flaming color.

Zendrak winced. "You hurt my eyes, Rowen."

Rowenaster pursed his lips and inclined his head toward

Janusin and Barlimo, whose hair echoed the professor's attire. "What's everybody so red about? Looks to me like Po's put on a nice pot of cocoa. We should be grateful for his thoughtfulness."

Po snorted. "I didn't put it on for any of *you*!"

"Exactly," said Barlimo. "And those are the only hot embers in the house. So we'll have to wait, I expect, for Po to clear out."

"Nonsense," remarked Zendrak. "Po will share."

Po scowled at his spiritual master. "It's three in the friggin' morning and you're going to turn *this* into a teaching situation? Give me a break, Zendrak. Give me a break."

Zendrak remained obdurate. "Po will share."

Po rolled his eyes, swore under his breath, and left the kitchen. They heard the door to his first-floor room slam shut.

Zendrak shrugged. "He'll be back."

Everyone in the room knew Zendrak was right. Although Po's temper exploded more often than anyone else's at the Kaleidicopia, his foul humors blew over equally fast.

Barlimo stirred the cocoa and muttered, "I wonder if Po washed this pot before he used it?"

"Better wonder if he washed his *hands*," retorted Janusin.

At the Kaleidicopia, as Yafatah had pointed out in her letter to her mother, Po's housekeeping habits were often the irate topic of the monthly house meeting that all Kaleidicopians were obliged to attend. If you didn't attend, you moved out. Very simple. Barlimo often said the Kaleidicopia was not a democracy. It operated more like a federation of *landdraws*. Everyone had a vote, but Barlimo could ask you to leave. Or stay. Since Barlimo was an eminently fair person, this system functioned quite well. Zendrak's presence in the house, however, had thrown a little confusion into the lines of command recently. Unknown to the rest of the members of the Kaleidicopia until the last year, Barlimo did not own the boarding house. She had designed and built it, yes, but she had done so according to the requirements of Zendrak. And Zendrak was following Greatkin Rimble's orders.

Yafatah pushed through the swinging door into the crowded kitchen. Yawning, the young Tammirring girl said, "Anybody found the dog?"

Zendrak glanced at Yafatah and said, "I think he's gone off again. He does that. Maybe for weeks at a time."

Yafatah scowled.

Janusin, who had not seen Yafatah for two days, stared at the sixteen-year-old's swollen face and hands. "You look *awful*. What happened to you?"

"Thanks," muttered Yafatah through fat lips.

"A swarm of uni—univer—whatever they are—got her," said Tree.

"Univer'silsila," corrected Barlimo and Rowenaster together.

Rowenaster began pouring everyone mugs of cocoa, being careful to leave enough in the pot for Podiddley when he returned from sulking. As he got to Zendrak, the Saämbolin professor said, "You and Kel must've had a dilly of a fight tonight. I've never seen her leave the house in such a state. Or with such haste."

"Where in the world will she go at this hour?" asked Janusin.

Zendrak set down his mug. "I had no idea she'd left the house. Blast!"

"Don't you ever get tired of chasing her?" asked Barlimo, stirring the cocoa.

"The truth? Yes. Tonight, I'm very tired of it. I take one step forward with her and three back." He left the room hurriedly, grabbing his dark green traveling cloak in the hallway. The door slammed behind him.

"I just doon't see why Kelandris has to take *everything* so personally," said Yafatah.

"She's in love," said Janusin.

Tree put his twiggy hands on his hips. "If she's in love, Jan, then she's only in love with herself."

Janusin sipped his cocoa out of a ceramic mug. "She's in love with Zendrak. Only she can't admit that. So she gets herself all upset so he'll have to comfort her. So she'll know that he loves her, too. Admittedly, a stupid system. But Kel's not exactly right in the head, if you know what I mean. So she does the best she can. We all do when it comes to love." .

Yafatah wasn't convinced. "Yeah, but what be so hard about saying you love someone? Timmer does it every time she writes a song. I love you. There. So what?"

Janusin's Jinnjirri hair turned a philosophical silver-gray.

"Uh-oh," said Tree. "*Now* you've done it, Ya. You've got him going on his favorite subject: love."

Janusin gave Tree a sickly-sweet smile and ignored him. Turning back to Yafatah, Janusin said, "I suppose the words 'I love you' *are* quite easy for anyone in this room to say—"

"Not me," snapped Po, returning unannounced.

Barlimo batted her fifty-year-old eyelashes at the little middle-aged thief and said smoothly, "Well, you're our resident Contrary, Po. What's easy for us *has* to be hard for you."

She handed Po a full mug of cocoa.

Chapter Nine

IN THE STREET outside the Kaleidicopia, a figure in black hurried toward the public stables. It was Kelandris. The moon shone brightly overhead, casting a silver radiance over Kel's shadowy form and the darkened houses. It was close to four bell-morn, and everyone was asleep in the city. Kelandris neared the stables. She knew that most of the horses were stabled inside this time of year. The weather had remained well below freezing for weeks now. Such temperatures made it mandatory to blanket the animals. Kelandris climbed under a cloth stable guard and hastily unbuckled the blanket on the black horse inside the stall.

Like her brother, Zendrak, Kelandris was able to ride a horse without bridle or saddle and control it through her emotions. Unlike her brother, however, Kelandris was unable to call one of the horses from Neath, the Greatkin underworld, and ask it to carry her. She had never been granted this privilege. Not yet, anyway. So while Zendrak got around the world on the back of his black mare, Further, Kelandris made do with the mortal variety of steed.

Kelandris stroked the neck of the black gelding and unhooked the stable guard. The gelding snorted as she made contact with his animal mind. Calming him, she grabbed a handful of mane and jumped on his furry back. The gelding wore a thick winter coat, nature's indicator of a continued tough winter. Kelandris commanded the gelding to leave the city at a slow canter. She realized that if Zendrak decided to follow her on Further, she had little hope of outrunning him. Still, it was worth a try. She had to get to Suxonli. She had to finish what was begun there eighteen years ago.

Black on black, the night hid both the rider and the ridden. Urging the gelding into a gallop, Kelandris turned the horse north. They approached the five-foot gate that led out of the city. Hunching over, she asked the horse to jump it. She did not wish to get stopped at the gate. She had no papers or pass to hand to the sleepy Saämbolin guard who would require them. If Saämbolin bureaucracy got hold of her, she would *never* escape Speakinghast before Zendrak caught up with her. The gelding gathered himself for the jump. He cleared it safely. Kelandris heard the astonished shout of the Saämbolin guard behind her calling for her to stop. She ignored him. Horse and rider sped north.

Zendrak reached the stable too late to catch Kelandris. Sniffing the air, Zendrak tested Kel's scent on the wind. He grunted. He had her. She was heading north at a fast clip. He swore loudly. He was certain her destination was Suxonli Village. And Elder Hennin.

Walking behind the public stable, Zendrak looked to see if any of the pastures were empty. They all were. Zendrak ran his fingers through his shoulder-length black hair. He needed a large open space, preferably one that held no people or animals. He intended to call Further from the stables of Neath. Her sudden appearance out of thin air would terrify two-leggeds and four-leggeds alike. Also, this was Speakinghast, stronghold of the Saämbolin. The psychology of this city did not lend itself to ready explanations of the impossible. Zendrak closed his eyes and called Further to him from the Greatkin underworld.

Based on five hundred years of trust between them, the mare came as soon as she was bid. Thundering out of the east, she galloped over rolling pasture covered with hardened snow, her body shimmering with blue-black power in the moonlight. Steam rose from her back, and her blue eyes glittered. Slowly she approached Zendrak. Standing on the snow of Saämbolin as easily as if it was a sandbar, she snorted at the man in green, throwing her head up and down. Were they about to have an adventure? she wanted to know. If so, she continued, she was fit to travel and full of spirit.

Zendrak smiled at her eagerness and patted her velvet nose. She smelled pungently of warm, furry horse. Zendrak jumped from the ground to her broad back. Then guiding her with pressure from his legs, they turned north. The mare gathered speed, shimmered, and entered Overneath time. They would reach Kelandris in a matter of moments.

Such was the power of Further.

Before Kelandris had gone a mile north of Speakinghast, Zendrak intercepted her, his large black mare blocking the road as she galloped through a wooded glen. Kel's gelding shied when he saw Further. Further was a power of the Fertile Dark. Kel's gelding sensed Further's Neathian nativity and was terrified at this unexpected encounter. Kelandris nearly fell off as the gelding veered to the right. Swearing, she regained her balance and yelled, "Get out of my way, Zendrak!"

He rode toward her slowly, his hands crossed over his chest, his legs loose around the barrel of Further's belly. "What now, Kel? Are you running away from home? Or our bed?"

Kelandris stiffened. She glared at him, pulling her black bathrobe tighter across her bosom. She had left the Kaleidicopia in such a hurry she had not had time to put on proper riding attire. Now she remembered what she was wearing and felt stupid. She noticed Zendrak wore pants, boots, and a tunic. She lifted her chin and said, "As a matter of fact, Zendrak, I'm running *toward* something for once. I'm running toward my destiny—I'm going to Suxonli to finish Hennin."

"To commit murder?"

"What does it matter, Zendrak? Suxonli already accused me of that. And 'proved' it," she added harshly, referring to the sad excuse of a trial that had preceded the Ritual of

Akindo. Kelandris shrugged. "So if I kill again, what can they do to me? They have already done their worst. I took their cup of bitter poison and survived. Hennin can't hurt me now, Zendrak. Get out of my way so *she* can feel the rage of Rimble's wasp queen."

"And if she finds a way to do you in?" asked Zendrak softly.

"Then I'm done in," snapped Kelandris. "But at least I'll be done in doing the right thing. At least I'll be done in fighting the bitch instead of sitting on my ass in Speaking-hast waiting for *you* to take her by the hinder and wallop her."

"After tonight, I know you don't have a very high opinion of me," said Zendrak with a small grimace. "Still—"

"You're quite right. I have a lousy opinion of you. Hennin and Cobeth both tried to kill me, Zendrak. Well, I would think that's cause for some pretty powerful outrage on your part. That's usually how real lovers are, you know. They don't just let the assholes of the world hurt their beloved and do *nothing*."

If Zendrak was aggravated by Kel's condemnation of him, he did not show it. He appeared to be listening intently, however. Finally he said, "Are we real lovers, then?"

There was dead silence.

Kelandris put her hand to her mouth, her eyes betraying her confusion. "No. I mean, yes." Furious, she added, "Don't change the subject!" Swearing, she kicked her gelding toward the woods.

Zendrak raised his eyebrows in surprise. "Where are you going now?"

"This damn horse is afraid of you. I can't get past you on the road, so I'm taking to the woods. I am *going* to Suxonli, Zendrak. And that's final!"

Zendrak hastily whispered something to Further. The mare let out a scream, horse fashion. The result was instant. Kel's gelding shied and bolted all at once. Kelandris fell off, landing in a bush. The gelding took off at a run in a southerly direction, heading home to Speakinghast. Kelandris was so surprised at her horseless condition, she was speechless. Zendrak jumped off Further and broke his way through the brambles where Kelandris lay in a black heap. Kelandris looked up at him, her eyes dangerous. Zendrak offered her a hand up. As far as Kelandris was concerned, his gesture was insulting. She spit on his hand.

Wiping the spittle off his palm, he offered her his hand again, saying, "In any good battle, Kelandris, there is strategy. Successful strategy is often made up of two things: patience and timing. If you go after Hennin now, you'll fail."

"How do you know?" she retorted, refusing to take his hand.

"I know something about Hennin that you don't know."

"What's that?"

"Elder Hennin is a high-ranking Mayanabi Nomad gone renegade. Do you know what that means, Kel? To go renegade?"

Kel's jaw dropped. "I don't *care* what it means, Zendrak. The Order of the Mayanabi Nomads is your business, not mine. If someone like Hennin is one of them, then you better do some housecleaning." She shivered involuntarily, remembering the look of enjoyment on Hennin's face when she had beat Kelandris during the Ritual of Akindo. The woman was the village disciplinarian, yes; she was also a first-class sadist.

Zendrak dropped his hand and knelt beside Kelandris. "You *better* care what it means, dear heart. Hennin has power—focused and malicious. She's the real adversary of Jinnaeon. Not Cobeth. She's a user."

"They all take drugs in Suxonli," muttered Kel.

"Yes. But she's also a user of people. She used to have Cobeth in her thrall. She promised him the world, and the poor sod thought he was going to get it. He would've been happy being an artist, Kel. He was a Jinn. But he got lost from his parents and grew up in Suxonli—"

"So did I!" she retorted. "And I don't go around claiming to be Rimble's emissary, or start drug cults like Cobeth did."

Zendrak regarded her reprovingly. "There's a reason for that. Want to hear it?"

"Yes."

"You don't need to make claims like Cobeth's. You're Rimble's daughter. You carry his blood in you. You're also Themyth's daughter. Even if you do nothing, Kelandris, you will affect civilization. You can't help it. Neither can I. Cobeth had no destiny like this. His own, however, should have been precious enough to him. Unfortunately, Elder Hennin convinced him that who and what he could be weren't enough. She gave him an impossible dream. The more he failed at it, the more dependent he became on her. As she wished him to be. You have to understand something about Elder Hennin, Kel. She's a spiritual warrior."

"So?"

"So, *she* understands the importance of patience and timing."

"So *what!*"

Zendrak cursed under his breath. Glancing at Kelandris in the darkness, he said, "Don't you know who Hennin's really after, Kel? It's *you*. Suxonli was a *political* move, Kel. She didn't know what you were then, but she certainly suspected. Like I told you, Hennin is ambitious. Spiritually ambitious. Never forget that. She wants your power. Mine, too, if she can figure out a way to get it. You go to her now, and she'll break you like dry leaves in the wind. Go to her now, and there will be no winterbloom."

Kelandris said nothing, holding her bathrobe close to her bosom again. The winter wind blew down her front and made her shiver. Seeing this, Zendrak offered Kelandris a hand up once more. This time she took it. The man in green guided her out of the brambles of the dark forest and gave her a leg up on Further. Then he pulled himself up behind her.

Kelandris turned to him and said, "We're going back to Speakinghast, aren't we?" She sounded disgusted.

"I think it's best at this time."

Kelandris shrugged. "But you do intend to do something about Hennin?"

"Presence willing, something will be done about Hennin."

Zendrak turned Further south with his legs, and they rode slowly back to the sleeping city. As they rode, Kelandris leaned back against Zendrak's chest and dozed off and on. Feeling Zendrak's belt buckle against the small of her back, she muttered:

"How did you have time to dress?"

Zendrak smiled but said nothing. They rode in silence, both Greatkin too exhausted from fighting with each other to even speak. Their exhaustion had also dulled their psychic senses. Neither Zendrak nor Kelandris felt a bitter wind blast them from the north.

Nor did they sense the silent outcry of Speakinghast as Elder Hennin's Akindo entered the city limits.

Panthe'kinarok Interlogue

RIMBLE'S INDIGNANT SCREAM in the kitchen at Eranossa brought all conversation at the dinner table to a stop. The table, which was alive, quivered. Ice cubes in crystal glasses tinkled while fruit again poured out of the silver cornucopia in the middle. All the Greatkin present scrambled to keep things from falling to the floor, especially Sathmadd, the Patron of Organization. Fuming at Rimble under her breath, she straightened fallen place cards that she had so carefully calligraphied the evening previous to the commencement of the Panthe'kinarok. When she came around to where Themyth was sitting, Sathmadd grumbled at Themyth for her bad taste in bed partners, specifically Rimble. Themyth smiled enigmatically and poured herself a fresh glass of sweet black-currant wine. The wine had been a gift to Themyth from Phebene, the Patron of Love. As Themyth put her wineglass down on the now stabilized table, she turned to Sathmadd and said, "Relax, Maddi, dear. Everything will turn out all right in the end."

"Not so long as those Neathian *nuts* are in charge," snapped Sathmadd in a low voice. "Just look at them. Every face is smug—and not one of *them* has gone to find out what's wrong in the kitchen. Know why? Because they're waiting for one of us from Eranossa to walk in there with Rimble. What do they think we are? Stupid?"

"Maybe just compassionate," whispered Themyth, patting Sathmadd's hand like a favorite grandmother.

Sathmadd snorted and bustled off.

Themyth surveyed the twenty-six faces around the table in front of her. Several of Rimble's brothers and sisters glanced nervously at the closed door to the kitchen. A few rolled their eyes. Others slumped in their chairs. It was clear to Themyth that no one in the room relished the idea of playing the dupe to Rimble's crafty intelligence. Themyth listened as throats cleared and conversation resumed. Smiles were forced, she noted. It seemed that all of them were trying to keep their eyes on their dinner partners and off the door to the ominously silent kitchen.

Themyth decided to help Rimble along with his schemes. Leaning toward Jinndaven, the Greatkin of Imagination, she planted an idea in his very fertile mind. "Jinn, sweetheart—you don't think Rimble is in *real* trouble, do you? I mean, I can't *imagine* what made your little brother scream like that."

"I know, I know," sighed Jinndaven. "I've been trying not to worry about it." Looking heavenward, Jinndaven threw his linen napkin on the table and got to his feet.

Before Jinndaven could leave the table, however, Greatkin Mattermat intercepted him. Grabbing Jinndaven by the arm, the Greatkin of All Things That Matter asked, "Why do you always defend the little brat? Why do you always help Trickster?"

Jinndaven pulled his arm away from Mattermat's grip, his expression annoyed. Straightening his crumpled, filmy, mauve sleeve, Jinndaven shrugged defensively and said, "I don't know. I just do. I *like* Rimble, I suppose."

Mattermat and Nessi'gobahn, the Patron of Humor, roared with derisive laughter. Mattermat wiped tears away from his eyes and said, "Well, there's no accounting for taste, is there?"

Jinndaven crossed his arms over his chest and glared at his enormous brother. "Rimble uses my ideas," snapped Jinndaven. "Even the bad ones. He can make a go of even my most mediocre creativity. That *matters* to me. Certainly more than it matters to you, Mattermat."

Mattermat helped himself to another serving of bread and

butter. "Fortunately for me, Jinndaven, I don't have to depend on anyone to exist. I simply *am*."

Conversation at the table came to an abrupt halt. Themyth was so shocked by Mattermat's statement that she began coughing and choking on the wine in her mouth. Phebene ran to the crone's side and patted her back vigorously. When Themyth had regained her composure, she thanked the Greatkin of Love for her assistance and turned to Mattermat, her expression hard. Then Themyth said, "We're all interdependent here, Mattermat. As Phebene has just illustrated by coming to my side when I choked on my wine, we're here to cooperate and help one another. Always."

Mattermat scowled at the cheery rainbow attire of Phebene. Then he said sarcastically, "I'm a realist. Not a ridiculous romantic—"

"Maybe I had better sit next to him," said Phebene to Themyth in a seductive voice. "Might improve his temper—"

Mattermat got to his feet. "And listen to your sickeningly sweet conversation through the next three courses of dinner? Not a chance of that, sister. Not a chance."

Jinndaven went quickly to Phebene's side and put his arm around her. Materializing a handkerchief out of the air, Phebene began to weep copiously. "Boo-h*ooooo*," she cried, "Boo-h*oooo*."

Phebene made so much noise that she brought Rimble running from the kitchen, his plan to lure Jinndaven and ultimately Themyth in there completely foiled. The little Greatkin burst through the kitchen door, his expression one of genuine alarm. Seeing that Phebene was on the brink of dissolving into a literal puddle of tears for the second time this Panthe'kinarok, Rimble walked up to Mattermat and said, "What did you say to Phebes? What did you say to her?"

"Interesting how he always blames me—" began Mattermat, his posture defensive.

"Well?" retorted Jinndaven. "He's right to blame you, you big lout!"

During a disagreeable pause, Themyth nodded at Rimble, her voice jovial. "Rimble, dear—what happened in the kitchen? Jinn was just on his way to find out. We were a little worried."

Rimble regarded Themyth with a mixture of affection and irritation. He knew Themyth was trying to be helpful, but he didn't need or want her help at present. His plans were going through Neath, not Eranossa. Trickster cleared his throat and smiled benignly at Themyth. "Why don't you come into the kitchen, then, Themyth? If you're so worried as all that."

No one thought this was a good idea, not even Themyth. However, Themyth thought it might keep the peace at the table if she humored Rimble at this point. The crone got to her feet stiffly, her patchwork quilt falling to one side of her body. She accompanied Trickster to the door of the kitchen, her aged hand held tightly by his strong fingers. This time when Trickster opened the kitchen door, smoke billowed out, engulfing Themyth. Her eyes smarting, her throat burning, the Greatkin of Civilization staggered backward. Jinndaven and Phebene caught her as she started to fall.

Themyth blinked, her expression one of incredulity and betrayal. "What are you trying to do, Rimble?" she whispered hoarsely. "Destroy civilization?"

"Not at all," said Greatkin Troth, the Patron of Death, as he stepped out of the kitchen, the colorful glass beads in his dark hair glinting in the light from the candles decorating the table. "We're just trying to shake you up, that's all. Did we succeed?"

Themyth gave both brothers an exasperated look. "Yes," she snapped.

Now seated at the table, Sathmadd raised a gray eyebrow, folded her hands primly in her lap, and said under her breath, "*Will* everything turn out all right in the end? I wonder."

Rimble, who had uncommonly good hearing when he wanted to, grinned at Sathmadd. Realizing that Trickster had heard her comments, the Greatkin of Organization turned scarlet with embarrassment. Trickster continued to grin—leer, really—and said, "You're spozed to wonder, Maddi, dearest." Suddenly changing his mood as quickly as he was apt to change his costume, Trickster bowed to the elite company assembled at the table and added, "Well, I'm off."

"Off where?" asked Jinndaven. He peered at Trickster, noting his brother still wore furs, gourd rattles, and black and yellow paint.

"To a Distant Place."

"What're you going to do there, Rimble?" asked Phebene between sniffles.

"I'm going to market my name."

Mattermat scowled. "Speak Oldspeech, will you? 'Market your name'—what in Neath does *that* mean?"

"Wouldn't you like to know?" sniggered Trickster.

"Yes, I would!" shouted Mattermat, rightly suspecting Rimble of some new mischief. "What's this Distant Place called? Is it on Mnemlith?"

"Nope. It's in Milwaukee."

There was a bewildered silence.

"Never heard of it," said Sathmadd, quickly scanning every place name in her prodigious memory. "Never heard of a Milwaukee."

Chapter Ten

As THE RESIDENTS of Milwaukee, Wisconsin, often said, this lovely city was the best kept secret in the Midwest. Made famous by the beer breweries that once heavily populated Milwaukee's precincts, in recent years Milwaukee had broadened its business base and begun attracting people interested in the computer industry. Influenced by its large German and Polish constituency, the city favored the ethic of hard work. Unlike its university sister city of Madison, Milwaukee excelled at being conservative—except in summer. In June, when native Milwaukeeans were digging themselves out of their six-month winter hibernation—and residual cabin fever—the city cut loose with fireworks. Literally. By the time the Fourth of July rolled around, the fireworks display held on the banks of Lake Michigan was almost anticlimactic.

Ethnic festivals abounded in Milwaukee throughout the summer. Each weekend hosted a different country. Bastille Day enlivened the downtown area in mid-July, culminating in the Great Circus Parade that strutted down Wisconsin Avenue complete with hundred-year-old wagons brought by train from Baraboo, Wisconsin, and unloaded by horses in the train yard to the delight of scores of cheering children and equally happy grown-ups.

Centuries ago, long before the Europeans set foot on the land, Milwaukee was famous for something besides beer and festivals; it was a peace center for many of the Native American tribes in the area. Many street names in the city were of Indian origin, Milwaukee itself meaning "at the gathering of the waters." In the 1980s Milwaukee had become more conscious of its Native American roots and had invited Indians of the area to host an early fall weekend entitled Indian Summer. The festival was well attended by local Indians and members of tribes living as far west as the Dakotas. In like spirit, when the city decided to reinstate the Great Circus Parade as one of its yearly festivals, local Indians were asked to join in the fun. Trickster thought this was grand, and being partial to the Native Americans for giving him so many names—Old Man Coyote, Bluejay, Raven, Moon, Hare, Mink, Nanabozho—*and* remembering them even into the present day, Trickster decided to pay his respects to the Menominee in Milwaukee and make sure they made room for him in their part of the parade. The medicine woman of the Menominee was an elder in her seventies who invited Trickster into her house immediately, promptly cuffed the little rogue on the back of the neck, and offered him tobacco. Trickster grinned, then settled into her house until time for the parade in downtown Milwaukee to begin.

The day was sunny, the sky nearly cloudless. As Trickster danced and pranced his stuff—goosing and rattling the people lined up on either side of the street with great enthusiasm—he kept an eye out for someone he affectionately called "the Obstinate Woman of Park and Shepard." She was not Indian, but white—blonde and blue-eyed, as a matter of fact. Trickster had first made her acquaintance in California and had kept track of her changes of residence. You may wonder why? Well, in California Trickster had told this woman his Greatkin name, Rimble. Then he had asked her to write some books using that name. Being a contrary sort of person herself, the Obstinate Woman had refused. She said she didn't want any part of Trickster's doings. She was certain she would never be the same if she got involved with Rimble.

"Right you are, girlie. So what d'ya want to be the same for, anyway?" argued Trickster, one rainy day in northern California.

"Don't press me, buster—"

Rimble winked at her and began humming to himself. After a few minutes, Trickster said, "I could make you famous."

"Not interested."

"Hey, hey—I'm a myth whose time has come. I'm telling you Coyote will be 'in' soon. Catch the wave, sweetheart. Catch the wave—"

"Nope."

Trickster pursed his lips. Then, giving the Obstinate Woman a sidelong glance, he said, "Why not?"

"I just told you why not."

"Tell me again."

The Obstinate Woman took a deep breath. "If I write for you, Rimble, my life will get turned upside down—"

"And inside inside out—don't forget that part."

The Obstinate Woman smiled thinly and went back to washing the dishes in the sink at her Berkeley duplex. When she didn't hear anything more from Rimble, she turned around to see if he was still there. He wasn't. The Obstinate Woman felt relieved at first. She congratulated herself on being wise. No one in his or her right mind would write for an archetype like Trickster, she told herself. She bit her lower lip.

"Then why am I standing here being disappointed that he didn't talk me into it?" she asked out loud. Rolling her eyes, the Obstinate Woman poured more soap in the sink and watched it bubble.

Of course, being Rimble (and absolutely ubiquitous), Rimble heard her final remark to herself at the sink. Cackling gleefully, he made plans for the marketing of his name through the Obstinate Woman's book publisher in New York City. Now, a few years later, Rimble had come to Milwaukee to check on the progress of this venture. Six months earlier, the Obstinate Woman had left California to return to an area of the United States which still believed in wholesome things like milk, mothers, and marriage. Milwaukee had fit this description, and so the Obstinate Woman had settled there. At present, she was sitting high on a bleacher overlooking the circus parade, wearing mirrored eyeglasses and a silly straw hat. As the Native American segment of the Great Circus Parade marched by, the Obstinate Woman's jaw dropped. There in plain sight of thousands was Rimble weaving in and out of the crowd.

"Shit!" she said nervously, and looked for a convenient way to escape. Unfortunately, the bleacher was packed and she sat at its highest point. In the street, Rimble waved gaily at her.

"*Shit!*" she repeated, and started climbing over people. .Scrambling between sunburnt children and beer-drinking college students, the Obstinate Woman made her way to the bottom of the bleacher. To her relief she saw that the Native American section of the parade was turning left on Water Street. Mercifully, Trickster was nowhere to be found. Deciding that she must have seen a hallucination of Rimble—no doubt brought on by the searing summer sun and ninety-four-degree heat—the Obstinate Woman decided to go in search of a soda. When she walked up to a nearby concession stand on the corner of Wisconsin and Jackson streets, the soda man had his back to her. The Obstinate Woman cleared her throat.

"May I have a Coke, please? Not diet. I like my caffeine and sugar straight up," she added with a grin.

The soda man turned around, his swarthy face reflecting in her dark glasses. It was Trickster, of course, his Indian costume gone. In its place he wore a red bandana, a candy-striped shirt, rainbow suspenders, and baggy white pants. Trickster guffawed rudely and said, "Rimble-Rimble, girlie."

The Obstinate Woman rolled her eyes and grabbed the unopened soda out of Trickster's proffered hand. "This better be on the house," she snapped at him as she peeled off the aluminum sticker on the Coca-Cola can.

"But of course," said Rimble, adopting a French accent

for the moment. "Bastille Days," he added. "Zey bring out ze French in *moi*."

"What *do* you want?"

"Just checking up on the books. Where are they? Don't see a single one down at Webster's or Schwartz's—"

"They're not *out* yet, Rimble. Takes time to make a book in New York."

"Well, well. We'll just have to remedy that, won't we?"

"I should never have agreed to write for you. Never, never, never—"

"No whining. Makes you unattractive, you know. Ask Barlimo. She'd tell you that in a minute."

The Obstinate Woman took a sip of Coke and swallowed it. "Now I suppose you'll tell me my own characters get to boss me around?"

Trickster yawned. "She thinks I'm not *real*," he said to a passerby.

The passerby, who turned out to be a weird mix of Brady Street aging hippie and Downer Avenue skateboard punk, smiled disagreeably at the Obstinate Woman. Clad in studs, leather, peace symbols, and embroidered patches, the passerby said, "Life's a bitch and then you die. So fuck the world, let's all get high." The fellow skateboarded away, his studs glinting in the two o'clock sun.

"I'm going home," muttered the Obstinate Woman.

And she did.

A bus ride later, the Obstinate Woman soon rounded the corner of Park and Shepard. As she did so, Trickster jumped out at her from behind a maple tree. He was dressed just like the skateboarder from downtown, his black hair sticking straight up, garish earrings swinging from his right ear. Grinning, Trickster said, "*This* more real to you, girlie?"

"Go away," said the Obstinate Woman. "And phew, what is that smell—"

"Week-old sweat. Like it?"

"Get out of my way!"

Trickster looped his arm in hers. "Come on, girlie. We're going for some coffee at the Downer Cafe.

"Not dressed like that, you're not—"

"Relax, will you? There. Smell's gone. Happy?"

"I would hardly call it that," she grumbled, slinging her purse over her shoulder and turning back the way she had just come. Miserable and certain that this meeting with Trickster would end in disaster, the Obstinate Woman walked toward Downer Avenue, Trickster jabbering merrily in her ear.

Greatkin Rimble and the Obstinate Woman took a window table for two at the restaurant. Airy fans rotated above their heads while the espresso machine bubbled and frothed behind the hardwood bar. Trickster ordered iced coffee. The Obstinate Woman ordered a tall iced tea. She dumped cream into it. Trickster watched her and grimaced.

Seeing his expression of disapproval, the Obstinate Woman began to laugh. "Don't say a word about *my* table manners, Rimble. I know all about yours at the Panthe'ki-narok."

Trickster dabbed his lips primly with his paper napkin and said nothing.

"So what's this about? Why do you want to see me?"

Rimble took a deep sigh, his expression unexpectedly tired. "I want you to put my name on the cover of your books. Doesn't have to be in the title. See, the more my name is known, the more the myth will change reality. And the more I will matter."

Rimble snorted haughtily. "Nobody knows it *here*. And nobody remembers it *there*."

"You exaggerate," replied the Obstinate Woman, clearly unimpressed.

"Of course, I exaggerate!" said Rimble. "Nobody pays any attention unless I exaggerate. Watch, I'll show you." Before the Obstinate Woman could stop Rimble, he flagged down the wait-person for their table. Scanning the menu, Rimble ordered a certain breakfast item that was only served between seven and eleven. It was now three o'clock in the afternoon. As expected, the wait-person told Trickster he couldn't have Benedict Oscar at this hour. Trickster nodded and let her go on to the next table.

"So?" said the Obstinate Woman.

"So watch *this,*" said Trickster. Flagging down a different wait-person, he repeated his request all over again. The wait-person started to tell Trickster that he couldn't have Benedict Oscar. Before she had gotten the sentence out of her mouth, Trickster's lower lip began to tremble. His eyes went mournful. Great crocodile tears dripped from his nose. He bawled loudly.

Heads turned in the restaurant.

"They won't give me my Benedict Oscar. They won't serve me because I'm a punk. Boo-hooooo," he added in perfect mimicry of Greatkin Phebene.

Both the wait-person and the Obstinate Woman were mortified and scandalized by Trickster's performance. The wait-person tried to assure Rimble that she liked him just fine as a skateboarding punk and was happy to serve him.

"No, you're not. I know you don't like me one bit. Boo-hoooo."

"Rimble—good God. Shut *up*!" hissed the Obstinate Woman.

"Prove you like punks," cried Trickster, his voice growing louder by the moment. "Make me a Benedict Oscar. Please?" he asked, now smiling in his most friendly manner.

Licking her lips nervously, the girl went to the kitchen. Within minutes the cooks prepared the most scrumptious Benedict Oscar imaginable, the eggs fluffy, the crab meat delectable. As the wait-person set the steaming plate on the table, Rimble leaned toward the Obstinate Woman and said, "See? Just asking for what you want doesn't carry any punch. Now I've made a splendid scene. I've exaggerated the wait-person's fears as well as the problem. And look what happened. I got Benedict Oscar at the wrong time of day."

"You also got the Downer Cafe manager," said the Obstinate Woman, as a thin, officious-looking man approached their table, his expression far from pleased.

Rimble-Rimble.

Chapter Eleven

ALTHOUGH IT WAS a searing summer's day in Milwaukee, it was a brutally cold night in Speakinghast, the wind chill bringing the temperature to well below zero. Cold of such caliber was expected this time of year. At least the physical cold was. However, no one in the city, including Zendrak, expected the emotional freeze that accompanied the gusting winds. Enter Elder Hennin's wasp-keeper, the perversion of Suxonli's *draw*—gray-robed, shuffling Akindo.

Horses shied and bolted when Akindo passed them. Children woke crying fitfully in their beds. Lovers broke off lovemaking. Politicians had nightmares. In short, the whole city of Speakinghast was affected by the monster. Wherever Akindo walked, he brought despair of the worst kind. Hope shattered in his presence, love fled. No one was immune to Akindo except one person: young Yafatah.

The univer'silsila wasps had done their job well. They had immunized the Tammirring child from Akindo and the deadly holovespa hive he carried on his back. She alone would remain unharmed through the next few days. Rimble had followed the mythmaking orders of the Mythrrim; he had created an antidote to despair—the univer'silsila. As much part of nature as Akindo was part of the cursed *draw* of Suxonli, the univer'silsila preyed on the feelings that Akindo inspired. Where Akindo brought pain, the univer'silsila brought pardon and healing. Unfortunately for the city of Speakinghast, however, the wasps under Akindo's control had a wasp queen, Elder Hennin. The univer'silsila were as yet without a queen, and were therefore unorganized, the good they did random and occasional. Akindo's holovespa were directed—powerfully.

Akindo made his way to the Jinnjirri Quarter. He did not head in the direction of the Kaleidicopia at this time. Instead, Akindo passed the playhouse belonging to the all-Jinnjirri acting troupe called the Merry Pricksters. He shuffled and drooled down Renegade Road toward Rhu's house.

Until his death the previous fall, Cobeth had lived at this residence with Rhu. Cobeth and Rhu had been lovers. Rhu was Jinnjirri-born and was employed as the stage manager for the Merry Pricksters when Cobeth directed and acted for them. After Cobeth's death, the troupe seemingly lost a lot of its political momentum. This had made Guildmaster Gadorian happy, as he had perceived the Pricksters as a potential hotbed of radicals and dissidents. Like the rest of the Pricksters, Rhu kept a low profile during the scant three months following Cobeth's drug overdose at the Kaleidicopia; no one wanted the Guild to investigate the Pricksters. If the Saämbolin Guild had done so, it would have discovered that the Pricksters were a front for some of the most notorious dope dealers in all Speakinghast, the props and powders used by the special-effects personnel in the troupe cut with holovespa and royal sabbanac from the north. Tree was blissfully unaware of this side of the Pricksters while he worked for them, the pushers always opening the shipments before he did. Cobeth had been a master of trickery and stealth. As long as Cobeth lived, he had never been caught. Rhu, his second-in-command, wanted to keep it that way, so she had cleared every drug out of the playhouse. Now the guild could search all it wished; it would find nothing.

Akindo stood outside Rhu's house, the bitter cold not affecting his skin. He made sure the holovespa swarm on his back stayed covered. He could hear the wasps buzzing angrily inside. These wasps acted this way all the time, their level of activity agitated and somewhat ferocious. The winter should have killed them. However, Elder Hennin's poison had raised their metabolic rate, giving them a nastier temper and making them more difficult to destroy.

Akindo let one worker-wasp free from the hive. It flew into the house. Tracking Rhu's body scent like a bloodhound, the wasp found its intended target sound asleep in her bed. The holovespa worker-wasp stung Rhu on the neck. Unlike Aunt, Rhu did not have an allergic reaction to the wasp. Aunt had been a person who rejected the kind of despair these wasps inflicted on their victims. In rejecting the despair, Aunt had also rejected Elder Hennin's bid for control over her. When the holovespa stung someone, the wasp opened a psychic back door to the wasp queen of Suxonli. From that moment on, the victim was expected to do the bidding of the queen. If you were not working for Hennin's cause and part of her growing hive-mind, then you were a drone—dispensable. Aunt's will had put her in this latter category. She had resisted Hennin to the last, her Mayanabi loyalties preventing Aunt from falling to Hennin's designs.

Rhu woke from her sleep with a start. Feeling the sting on her neck, she was incredulous. The poison began to work in her system almost instantly. Rhu got out of bed, feeling more and more depressed by the moment. She took an artist's rendering of Cobeth down from the wall. Seeing his face, she wept tears of longing for him. Rhu walked over to her desk. She pulled open a desk drawer, her expression angry. Rhu reached for a piece of folded paper. She opened the paper and read the words printed on it:

Cobeth, you bastard—
We've taken Mab back to the Kaleidicopia. Used your bathrobe. You want it back? Come and get it if you dare. Doogat'll be waiting for you—not to mention the whole house. See you at the Hallows.
Love and kisses,
your ex-housemate,
Timmer

Rhu reread the note several times. As far as she could make out, Timmer, Mab, and Doogat had all been present the night of a Saämbolin drug raid on her house last autumn. Cobeth had made nothing of this at the time; he hadn't wanted the Guild authorities to close the Kaleidicopia on suspicion of drug dealings before he had a chance to get even with the Kaleidicopians—his way. His way entailed dropping a hefty dose of hallucinogenic holovespa into the punch at the Rimble's Revel, which the house sponsored annually. After everyone was thoroughly dosed and flying, *then* he would go get the Guild. But Cobeth's plans had failed that night; Rimble himself had killed the scrawny Jinn actor through the touch of his famous "chaos thumb." So the Guild had never figured out that anyone at the "K" knew Cobeth, much less had ever lived with him.

Rhu would fix that now.

Smiling, Rhu climbed back into bed to wait until sunrise.

Chapter Twelve

THE GUILDMASTER AND his wife, Sirrefene, had been arguing since dawn. Gadorian had waked with the conviction that he should and would close down the Kaleidiscopia Boarding House. He was suddenly certain that this house was the root of all civil unrest in the city. United under one roof, the residents could meet whenever they wished and hatch plots to overthrow his governance in Speakinghast. Worse, the house rested in the Jinnjirri Quarter, a section of the city famous for its politically anarchistic ideas and intemperance. Gadorian had told Sirrefene his decision while he sat up in bed and rubbed the sleep from his eyes. Sirrefene had reacted negatively. Gadorian had been shocked. Astounded at his wife's vehement defense of Janusin, Rowenaster, and the rest of the residents of the "K," Gadorian now sulked in his pillow, the sheets pulled over his head.

Sirrefene wagged a finger at her husband, her wavy, dark tresses tumbling down her back. When she had finished her tirade, she reached to the end table nearest her and picked up a blue ceramic jar of hand cream. She put a dollop of sweet-smelling goo on her dark-skinned hands and rubbed vigorously, her motions angry, her expression stern.

Gadorian grumbled under the blanket, his words muffled.

"What did you say?"

Gadorian threw off the blanket. "I said—I don't know *why* you're sticking up for the residents of that house. What *is* it with the Kaleidicopia, anyway?" he asked the universe-at-large. "Why can't I close it down? I'm the Guildmaster. It's my job to close down houses like that one."

Sirrefene shrugged. "Rimble-Rimble."

Gadorian snorted. "That's *exactly* my point. The 'K' celebrates revels to the Patron of Deviance! It's a cult, that's what it is. We should do a drug raid. *Then* we'll see something, Sirrey. You mark my words."

"Professor Rowenaster would never live in a house that had drugs in it. He's as clean as they come, Gad. You know that."

Gadorian grunted. "Including the new kid from Tammirring, Rowenaster lives with nine other people. Nine other people—three of them Jinn—are liable to do anything."

"Nonsense."

Gadorian glared at his forty-six-year-old wife. She was a beautiful woman, as lithe as he was obese. Scowling, he remembered the affair she had just before they were to be married—with a Jinnjirri! Scowling, he wondered just how deeply her Jinn sympathies went. Mostly, he didn't want to know. He was afraid the truth would destroy their marriage. Thanks to the efforts of the Merry Pricksters last fall, relations between the Saämbolin *draw* and the Jinnjirri *draw* were more than strained; they were potentially explosive. Gadorian no longer frequented any portion of the Jinnjirri Quarter without an armed escort. Politically speaking, he knew it was wise not to trust anyone—not even his wife. This thought hurt. Gadorian winced, and turned away from Sirrefene. The tensions between the Saäm and the Jinn perfectly reflected themselves in his marriage. It angered him that Sirrefene refused to stand by his decision to close the "K." Turning back to Sirrefene, the guildmaster repeated, "Why do you defend the people at the Kaleidicopia?"

"I hate scapegoating, Gad. My family has lived in this city for generations. I've got guildmasters galore on both sides of my family. I know this city. I know how it gets when it gets scared. And right now Speakinghast is scared."

"The whole city? Oh, come *on*—"

Sirrefene nodded, her expression grim. "The weather's

all wrong. It's made everyone's internal rhythm go weird. In a situation like this, people react blindly. But whatever's amiss in Speakinghast, I'll wager many silivrain you won't be able to control it, Gadorian. The changes afoot are bigger than you—"

Regarding his great belly, Gadorian chuckled and said, "Nothing's bigger than me in this city."

"Rimble is."

Gadorian laughed derisively now. "Well, you've certainly got *that* wrong. The one thing I do recall about Greatkin Rimble is that he's uncommonly short."

"That's not the kind of size I meant."

There was a short silence.

Gadorian pursed his lips. Then he said suspiciously, "How come you know so much about Rimble, Sirrey?"

Sirrefene snorted. "Meaning what? You think I'm part of some cult, too? Gadorian—you're so predictable."

"I'm Saämbolin! I'm supposed to be predictable! You're Saämbolin! *You're* supposed to be predictable, too, Sirrefene! What's *wrong* with you?"

Sirrefene lost her temper for the countless time that morning. "How do I know so much about the Greatkin? Because I took Rowen's course. And I passed it, Gadorian. Passed it with high marks."

"Are you saying you think I'm stupid? Because I didn't ?"

"No! And don't change the subject." Master Curator Sirrefene got out of bed. She went to the closet and pulled on a warm, golden-colored bathrobe. It had fur around the neck and cuffs. Her expression now imperious, Sirrefene looked like a queen about to give orders. Whirling on her husband, she snapped, "Twenty some years ago, you screwed up that course, Gadorian. Why? Because you thought I was having an affair—"

"You *were* having an affair! I caught you naked in that Jinn's room!"

"He was an artist! I was his model! He was telling me

where he wanted me to sit! Damn it to Neath! How many times do I have to tell you this? You and your murderous paranoia! I hate you, Gadorian! I hate you!" she repeated, beginning to weep. Struggling to speak, Sirrefene added, "The truth? You blamed me for something *you* were doing—"

"Are you mad? I had no affairs—"

"Liar! You think *I'm* stupid? I knew what kind of man you were when I married you, Gadorian. You have an appetite for a great many things. One of them is women."

"Oh, yeah? Then why did you marry me? Never mind, I know why. Some political convenience of your mother's, no doubt." he said referring to the fact that the previous guildmaster was Sirrefene's mother.

"No!" she shouted. "I married you because I loved you!"

There was a long, painful silence.

"*That* was stupid, Sirrey. No one in your position ever marries for love."

"Well, I did!"

Sirrefene went into the bathroom and slammed the door. Gadorian could hear her sobs. He got up slowly. He went to the solid oak door and knocked on it. "Sirrey, come out, will you?"

"No!"

Gadorian sighed. Leaning against the door, he spoke to Sirrefene from where he stood. "A man has pride, Sirrefene—"

"Fuck your pride! A woman has pride, too!"

Gadorian winced and tried again. "It wasn't seemly for you to be modeling in the nude for a *shift*," said Gadorian, using the pejorative term for a Jinnjirri-born. "You were the guildmaster's daughter. You were consorting with the worst sort of people—intellectuals and artists. It made you look bad. It made your whole family look bad. And because I was your fiancé, it made me look bad, too. You were a hot-head, Sirrey. A libertine by Saäm standards.

Why shouldn't I have thought you cuckolded me? Your mother—"

The door flew open. "Yes, and I expect *she* was the one who told you I was having the affair. Well, she must've told Rowenaster, too. I had lunch with him the other day and he confided he knew about my affair." Sirrefene swore. "It would've been just *like* Mother to conclude something like that. As a child, I was good at climbing out of three-storey windows, you know. And picking the locks on iron gates." Sirrefene blew her nose on a handkerchief she found in her bathrobe pocket. "Why? Because I spent my teen years escaping my home!"

"You were the guildmaster's daughter," repeated Gadorian softly.

"So what? Did that mean I wasn't to live, Gad?" she shouted, crying fresh tears.

"It meant you had a certain standard to uphold. A certain Saämbolin dignity—"

Sirrefene spat on the rug. "I was and *am* a daughter of this city. This *whole* city. That means I care about all the *draws* that live here. it means I honor their gifts. And make use of them for the benefit of Speakinghast. That's why I commissioned Master Janusin to do those statues of the Greatkin. Because Janusin is the best. Not because I love the Kaleidicopia. You're just like Mother, Gadorian. You believe in partisan politics. Those days are *over*, Gadorian! Over! This is the Jinnaeon! If *you* consorted with someone other than your own *draw*, you'd know the Tammirring prophesies about this time period." She glared at her husband. "You're lucky you have me, Gadorian. You're lucky you have someone to keep you informed!"

Gadorian pursed his lips. This conversation wasn't going the way he had planned. Running his fingers through his thinning hair, the guildmaster asked, "What prophesies?"

"Ask Rowen. He'll tell you."

"He's not speaking to me."

"I'm not surprised."

* * *

Professor Rowenaster stepped outside his classroom as the noon bell tolled for lunch. The hallways flooded with university students, all of them talking or laughing. As the professor made his way down the crowded stairs, he saw Guildmaster Gadorian cut through the throng. It appeared the Saämbolin official wished to speak to him. Rowen sighed with displeasure. He was supposed to meet Janusin for lunch. After Gadorian's outrageous display of *landdraw* bigotry in his class recently, Rowenaster had little interest in inviting Gadorian to join him and a *shift* for a noonday meal. Rowenaster waited for Gadorian to catch up to him, and smiled as pleasantly as he could manage when Gadorian bid him good day.

"Good day to you as well," said the professor.

"What're you doing for lunch?"

"I'm eating it with Master Janusin."

Gadorian hesitated. "Mind if I join you?"

"You want the truth?"

"I see." Gadorian stuffed his hands in the pockets of his orange velvet robe. "Say, I'm sorry for what I said in class yesterday. I was out of line. I'm just the guildmaster. I've no say in what goes on at Speakinghast University." He smiled weakly. "Separate but equal, you know."

Rowenaster raised an eyebrow. "What happened, Gad? Did Sirrey tell you to keep your nose out of her territory?" he asked. Master Curator Sirrefene was the official head of the University of Speakinghast as well as the Great Library grounds. Rowen paused. "I had an interesting lunch with her the other day. Did she tell you about it?"

"Yes."

"Seems I've been holding a gross misconception about your wife. And to think I took pity on you, Gadorian— letting you pass my course because I felt sorry for your poor nerves. Newly engaged and already Sirrey was unfaithful? Wasn't that what you told me?" Rowenaster studied the guildmaster's averted face. "You know, we don't have a statute of limitations at the university. I could pull your old records. Make you take that course again. It was mandatory then to graduate. It still is. Can't be guildmaster, Gadorian, without that prized Saämbolin degree."

There was dead silence.

"Are you threatening me?" asked Gadorian, his voice disbelieving.

"Throw me out of my house, Gad, and I'd have to go through a lot of boxes. To decide what I'd be taking with me, you understand. I might come across some old correspondence. Seems to me I recall you swearing that Sirrefene had slept with a Jinn artist—"

"At that time, I thought she *had*!" yelled Gadorian.

Students' heads turned in their direction.

Gadorian bit his lip and lowered his voice. "What I wrote you, I believed. Sirrefene's mother told me—"

"What you wanted to hear? What you wanted to believe?" Rowen shook his head. "And to think I listened to you. And gossiped about it to Barlimo last fall! Sirrey says you never asked for *her* version. Much less the artist's."

Gadorian rolled his eyes. "I didn't have to ask the *shift*. Sirrey's a beautiful woman. We all know beautiful women aren't faithful. How can they be? They have men after them day and night—"

Rowenaster stared at Gadorian. "You don't deserve Sirrefene."

There was a long pause.

Gadorian knew he possessed more political clout in the city than Rowenaster. If Rowen chose to threaten him with regard to a twenty-year-old grade point, Gadorian would return the threat by draining certain funds out of the university financial office. Fair was fair, thought Gadorian. He suspected Rowenaster was bluffing, and indeed, Rowenaster was.

Rowenaster thumbed through the stack of papers in his

arms. "What did you want to see me about, Gadorian? I'm a very busy man—"

"Nothing," snapped the guildmaster, suddenly deciding not to ask the professor to tell him about the Tammirring prophecies. He was mad now. Mad at the world. At that moment, Rhu walked up. She handed Gadorian the note Timmer had written Cobeth last fall just before the drug raid at Rhu's house. She had written the note at Zendrak's request. If Zendrak had thought it through that fateful night, he would never have told Timmer to write it; however, he was hung over from a rich meal he had shared with the Greatkin of Love at the time, and so was thinking fuzzily. Now Rhu presented all the evidence Gadorian needed to shut down the Kaleidicopia. It didn't matter if the evidence was shaky or not; at this point, Gadorian only needed an excuse. Gadorian took the note roughly, hating Rhu for being Jinnjirri.

"I thought you might want to see this," she said calmly.

Timmer's handwriting was distinctive. Catching sight of it out of the corner of his eye, Rowenaster felt goose bumps crawl along his spine. "What is it?" he asked Rhu, speaking as amiably as possible.

Rhu smiled coldly at the Kaleidicopian.

Gadorian turned to Rowenaster. "Cobeth was a *house-mate* of yours?"

Rowenaster cleared his throat, but said nothing.

Outside in the city streets, Akindo crossed the university campus. He turned at the campanile. He was now heading for the Jinnjirri Quarter of the city. In half an hour, Akindo would reach the Kaleidicopia.

Chapter Thirteen

ALTHOUGH IT WAS now well past noon, Zendrak and Kelandris had only just returned to the Kaleidicopia after Kel's injudicious attempt to ride to Suxonli Village late last night. The two Greatkin had been so tired that instead of asking Further to deposit them speedily back at the "K's" front door—where they would no doubt run into half the house still drinking cocoa in the kitchen—Zendrak and Kel had decided to spend the night at a Saämbolin inn on the outskirts of Speakinghast. At four bell-morn, the two Greatkin had finally fallen asleep in each other's arms, both too exhausted to consider the possibility of making love. At dawn, they made their way back to the city with Further's help, thus avoiding any questions by disgruntled Saämbolin gate guards. Such as, "How did you leave the city without a proper pass?"

Famished, the two Greatkin rummaged in Barlimo's well-stocked kitchen for lunch. Finding cheese, bread, wine, and apples, Kelandris washed the fruit while Zendrak cut the bread. As Kelandris handed Zendrak a clean plate, Mab entered the kitchen.

"Give me one, too," said the little Piedmerri, extending her hand to Kelandris. "I've got to eat and run. Classes, you know."

Mab was a straight-A student at Speakinghast University. Nineteen and plump, Mab was Piedmerri through and through. Naturally interested in children, she intended to teach elementary grades when she graduated. The billowing tunic she wore hid her ample bosom and lap. Plopping down beside Zendrak—who smiled at her—she eyed the sweet cheese under his knife.

"Want some?"

Mab beamed at him and held out her plate.

"Bread?" asked Kelandris, handing her two slices.

Mab grinned and began buttering them lavishly. "What a morning," she said conversationally. "Everything that could've gone wrong did. And wasn't Rowen in a poor mood! He snapped at everybody in class this morning. Then I lost my term paper in the wind. Presence, it's cold! Anyway, after that all happened, the happincabby I hailed took me the long way around. Wasn't watching out the window. I've this test tomorrow so I was reading. Guess the stupid Saäm driver thought I was from out of town or something. He charged me for his thievery. Couldn't talk him out of it. That was my book money, too," she added with a woeful sigh.

Zendrak grinned. Mab's fondness for penny romances was well known at the "K." Offering Mab half an apple, he asked, "I assume you slept through all the excitement last night?"

"Like a log. You know me, Zendrak. Nothing wakes me up. Well, except earthquakes and Jinnjirri arguing outside my door. That *always* wakes me up," she added, rolling her eyes. "Left over from childhood, I guess. Raw nerves. Wish I weren't so weird."

"No one in this house is normal, Mab," said Zendrak reassuringly. "The fact that you grew up in the northwest border of Jinnjirri—"

"And survived it," laughed Kelandris.

"—is to your credit," continued Zendrak, He referred to the fact that placid, stable Piedmerri liked the ground stationary under their wide feet. The northwest border of Jinnjirri was particularly earthquake-prone. After her birth in Piedmerri, Mab had spent the eighteen years of her life in this treacherous corner of the world. Both of her parents were Jinnjirri. They had been vacationing in Piedmerri when Mab's mother "caught."

Mab shrugged. "I suppose. Still, I wish I could've grown up in Piedmerri."

"What, and miss the opportunity of coming here?" said Zendrak.

"What do you mean?" asked Mab, her mouth full of bread and cheese.

"If you'd been raised in Piedmerri, you would've been too wholesome for the rest of us at the Kaleidicopia," said Kelandris, pulling up a chair and sitting down in it. "I'd have thrown you out personally."

Mab scowled at the tall Greatkin. "Considering *I* got here before you did, Kel, I'd have had seniority over anything *you* wanted—

Kelandris stiffened, clearly ready to argue the point. Zendrak put up his hands in a placating gesture. "Dear ones—please. Can we eat in peace?"

So they did.

As each person was finishing his or her last bite, Kelandris suddenly jumped to her feet, her eyes wide with fear. Holding her hands open in front of her, she shut her green eyes and reached with her Tammirring-born senses to find what threatened her. Zendrak watched his sister with interest.

"What's wrong, Kel?" he said softly.

"I don't know. Something. I've felt it before. Reminds me of Suxonli." Kelandris backed up, her hands pressing against both ears. "Something's outside the house, Zendrak. I can hear it breathing."

Before Kelandris could stop Zendrak, he was on his feet, running to the front door of the Kaleidicopia. Kelandris called after him to stop. He ignored her pleas. Stepping outside the large house, Zendrak was the first of Rimble's Nine to be stung by one of Elder Hennin's poisoned holovespa wasps. Zendrak flung the wasp away with anger in much the same way Aunt had done. Zendrak was

Rimble's own child—the son of the Old Yellow Jacket himself—so he expected no ill effects from the wasp. Still, it perplexed him why he had been stung. Walking over to where he had cast the wasp, he was amazed to find it still alive. Although he hadn't meant to throw the wasp away from him with such force, the surprise of the sting had caused him to react without thinking. Kneeling by the yellow jacket, he spoke to the wasp in its own tongue, apologizing for hitting it.

The wasp responded by hurling itself at Zendrak for another go at him. This time Zendrak was ready for the wasp. Using the brunt of his coat arm, he smacked the wasp against the front entrance to the Kaleidicopia. Its guts exploded on the fuchsia-colored door. The wasp died promptly. Zendrak scraped the insect off the door and crushed the remains under his green boot.

"Why did you do that?" asked Kelandris, horrified to see him kill one of the symbolic representatives of Trickster. In Suxonli all wasps and hornets were revered as message bearers from Rimble and therefore from the Presence.

Zendrak shook his head. "I'm not sure."

"What do you mean?" asked Mab nervously, standing on the doorsill behind Zendrak.

"I'm not sure," he repeated, touching the part of his neck where the wasp had stung him. "It was drunk," he added.

"Drunk?" said Kelandris.

"Drunk. It sounded drunk. I spoke to it. Something—oh, I don't know. It probably means nothing. Why bother going on about it?" he added angrily, and started back into the house.

Kelandris frowned. As she turned to follow him, the holovespa wasp meant for her flew toward her with unusual speed. Before it could reach her, however, a lone univer-'silsila wasp intercepted it. Both wasps stung each other to death. Seeing this, Kelandris pushed Mab inside the safety of the Kaleidicopia and slammed the door.

"You don't have to be so rough—" began Mab plaintively.

"Shut up, Mab," snapped Kelandris. Before the little Piedmerri could retort, Kelandris left the hallway in search of Zendrak. Kelandris found him in their bedroom.

He was dying.

Panthe'kinarok Interlogue

GREATKIN PHEBENE TOOK off her garland of green roses and threw it like a weapon at Greatkin Mattermat, who sat across the table from her at the Panthe'kinarok. He was munching complacently on a breadstick. The garland, briars and all, hit Mattermat square on the forehead and made him bleed. Mattermat was so surprised by this act of hostility from his sweet and gentle sister that he was speechless. So was everyone else at that table.

"What was that for?" asked Jinndaven in a whisper to Phebene.

Phebene answered Jinndaven shrilly, her voice audible to all. "He's killing Zendrak! The bastard is killing Zendrak! I'll have you to know, Mattie, the love interest in the story is *my* department! You're on shaky ground, buster! Make no mistake about it!"

Mattermat chuckled, using the half-eaten breadstick in his right hand like a pointer from a classroom as he spoke to Phebene. "I can't possibly be on shaky ground, Pehbene. I *am* the ground, and I'm *not* shaking."

"Well, you will be!" countered the Greatkin of Tender Trysts and Great Loves. "You *will* be! You think Rimble is a handful when he's mad? You haven't seen anything until you've seen the agony of love denied. It can move mountains—without *your* permission!" added Phebene furiously.

Mattermat yawned and continued eating his breadstick.

Phebene turned to Jinndaven. "Where are Troth and Rimble?"

"In the kitchen. Or in Milwaukee. Maybe both."

"See you," she said, standing up.

"Where are you going?"

"To find the Greatkin of the impossible possibility: Rimble. After that, I'll visit Neath. Troth and me go back a long ways. I'll fix you, Mattermat, I will!"

Before Phebene could dematerialize, however, Greatkin Themyth interrupted, her voice commanding. "Phebene! Come to my side this instant!"

Hearing this, Mattermat began to laugh. "She'll tie your hands for sure, Phebes. Civilization always does when it comes to love."

"Rimble is the Patron of Exceptions. And *he's* Zendrak's father. So I've nothing to worry about," snapped Phebene, leaving her seat and going to stand beside Themyth.

The Greatkin of Civilization motioned Phebene to come closer. Phebene did so. Whispering in her right ear, Themyth grinned and said, "Whatever Rimble decides— count me in. Oh, and take Jinndaven with you, hmmm? He could use the exercise."

And this was how Love and Imagination came to Milwaukee in the 1980s.

Chapter Fourteen

TRICKSTER AND THE Obstinate Woman were still at the Downer Cafe when Jinndaven and Phebene arrived. At present, Rimble was doing his best to reassure the restaurant manager that he'd only been trying to illustrate a point by ordering Benedict Oscar in the middle of the afternoon. So far, the manager remained unconvinced. The fellow was just on the verge of asking Rimble to leave the cafe when Phebene sidled up to the manager and reminded the poor man that he had forgotten to buy his wife an anniversary present. In actual fact, the manager's anniversary wasn't until next week, but momentary confusion had its uses. The thin little man's face turned ashen. Without further comment to Trickster—who looked visibly relieved—the cafe manager hurried away, intending to use the office phone downstairs.

Grinning at Love and Imagination, Trickster said, "Just in the nick of time, kiddos. Just in the nick of time. These third-generation types have *no* sense of humor. I prefer the natives."

"Now you're really in trouble, Rimble," said the Obstinate Woman. "You think anybody's going to want to read about you when you say things like that? Milwaukee is a very fine, old city. Lots of third-generation folks settled around this lake. You better apologize."

Trickster rolled his eyes. "Okay, so like I'm *sorrrry.* Okay?"

The Obstinate Woman took a deep breath of exasperation. Turning now to the two Greatkin standing on either side of Rimble, she asked, "Who are these people?"

"Phebene and Jinndaven." Rimble wagged a finger in the face of the Obstinate Woman. "You should know that. *You* wrote about them—"

"Where's her garland? And where are his silver slippers?"

"I threw my garland in Mattermat's face and Jim lost his slippers in the Everywhen," replied Phebene. "We thought we'd try for something a little more contemporary," she added, pointing to her wide-brimmed pink hat and the Birkenstock sandals on Jinndaven's feet. "Sorry we made it hard for you to recognize us."

Rimble interrupted her. "You threw your garland in Mattie's face?" Trickster cackled with glee. "Oooh, I would've liked to see that."

"It was a good throw," reported Jinndaven. "Hit him square in the forehead."

The Obstinate Woman groaned. "Oh, great. Can't wait 'til *that* translates here. I can just imagine what the New Age community will do with it. Probably package 'Third-eye Busters.'"

Jinndaven considered the possibility. "She may be right."

"I *wish* you guys would be more careful at that dinner of yours," the Obstinate Woman complained. "Mortals have it tough enough as it is."

Phebene winced. "We'll try, dear."

Rimble scanned the tables around the cafe. All of them were full with talkative and fashionable East Siders. "Can't sit here. This table's for two. Let's pay the bill before the manager remembers I'm still here, shall we? We can all go back to *her* house," he added, nodding at the Obstinate Woman.

"We can?" she asked, trying not to imagine what might happen if she took them into the boarding house where she lived. Like the Kaleidicopia, her home was a trifle on the peculiar side. Many of the members of the household belonged to the Society for Creative Anachronism. They often wore swords and capes. What would the three Greatkin think? What if the Greatkin thought the swords were real? Somebody could get seriously misunderstood, if not hurt.

Reading her mind, Jinndaven nodded. "Anything's possible with Rimble here. Anything at all."

Thinking quickly, the Obstinate Woman suggested they visit Lake Michigan instead. "We can sit on the rocks and bake," she added.

"Bake?" asked Phebene. "Why would we want to do that?"

Rimble's eyes widened. "My roast!" he yelled. Before anyone could stop him, Rimble returned to Eranossa's kitchen to salvage his forgotten entree for the Panthe'kinarok.

Phebene bit her lower lip. "I didn't even have time to tell him his son was dying."

"I think he knows," said Jinndaven. "The kitchen's full of real smoke this time," he added, pointing to the gray clouds now billowing out of the kitchen at the Downer Cafe. Restaurant personnel hurried their customers into the street. Fire engines screamed as they approached the burning building.

The Obstinate Woman regarded Phebene and Jinndaven earnestly. "Zendrak *is* going to live, isn't he? I mean, what about Kelandris? She'll go after Hennin if he dies. And then where will you be? A story without a love interest will get shelved, guys. Love is 'in' in New York."

Phebene nodded, watching smoke pour out of the Downer Cafe. "Time to visit Neath, Jinn. Come on."

"Good luck," said the Obstinate Woman. "Let me know what happens, will you? Otherwise, I won't know what to put in the sequel."

Jinndaven smiled raggedly and shivered. "Won't be much, I can assure you. Neath chills me." Turning to Phebene, Jinndaven added, "Why Themyth thought *I* should accompany you is beyond my understanding. That

Rimble. This is all his fault. When we get back—"
Jinndaven's monologue broke off as he and Phebene dematerialized in broad daylight in Milwaukee.

A jogger in pink running shoes, a pair of shorts that barely covered her, and a T-shirt with the words "Udderly Cool" strategically placed over her breasts, shrieked. And fainted.

People said it must've been the ninety-four-degree heat.

The Obstinate Woman knew better.

Chapter Fifteen

POISONED BY ELDER Hennin's holovespa, Zendrak rapidly slipped into physical and emotional shock. Of the two, the latter was the worse. Zendrak had been alive for more than five hundred years, his Soaringsea *landdraw* and Greatkin inheritance blessing him with an unusually long life span. It was the Mythrrim in him, however, that made him mortal enough to die. Even though he knew he was mortal, the reality of this fact had never before confronted him with such finality. Zendrak swallowed thickly, his breathing irregular. He tried to smile at Kelandris, who was seated near him, her expression one of growing horror. Zendrak shut his dark eyes. A wave of despair hit him. And again.

"All for nothing," he whispered.

"What?"

Zendrak tried to speak again but found the effort too taxing. He closed his lips and attempted to reach Rimble with his mind. He was met with silence. Zendrak tried again. Rimble still failed to respond. Feeling angry and abandoned, Zendrak's despair deepened. Reflecting on his life, he felt dissatisfied with it. He had worked for Trickster for five centuries, acting the role of Rimble's emissary, subordinating his personal needs so that he might better serve the world of Mnemlith.

Zendrak opened his eyes with difficulty, his gaze resting on Kel's unveiled and anxious face. Seeing Zendrak looking at her, she reached over and stroked his black hair. Tears sprang to her eyes. In silence she took Zendrak's hand and clasped it to her heart. Zendrak felt a devastating pain in his own heart, her feelings reflected in his.

"Elder Hennin," he whispered.

"I'll kill her."

"Get the Mayanabi to help you. Don't try it alone. Clear?"

Kelandris nodded.

Zendrak swallowed with difficulty. His body felt bloated and distant. "Ask Po. Contact Himayat. Depend on Po, okay?"

"Okay."

Zendrak stopped speaking. His feet felt as though they were asleep. He stared at the ceiling. *I'm dying*, he thought. Rage at his fate burned in his throat. He grit his teeth, trying to hold on to life. The poison claimed more and more of his body with each passing moment. Turning his head so he could look at Kelandris one last time, he whispered, "You know I love you, don't you?"

Kelandris nodded, tears streaming from her eyes. A sob escaped her. "How can this be? How can you be dying?"

"Mattermat," replied Zendrak. "He's winning."

Kelandris made a fist. "I'll fight him, Zendrak. If I have to go to Neath itself and wrestle Death to the ground, Mattermat won't win."

"Everyone dies—" began Zendrak.

"Don't give in! Can't you understand? You have to fight Mattermat! He's the Patron of Inertia. He wants you to think like this. He wants you to give up hope. And you mustn't. You mustn't."

"This is death, sweetheart. You have to face—"

"No!" she yelled at Zendrak. "It's Death who'll have to face me!"

And so, as he had lived, Zendrak died arguing with Kelandris. Kelandris felt life leave Zendrak through the hand she held. One moment Zendrak was touching her, his fingers strong, and the next he was not, his fingers limp. It happened so fast, it was hard to believe he was dead. Yet, he undeniably was—his dark eyes open, his chest motionless. With a small cry of despair, Kelandris stood up. She fell over the chair she had been sitting in and scrambled awkwardly to her feet. Yafatah heard the commotion and came running into the room. Seeing that Zendrak was dead, the young girl put her hand to her mouth. Tears filled her eyes. Kelandris knelt beside her.

"I'm going to Neath."

"What for?" asked Yafatah through her tears.

"To bring Zendrak back from the dead."

"Can—can you *do* that?"

"Don't know," she admitted. "But I'm going to try."

Someone knocked on the door. It was Barlimo. When she saw Zendrak, her hair turned dark blue. She said nothing, her expression sad.

"Kel's going to Neath," said Yafatah confidently. "She be going to bring Zendrak back from the dead."

Barlimo touched Yafatah's cheek. "Sure, she will, honey." Glancing at Kelandris as though she thought the Greatkin was crazy, she told Yafatah to join her downstairs. "Kelandris might need some alone time with Zendrak."

Kelandris snorted. "Zendrak's not *here*. He's dead."

"I'm glad you realize that," remarked Barlimo drily. "Come on, Ya."

Kelandris put her hand on Yafatah's arm. "You think I've lied to the child, don't you? You think I'm giving her hope when I should be giving her reality?"

"That's right," said Barlimo coolly.

"You don't believe that I can bring Zendrak back?"

"Nope. Dead is dead, Kelandris. Everyone has a time for this—even the Greatkin."

Kelandris bit her lower lip, her hands clenched with anger. Truth to tell, she wasn't sure if she could bring Zendrak back or not. She had never been to Neath before. She assumed there were rules for death and dying. She had never met Troth, the Greatkin of Death—nor did she relish the prospect. Zendrak had once described him to her as "a stern bastard."

"Well, I'll prove you wrong, then," said Kelandris boldly.

"Do what you like, Kel," said Barlimo, her voice tired.
"You never listen to me, anyway. Why start now?"

Kelandris raised her hand about to strike Barlimo. Yafatah stepped between the Jinnjirri and the Greatkin. "Zendrak be barely dead. Me ma says we must be respectful of
the dead—please. Please doon't fight."

Kelandris lowered her hand, her green eyes furious.

Barlimo stood her ground, her arm around Yafatah
protectively.

Yafatah looked up at Kelandris. "I do believe you,
Kelandris. I do believe you'll bring him back."

"Hush, child," said Barlimo.

Kelandris pulled her veil over her head. When she spoke
again, the soft black material fluttered with her breath. "I
promise you this, Ya. I'll bring him back physically or in
spirit. But I will bring him back."

As Kelandris walked out of her bedroom, she passed
Janusin standing in the hall. Clearly he had been eavesdrop-
ping, his hair a frosted sad blue.

"Well, now you know everything," she snapped at him.

"Kel, I'm so sorry Zendrak is—"

"Shut up. Just shut up."

Running into an open field near the public stables,
Trickster's daughter called Further. The blue-black mare
answered instantly, her wild heart alive with Kel's passion
and the news of Zendrak's death. Kelandris jumped on
Further's broad back. Wheeling, the mare jumped the lines
of coincidence. Horse and rider shimmered. Sparks flew,
hoof against stone. There was a whooshing sound, a
crushing cold, and finally utter silence. They had entered
the Everywhen of the Presence. Soon they would be at the
tall black gates of the underworld. Here souls roamed
compassionate corridors and waited for their next incarna-
tion. Further slowed, barely winded by the journey. Kelandris dismounted. Turning around to face the gates of Neath,
Kelandris came to an abrupt stop. Heart beating wildly, her

hands grew cold with fear. She could not believe what she saw.

It was Cobeth come to greet her.

Just dead these past three months, it seemed Cobeth had been put through a strict examination of conscience during his stay in Neath. Gone were Cobeth's smug smile and overwhelming arrogance. In fact, *this* Cobeth looked like the brother Kelandris had once loved as a young child. Kelandris peered at the Jinnjirri shade thoughtfully. It was Cobeth who broke the silence.

"Hello."

"Hello."

"Troth sent me to meet you."

"Nice of him."

Cobeth shrugged. "He thought you might want to see me again."

"Actually, I'd rather see Zendrak," Kelandris said coldly.

Cobeth stuffed his hands in his black tunic. "He's with Troth. So's Phebene, Jinndaven, and Rimble. They said I was to escort you to Troth's place. You willing to come, or not?"

"Maybe I could find my own way."

"Not likely. Neath's a labyrinth."

"Oh."

There was an uncomfortable silence.

Cobeth cleared his throat. "Kel?"

"What?"

"I'm sorry for what happened in Suxonli. Giving you the drugs and all."

"*And* ratting on me to Elder Hennin!" Kelandris snapped.

"Oh, yeah. Forgot about that part." He smiled sheepishly. "I was really mad you got to turn at the revel instead of me. Finding your bloody underwear—I knew you'd broken the Blood Day Rule. Danced on your menses. It was too good an opportunity to miss. For getting even, I mean.

Hennin was always comparing me to you, and finding me wanting. She knew you were a Greatkin. Wish I had known, too."

"Would you have acted differently?" asked Kelandris, her voice skeptical.

"Probably not," he admitted. "Hennin had me going, see. All I wanted was to have her think I was as good as you. Impossible, of course. Made me crazy. Made me want to kill you and your blasted inspiration."

"Yeah. I remember that part," replied Kel drily.

There was another long silence.

"So are you going to forgive me, or what?" asked Cobeth.

"Don't see why I should."

Cobeth shrugged. "It would be nice if you did."

Kelandris rolled her eyes. "Having trouble sleeping, are you?"

"Ghosts don't sleep much. Don't need to."

"I suppose."

Cobeth sighed. "Come on, Kel. We *used* to be friends."

"When you were Yonneth. Not Cobeth."

Cobeth nodded. "So call me Yonneth again. We can start over maybe."

"You're dead, Yonneth. I think that changes things."

"I guess I was a pretty rotten person." Yonneth brightened. "Maybe I could be a good ghost."

Kelandris swore several times. "Look, Yon," she said, her voice as impatient as it used to be when she was Yonneth's sister in Suxonli. "I came here to find Troth. I came here to fight Mattermat. I came here to save Zendrak. In short, I came here to *do* something. I did *not* come here to chat with *you*."

Cobeth said nothing for a few minutes. When he spoke again, his voice took on more authority. In fact, Cobeth's voice changed so dramatically that Kelandris stared at the Jinnjirri shade, wondering if he really was Cobeth after all.

"Say that again," said Kelandris.

Cobeth shrugged. "I said—don't you know every under-world has a guardian whose test you have to pass?"

"Meaning what?"

Cobeth's form shimmered. Then it shifted and darkened. In front of her stood Troth, the Greatkin of Death.

"You aren't Cobeth," she mumbled.

"No."

"Why did you trick me?"

"To see you."

Kelandris frowned. "And what do you see?"

"Resentment."

"So?" asked Kelandris, her expression indignant. "I've every right to feel resentful toward Cobeth. He ruined my life. He tried to *kill* me."

Troth shook his head sadly. "How can you hope to find love with resentment in your heart? As Cobeth I would've guided you to Phebene—and to Zendrak. But you refused to forgive. So now you get no guide. Good luck," he added, and disappeared. Literally.

Kelandris stood speechless in the shadows of Neath. Angry, she kicked a stone. And stubbed her toe. She sat down on a large rock, her head in her hands. She felt stupid. Here she was in Neath to fight for Zendrak's life and she couldn't even get past the front gate. She thought over all the things that Troth had said to her as Cobeth. She sighed ruefully. Troth was quite right. She hadn't forgiven Cobeth for his actions in Suxonli. Worse, she didn't *feel* like forgiving him, either. As far as she was concerned, the little bastard could rot in Neath's darkest pit. That's what he deserves, Kelandris thought.

The darkness surrounding Kelandris became so thick, it was palpable. She stumbled around in it for a while. Unable to find her way at all, she squatted against the front gate of Neath, her fists clasped to her stomach. She was afraid, and it was all she could do to admit it, much less find a way to corner it. Mist and strange blue lights advanced toward her. Seeing both phenomena, Kelandris shrieked and flattened against the gate. After a few moments of terror, Kelandris summoned the most honest part of herself.

"I'm leaving," she said brokenly. Turning to the dark maw of Neath, she added, "Zendrak, I don't know how to do this. I don't know how to find you. And I can't just forgive Cobeth. It would be nice if I could. But I'm not always very nice." Kelandris bowed her head, tears slipping down her cheeks. Now she faced the reality of returning to the world without a hope of ever seeing Zendrak again. The impact of his absence hit her hard. Turning away from Neath, Kelandris called Further.

The mare didn't respond.

"Oh, wonderful," muttered the distraught Greatkin. "Marooned as well, I expect."

"Maybe not," said a friendly voice behind Kelandris. She whirled around, this time drawing the knife she kept hidden in her right sleeve. Aunt—or someone who looked a whole lot like the Jinnjirri healer—smiled at Kelandris and added, "It really is me, Kel. No tricks this time."

"What do you want?" asked Kelandris suspiciously, studying the colorful attire of Aunt. The brightness of the Jinnjirri's clothing stood in sharp contrast to the dark shadows of Neath. "Are you dead?"

"Quite dead. Hennin got me. Fasilla's on her way to the Kaleidicopia to warn everyone."

Kelandris shook her head. "Hennin's wasps are already there—"

"Then we must act quickly."

Kelandris shrugged. "Can't. I failed Troth's test. He won't let me past the front gate. Wasn't forgiving enough, you know."

Aunt stepped closer to Kelandris, lowering her voice as she did so. "If you ask me, Death's a bit of a bastard. Thinks he owns Neath. Runs it like a little king." Aunt smiled. "So you failed his test. Well, you haven't failed mine."

Kelandris raised her eyebrows. "When did you test me?"

"I haven't given it to you yet. Feeling brave? No? It's okay. I used to test people in all sorts of states when I was a Mayanabi Nomad. Relax. This will be fun."

After the ordeal of getting through the front gate of Neath was over, Kelandris told Aunt privately that "fun" was not exactly the word she would've used to describe Aunt's test.

"Well, I didn't want to *scare* you, Kel," replied Aunt indignantly.

Chapter Sixteen

AKINDO WAS STILL lurking outside the Kaleidicopia when Fasilla arrived. At the last moment, Himayat had decided to accompany her to the house. He and the other Mayanabi Nomads at the Inn of the Guest had met in council until the wee hours of the morning. After much discussion and debate, everyone present concluded that Aunt's death had not been accidental. No one quite knew what to make of the lack of winterblooms in the Feyborne Mountains. Himayat decided to ride to the "K" and ask the only First Rank Mayanabi master in existence, Zendrak of Soaringsea. Surely, *he* would know what the others did not.

As Fasilla and Himayat came within half a block of Wise Whatsit Avenue, Himayat reined his Appaloosa to an abrupt stop. Motioning Fasilla to be quiet, the Mayanabi scanned the area with his Mayanabi senses. He couldn't interpret what he received. Shaking his head, the Asilliwir man said, "I don't understand it. I keep getting images of Tammirring landscape. This is Speakinghast, a Saämbolin city." Himayat tried again. "Well, whatever it is," he muttered, "something is dreadfully wrong around here. I suggest we arm ourselves," he added, reaching for a blowgun and pack of lethal darts. The blowguns were called akatikkis.

Fasilla removed hers, studying the busy streets carefully. Livestock ambled down an alley. As the sheep reached the corner of Wise Whatsit Avenue, they began to act in an agitated manner. The shepherd eventually lost control of the nervous animals, his sheepdogs bolting along with the sheep.

"Odd," said Fasilla under her breath.

Himayat suddenly whipped his head around. "We're being watched, Fasilla. We need to get rid of these horses. I don't like being in the open like this. Come on," he said hastily.

The two Asilliwir put away their blowguns and rode their mounts to a nearby public stable. They paid overnight charges, and hailed a happincabby. This was a carriage drawn by horse and driven—for the most part—by Saämbolin drivers. Before the man turned the happincabby on Wise Whatsit Avenue, Himayat told him to stop the horse. Giving the fellow a handful of coppers, Himayat and Fasilla jumped out and walked the rest of the way to the Kaleidicopia.

Every sense alert and armed once more, Himayat kept strict silence as he walked toward the three-storey monstrosity known as the "K." Peering upward at the gables, the tricolored roof, and the asymmetrical additions, he winced. "Very Jinn," he said.

"Think we should go in?" asked Fasilla.

Himayat frowned. "Someone has died."

Instantly thinking of Yafatah, Fasilla's face paled. Without considering her own safety, she tore across the street toward the Kaleidicopia. As she reached the lowest end of the front steps, Akindo loosed another holovespa wasp. As before in Kel's case, the holovespa was intercepted by the new breed of wasp from the south, the univer'silsila. Akindo loosed another holovespa, and another, and another. Soon the sky was buzzing with the furious creatures. They were met by more univer'silsila. The two swarms ripped into each other. Fasilla could not reach the top of the stairs leading to the Kaleidicopia. The sound of the wasps increased. Himayat pulled Fasilla away from the wasp swarm. Neither was stung.

The front door of the Kaleidicopia flew open. It was Yafatah. The holovespa fell on her, stinging the child venomously. She screamed, fighting off the attacking insects with her hands. Reaching blindly for the door, Yafatah threw off the last of the holovespa and stumbled into the safety of the Kaleidicopia. The door of the "K" slammed shut.

Unlike last time she was stung, Yafatah did not react to the stings of the holovespa wasps. Barlimo was surprised by this and said so. The rest of the house members gathered around Yafatah.

Examining Yafatah's head, Podiddley remarked, "Maybe they saved her life."

"What?" asked Barlimo.

"Immunized her," explained Po, reexamining Yafatah's stings. Each sting was red and had what healers called a local swelling. "But how would they know to do that? And why do it to Yafatah?"

No one had an answer for this.

Outside in the street, Akindo shuffled and drooled. Hundreds of dead holovespa wasps crunched under his feet. A battle had been waged. The holovespa wasps had lost, and at Eranossa, Greatkin Mattermat was no longer laughing at Rimble and his burnt roast. Why?

Because Rimble had salvaged it; the next generation of Rimble's own, represented by Yafatah, would now survive the Jinnaeon. Yafatah was immune to the despair of her Age.

Chapter Seventeen

KELANDRIS FOLLOWED AUNT in silence. The Jinnjirri shade walked effortlessly over the rough terrain of dark Neath. Watching Aunt negotiate a particularly steep incline with ease, Kelandris began to feel as though Aunt might prove to be a reliable guide in the "test" to come. Kelandris rolled her eyes. When *she* took *her* place at the Panthe'kinarok table, Kelandris decided she would propose the outlawing of Greatkin tests. They offended her sense of fair play. Kelandris sighed. Nevertheless, her rather strong feelings on the subject were not going to get her out of the ordeal ahead of her. Although Aunt had said the test to get into Neath would be fun, Kelandris suspected it would be anything but. After all, this was Neath. Nightmares came from Neath.

Aunt led Kelandris down a rocky ravine. As they reached a tiny rivulet at the ravine's bottom, Kelandris said, "I thought Troth said Neath was made up of corridors. Not open places."

"You're not in Neath proper yet, Kelandris. When you get inside, you'll see the corridors."

Kelandris stopped. "Then where are we going?"

"To the River of Memory."

"What are we going to do there?"

"Who knows?" said Aunt cryptically.

Kelandris swore, but continued to follow Aunt along the bank of the rivulet. In time, she heard a roaring sound. Probably waterfalls, she decided. And indeed they were. As Kelandris and Aunt slipped through a narrow place in the ravine, they came face-to-face with a thundering dark waterfall that was lit from within by blue-black light. The spray of the water dampened Kel's hair. The falls themselves were comparatively low—perhaps no more than ten feet in height. Kelandris frowned. How could such low falls make so much noise? She asked Aunt.

"When souls fall over the edge, they fall a great distance—morally speaking. Hence the sound."

"When *what* souls fall over—"

"Watch," directed Aunt, her voice crisp. The Jinnjirri healer pointed toward something bobbing up and down in the swiftly moving water. Squinting, Kelandris suddenly realized she was watching someone's head bobbing in the water. The man fell over the edge, his body lifeless. When he hit the pool below, he sank and did not rise.

"What happened?" asked Kelandris, wondering if she should dive in after him. Aunt held her back.

"That soul's future is of no concern to you."

"Maybe. Maybe not," snapped Kelandris. "I'm not going to stand on this bank and quibble over my responsibility or lack of it while someone drowns." She pulled away from Aunt.

"Stop!" commanded Aunt with such force that Kelandris came to a dead halt. Aunt pointed again to the waterfall. Another head bobbed up and down. This time it was a woman. She flailed helplessly and fell over the edge as the man before had done. Unlike her predecessor, the woman did not sink. She continued to float downstream.

"At least *she* can swim," muttered Kelandris.

"One's ability to swim is of no consequence in this river. The reason the woman did not sink is this: someone has forgiven her the thing that has made her forget herself. Someone has forgiven her the thing that has made her fall off the edge. No one has forgiven the man."

Kelandris stiffened. "That wasn't Cobeth, was it?"

Aunt shook her head. "No. But Cobeth will be along."

Kelandris stared at Aunt. "What do you mean he'll be along? Where?"

"There," said Aunt, pointing to the river again. "He falls off the edge several times a day. We can wait here and watch."

Kelandris said nothing. She saw what Aunt was doing; she saw only too clearly. And it angered her. If what the Jinnjirri shade said was true, then Cobeth would fall over the waterfall—and sink. It would be up to Kelandris to save him or not. Not that it really mattered, she reminded herself. After all, Cobeth was already dead. Drowning several times a day was simply anticlimactic. It was nothing to worry about. Of course, said Kelandris to herself, Cobeth had always had a terrible fear of water. Always. Kelandris winced. She turned to Aunt and asked, "What happens if we don't stay and watch?"

"Nothing. I go back to creating my next body and you return home to the Kaleidicopia."

"Without Zendrak."

Aunt nodded. "Can't be helped, I'm afraid. You can't save Zendrak without speaking directly to Troth and Phebene. True love is one of the few ways death can be overcome in this world." Aunt shrugged. "You see the situation, I think."

Kelandris crossed her arms over her chest. "I don't want to forgive Cobeth for what he did."

"Fine. Don't forgive him. I don't care. You can save his life without forgiving the bastard. You can save it not because he's Cobeth, but because he's a two-legged in trouble. You nearly did that for a stranger only moments ago."

Kelandris shrugged. "Cobeth's no stranger."

"But he *is* a two-legged. One who is lost and drowning—" Aunt broke off. Pointing, she added, "Here he comes now."

Kelandris swallowed, anger in her throat. Cobeth was screaming for help, his terror of the water surrounding him evident. Kelandris covered her ears. Cobeth's yells penetrated her fingers. "Shit," she said. "*Shit.*"

Unable to ignore Cobeth's pain, Greatkin Kelandris

jumped into the River of Memory as Cobeth went over the edge of the falls. Water filled her mouth, she began to cough. In horror, she realized her long robe was pulling her down. She fought for her own life as Cobeth came crashing down on top of her. As is the habit of most drowning persons, Cobeth latched on to Kelandris with a stranglehold. Kelandris started to kick him off her. She could not dislodge the Jinnjirri actor. Panic shot through her body. Unlike Cobeth, she was *not* dead. Summoning her will to live—the very will that Cobeth had tried to extinguish sixteen years ago—Kelandris thrashed toward the bank of the river, Cobeth clinging to her back like a barnacle. Coughing and gasping, Kelandris threw herself toward the muddy bank. Hands reached down to help her. They belonged to Troth and Phebene. Looking up, Kelandris muttered, "I've *hardly* saved his life, my dears. All I've really done is save my own. Surely I can't have passed the test."

Phebene laughed merrily. "Come, come, Kelandris. You could've thrown him off if you had wanted to do so. You're a Greatkin. Your strength far outstrips his. Remember, we're Greatkin, too. So you saved his soul—whether or not *you* want to admit it."

Troth grinned. "She's been living with two-leggeds so long, she thinks we're thick like them. How amusing."

Kelandris shut her eyes and lay in an exhausted heap on the riverbank. Cobeth crawled away from her, his mind suddenly filled with memories of his previous life. After a few moments, he said, "Where in Neath am I? What *is* this creepy place?"

Troth's laughter boomed out across the water. Aunt, who stood on the opposite bank, joined him with laughter of her own.

Kelandris was still wet when she was taken to Zendrak. Trickster's emissary stood up. He was no longer wearing green. Now he wore black, the color of the shades of Neath.

She became unexpectedly shy upon seeing him. She wondered if he was angry with her that she had come to fetch him from Neath. Maybe he wanted to die, she thought suddenly. After all, he was over five centuries old. Before Kelandris could think about it further, she heard Zendrak's voice inside her head.

Of course, I didn't want to die, Kel. Why would I want to leave you? Akindo had slipped into my heart, that's all. He got me once, but he won't get me again. I am indebted to you, sweetheart. So's the world. What you've done here took more courage than anyone will ever know. Now we must return to the lands of light and finish the shuffling bastard. Even now, he sucks hope and all other good things from the city. So we must hurry and save our hellos and kisses for tonight. We will attack Akindo and Hennin on the morrow. I must rest my body—assuming Troth gives me a new one.

He extended his hands toward Kelandris. Kelandris took them hesitantly, expecting his fingers to be cold like the grave. To her great surprise, Zendrak's fingers and palms were warm.

"How can this be?" she whispered. "Weren't you dead?"

"Your love for me has brought some warmth to my veins." He smiled reassuringly. "I know it sounds trite. But love often is on the surface. Really, nothing could be simpler than love. The desire of the heart is the strongest remedy there is. Nothing can block it. Not even Death."

"And not Mattermat!" cackled a familiar voice. It was Rimble come to join them. He looked insufferably pleased with himself. Clapping Kelandris on the lower back—because that was as far as he could reach—Trickster congratulated Kelandris on passing Aunt's test.

Kelandris rolled her eyes and reiterated the fact that she had not wanted to save Cobeth. She just hadn't been able to make herself throw him back into the river. "Where's the heroism in that?" she demanded.

Zendrak extended his arm. As he did so, Cobeth walked

into the room. This was the real article. The Jinnjirri regarded Kelandris thoughtfully. Licking his lips, he said, "I can't believe you saved my soul."

"Me neither," she snapped, wanting to conclude her business in Ncath, wanting to put her arms around Zendrak and cover him with kisses.

"I appreciate it," said Cobeth humbly.

"Who cares?"

"No—I really *do* appreciate it."

Kelandris said nothing, oddly moved by Cobeth's gratitude. She shifted her weight, hoping she wasn't losing her edge. Or her intelligence. The last thing she wanted to feel was generosity toward the man who had ruined her life in Suxonli.

Cobeth regarded Kelandris steadily. "You still don't trust me, do you?"

"Nope."

He shrugged. "Can't say as I blame you. I fucked things up for you pretty royally." Before she could retort, Cobeth added, "You sure took on a lot for us in Suxonli, Kelandris. I could never have done what you did. It's a good thing you turned instead of me."

Kelandris snorted. "Now he tells me! After sixteen years!"

Cobeth shrugged. "Maybe I didn't see it *to* tell you before now. So I'm slow, okay?"

Kelandris shook her head, her expression furious. "This apology is supposed to make everything all better?" she asked Zendrak. "Do *you* accept this muck he's speaking?"

Zendrak reached over and pulled a wet strand of dark hair out of Kel's face. Then he said, "You don't have to love who Cobeth was. You just have to let him be sorry for what he did. That's *his* healing, Kelandris. Surely you can grant him *that*."

Kelandris took a deep breath. "I don't want him doing this kind of thing again—when he next incarnates. Who will stop him if he starts to do so? Who will protect the innocent?"

Rimble spoke now. "Well, actually we don't have some-one to do that job. Unless you want to take it, of course," he added, giving his daughter a bored look.

Kelandris studied Trickster. "Meaning what?"

Rimble shrugged. "Nah. It was a dumb idea—"

"What was?" Kelandris demanded.

Rimble sneered at her. "To let *you* be the Patron of Innocence and Purity. For one thing you've taken to wearing black again. Like you're dead or something. For another, you don't believe in your own innocence—"

"But I *wasn't* innocent in Suxonli!" she shouted, tears starting to her eyes. "I killed eight people. I spoke the Mythrrim called *The Turn of Trickster's Daughter*. I know," she added with more emotion than she wanted anyone to see or hear. "*Shit!*" she muttered and averted her face, tears coming to her eyes.

"Perhaps you would repeat that particular verse for us, Kelandris," said Troth, who had been standing unseen in the shadows.

"Leave me alone!" she replied, her voice hoarse.

Zendrak touched the back of her shoulder. "Speak it, Kel. You might discover something worth knowing."

Kelandris swore. Then she shut her eyes, turning herself over to the Mythrrim consciousness in her being. Time fell away. Words rose in her mind. She coughed and cleared her throat. Finally, Kelandris said:

"Stumbling, the *he* lost control of Rimble's line;
Eight were too few to ground Yonneth's rage.
'Twas a bad beginning for Rimble's first nine.
As the minds of his circle began to cook and burn,
All Suxonli was swept into the searing rogue turn
Of Trickster's injured daughter."

There was a long silence.

Finally, Troth said, "I don't see anywhere in that verse where it says you intentionally killed eight people, Kel."

"I was supposed to hold the line!" she cried. "The *draw* got away from me."

Cobeth started laughing.

Kelandris stared at him. "I ought to slap your face!"

Cobeth immediately sobered. "I was laughing because you're being so stupid for a Greatkin. You still don't get it, do you? You still don't understand that the *draw* of Suxonli was under Elder Hennin's control even at that time. What happened in Suxonli was political, Kelandris. Hennin needed you to break the rhythm of the *draw* so she could get it under her control. When the power got loose and pandemonium erupted at Revel Rock, Hennin was ready for it. While everyone was blaming you, she grabbed the *draw*. No one noticed. I didn't find out myself until the following year. Of course, I played into it by discovering you had turned on your menses. Even if you hadn't gotten your bloodcycle that night, you would've lost control of the power. It was all rigged. You didn't have a chance. You were guilty with or without a trial, Kelandris. Hennin wanted power. She knew you had an overabundant supply. She used yours to secure her own." Cobeth shrugged. "So you see it's really stupid for you to keep thinking *you* killed all those people. You did—but only superficially. It was Hennin's will that caused the *draw* to run wild like that. You were young and untrained—she had seen to that. I know because she told me in later years when I used to go and apprentice with her in the summer. Despite the fact that you were a Greatkin, it was a fairly easy matter for her—a trained Mayanabi Nomad—to wrest control of the *draw* away from you."

Kelandris said nothing, her mind scrambling to make sense of all Cobeth had said. She rubbed her eyes tiredly and said, "You're saying I killed eight people, but I'm not to blame."

"He's saying it was an accident," replied Troth. "Your part, that is. Hennin's part was deliberate, of course."

"So I'm not a murderess?"

Rimble shrugged. "Not as far as the Greatkin are concerned. Especially us folks in Neath. Suxonli? Well, village laws are slow to change. And village justice is slow in coming. If I were you, daughter, I'd forget about the judgment at Suxonli."

Kelandris met Trickster's eyes evenly. "That's all very well, but you're forgetting one thing, aren't you? You're forgetting the eight people who died. Surely they would rather have lived. Surely *they* can't have forgiven my part in this."

Troth grinned. "Give a little, get a little."

"What?"

"Let's ask them, shall we?" said the Greatkin of Death, going to stand in the shadows. He made a swift gesture with his hand several times as if he were drawing something up from the ground. In moments, the eight villagers who had participated in the fateful turn sixteen years ago in Suxonli arrived.

Recognizing their faces, Kelandris stepped backward, her expression horrified. She expected them to accuse her anew of her crime. Instead, one of the dead handed her a written scroll. Kelandris took it gingerly. She opened it and stared at the words, her face paling with shock.

"What's it say?" asked Zendrak.

"It says that I am pardoned. In big letters," she added.

Cobeth smiled. "I'm glad, Kel. I'm really glad. It was a stupid business all the way around. Mostly you were an okay sister to have. You deserved better than what happened in Suxonli."

Zendrak tousled Kel's dark, damp hair. "How does it feel?"

"How does what feel?"

"To be pardoned?"

Kelandris shrugged. "I don't know. I'll have to get used to it, I guess." She paused. "It's a little like going into a wardrobe and finding out that all the clothes one wears most often have suddenly fallen apart at the seams—with no hope of repair. Makes me feel a little naked," she added, her posture clearly uncomfortable with the idea.

Zendrak smiled at her, his dark eyes kind.

Kelandris turned toward the eight shades who were still standing around her in silence. Gazing at each of them, Kelandris said, "Thank you."

The shades bowed to Greatkin Kelandris and departed.

There was a long silence.

After a few moments, Kel asked Zendrak if he was alive or not. And if he wasn't going to get a new body, she added to Troth, would it be possible for her to remain in Neath, too?

Rimble answered Kelandris. "He's about as dead as he's ever going to be. And about as alive as he's ever going to be. By this, I mean, Zendrak is mostly Greatkin. Being mostly Greatkin, Zendrak can decide if he wishes to incarnate again and in what form. And at what age." Rimble gestured at his son. "It's up to you, see. You want to go back with Kelandris?"

Zendrak nodded. "There's this little inn I know . . ." He wig-wagged his eyebrows.

Kelandris, who had been living like a celibate for the past six months, stiffened. "Uh—are you sure? Maybe it's too soon—"

Zendrak glared at Trickster's daughter. "You want me to stay in Neath? Without you?"

"Well, no, but I—"

Watching this exchange, Rimble broke into peals of laughter.

Chapter Eighteen

DRESSED IN HIS usual greens and Kel still in black, Zendrak and Kelandris rode back toward Speakinghast in silence. They had traveled the distance between the plane of Neath and the land of Saämbolin in a matter of a few minutes. Further walked slowly in the moonlit open road that would eventually lead to the North Gate of Speakinghast, the mare's coat shining in the silver light from above the two riders. Zendrak rode with his arms snugly wrapped around Kel's waist. Feeling weary from the physical shock of having gone swimming in the river of Neath, Kelandris leaned against Zendrak's chest, her eyes closed, rocked by the gentle motion of the mare's dawdling pace. Zendrak leaned forward and whispered, "You asleep?"

"No, but I'd like to be," she said, stifling a yawn.

Sleep in a comfortable bed felt very appealing to both Greatkin. Zendrak stabled Further at the next inn they passed. It was a large place with beds for twenty and ample food and pasture for the Greatkin mare. Zendrak jumped off and helped Kelandris down. The two Greatkin approached the front desk of the inn called "Mother's Milk and Breakfast." It was a cheery establishment run by a husband and wife team of Piedmerri-born.

The innkeeper took the pertinent information, Piedmerri style. "Any children traveling with you?"

Kelandris stiffened involuntarily. Zendrak put his arm around her waist protectively. Kelandris had said precious little about her feelings about never having had children, but he suspected she was feeling the loss of that opportunity deeply.

"No, no children," said Zendrak.

"Are you ringfasted?"

"No," said Zendrak. Then he smiled. "We're soulfasted."

The Piedmerri scratched his large belly, inclining his head. "So does that mean you'll be wanted a double bed? I mean, are you *legal*?"

Zendrak was taken aback by the bluntness of the question. "Since when do legalities interest the Piedmerri-born, sir?"

"We're in Saämbolin, mate. And in Saämbolin, you play by their rules or you get trounced—if you know what I mean."

"I know what you mean," said Kel unexpectedly.

"So are you legal?" continued the plump fellow.

Zendrak rolled his black eyes, wondering if they should've spent the night in Neath. "No," he said gruffly. "We're not legal."

The wife of the innkeeper, who had been listening to this conversation as she tidied a nearby closet, turned around and asked, "But are you in love, sir?"

"Now, Melli, what's that got to do with it?" demanded her husband.

"Everything," she said, grinning broadly, her plump cheeks as rosy as a blush apple. She toddled over. "So? Are you?" she asked, looking first at Zendrak and then at Kelandris. "Are you in love?"

Zendrak nodded his head. "Yes. But I don't know if—"

Kelandris cut him off. "Yes, we're in love. May we have the double bed, please?"

Zendrak stared at Kelandris, his expression a mixture of astonishment and undisguised delight. He paid the innkeeper the sum he required and added a little extra to cover their indiscretion. As Zendrak and Kelandris turned to go up the winding staircase, Zendrak said in a low voice that only Kelandris could hear:

"What made you say *that*?"

Kelandris shrugged. "It just sort of popped out. Maybe Neath had something to do with it. I don't know."

"Neath?"

Kelandris nodded almost shyly. "Phebene told me she

wanted us to get along. She wanted things to work out between us. She said she'd help. Maybe she just did."

Some time later when both Kelandris and Zendrak had scrubbed the grit out from behind their ears in a long, luxurious bath, the two Greatkin retired to their comfortable bedroom at the inn. The walls were covered with a delicate, floral wallpaper and dotted with pictures of calm countrysides hung with a decorator's eye for placement. Dried flowers adorned a small wooden dresser while the large bed was softened by the presence of a generous eiderdown comforter. A wood-burning stove crackled happily in the corner, a supply of wood and kindling stacked neatly beside the cast-iron fixture. Zendrak lit a candle, then, snuggling down into the bed, he opened his arms to Kelandris, who was still wandering about the room drying and combing her long black hair. She smiled slightly and came to the corner of the bed, a large yellow towel wrapped around her bosom and torso.

"Won't you come to bed now?" asked Zendrak gently.

Kelandris shrugged, fiddling with a fold in the towel. She said nothing, her posture slightly stiff. She was clearly ambivalent about doing anything more than sleeping next to Zendrak. Seeing this, Zendrak said, "You know, Kel—nothing has to happen."

"I know."

There was a long silence.

"Aren't you cold?" asked Zendrak. "The air in this room is hardly that of summer—even with the stove."

"Yes, I'm cold," said Kelandris, making no move to come any closer to her brother and old lover. Her lips parted, her eyes downcast. A tear slipped down her cheek.

"Would you like to talk for a while?"

Kelandris nodded dumbly. "You start."

Zendrak took a deep breath and brought the candle closer to the corner of the bedside table. He sat up in bed, propping several pillows behind him, the comforter pulled up to his neck. "Well," he said slowly, debating what to discuss with his sister. Finally, he decided to risk everything and speak of the time they had made love in Suxonli. But rather than have Kelandris get lost in the terrible things that happened later that night at the hands of Elder Hennin and Cobeth, he chose to remind Kelandris of the feelings of love he had had for her so long ago. "Kel?"

"Yes?"

"Things got very messy in Suxonli sixteen years ago. But before that happened, you and I shared something very special. Do you remember what that felt like?"

Kelandris turned to look at him, her expression wild and accusing. "I have never forgotten it."

Zendrak said nothing for a few moments. "You make me cold to look at you, Kel. Will you get under the covers?"

Kelandris, who was close to shivering now with both cold and fatigue, consented grudgingly. She slipped between the sheets and jumped when Zendrak reached for her and pulled her close to his warm body.

"You're like ice," he said.

"I didn't use to be," she snapped.

"I remember."

Kelandris met his eyes for a moment and looked away.

"I *do* remember, Kel. I remember a warm, loving woman who trusted me."

"I remember that, too," she said in a choked whisper, tears tumbling from her eyes now. Emotions that she had not felt in sixteen years welled up in her, and she collapsed sobbing against Zendrak's bare chest. While she cried, he kissed away her tears, his expression tender.

"Let's give ourselves a second chance, hmm?" he whispered.

"I don't know how," she bawled. Then she collected herself and said, "I mean, what if I don't know how? It's been so long—" She broke off, her eyes genuinely anxious.

Zendrak chuckled. "Well, there's one way to find out."

Kelandris swallowed.

Zendrak kissed her on the mouth. She responded only marginally. He pulled away, his expression thoughtful.

"Well?" she asked nervously.

"A little rusty," he agreed. "Better try again."

So they did.

"Well?" she asked, a bit more breathless this time.

"Needs improvement," he said, starting to chuckle again.

Kelandris swore and kissed Zendrak a third time. Suddenly there was emotional fire. Zendrak felt the change in her body. Gone was her wall. Her lips softened and her face flushed. Zendrak pulled away from her, his dark eyes impish.

"Well, that's enough for tonight," he said. He blew out the candle and turned over on his side.

Kelandris sat in stunned darkness, the faint light of the stove playing across her perplexed features. "I thought you wanted—"

"Changed my mind," said Trickster's son.

"I was that bad?" she asked, scandalized.

Zendrak glanced at her over his shoulder. "Too rich for my blood."

She grabbed him by the shoulders and made him face her. "Zendrak, did I do something wrong?"

"No, no, my dear. The fault's not in you. Not at all. That last kiss was scary."

"Scary?" Kelandris was having difficulty believing her ears.

Zendrak nodded. "I don't think I'd survive making love with you. The passion would be too much for both of us—"

"Speak for yourself!"

Zendrak shrugged unenthusiastically. "Really, Kel, I think it's best that we don't—"

"Zendrak," she said, her voice trembling with confusion, "what're you doing? I mean, are you refusing to make love with me?"

Zendrak turned over on his side again. "Remember, I only just started being alive again a few hours ago. I need more time to get used to my body."

"Sonofabitch," she muttered. There was a long silence. "Well, you could kiss me good night."

"I don't see what good—"

"Oh, Zendrak—just one kiss isn't going to kill you."

So Zendrak kissed her, and it was as passionate as the last time. When both had come up for air, Zendrak played with her mouth and said, "I think you'd like making love with me, Kelandris. Forget your bad memories of Suxonli, hmm? Forget the nightmare. Come into the present."

Tears started to her eyes as she lay against the pillow; making love was a pleasure she had given up after Suxonli. She had been convicted as a murderess; murderesses didn't deserve joy. Or second chances. Kelandris shook her head, the impression of the past still too strong upon her.

Zendrak caressed her breast slowly. "The judgment against you has been reversed. Give up the past, Kel."

"I'm afraid something will go wrong again. That you'll leave me."

"I know. That's the chance you'll have to take. And me? I have to take the chance that you won't bolt and break my heart into a thousand painful pieces." He traced a tear with his finger. "So is it a deal? My risk for yours?"

Kelandris winced, her heart beating with fear. She shut her eyes for a moment, trying to gain control of her emotions. She couldn't do it. "I'm so frightened," she whispered. Zendrak nodded and put her hand on his chest so that she could feel how quickly *his* heart was pounding. Kel opened her eyes, a flicker of compassion on her face. Then she said, "Okay. I promise. I'll leave Suxonli behind. For good."

Zendrak nodded, his face now contorting with the power of the emotions that he felt and had always felt toward Kelandris. His love and passion rose for her simultaneously. Kelandris met his feelings with her own. As they settled into a playful, physical exchange, Zendrak said, "One thing we'll have to be careful of, Kel."

"What's that?" she asked huskily.

"We mustn't,"—kiss—"set this place"—kiss—"on fire."

Kelandris smiled. "I love you," she whispered. "I always have."

"I know," he said matter-of-factly, and lowered himself on her gently.

Panthe'kinarok Interlogue

GREATKIN RIMBLE RETURNED to Eranossa with Phebene. Jinndaven met them at the front door. On Trickster's orders, the Greatkin of Imagination had parted company with Phebene and Rimble when Kelandris failed to get past Troth at the gate of Neath. Rimble had sent Jinndaven to Eranossa to see what was going on. Until that moment, Rimble had been under the impression that he had salvaged his roast and silenced Mattermat. Kel's refusal to forgive Cobeth indicated otherwise. Earth was the element that held the emotion of resentment. If Kelandris was still feeling resentful, then this meant Mattermat was talking to her—*and* she was listening. Still, Zendrak's recent return to the living should distract Kelandris, thought Rimble. Make her stop listening to Mattermat altogether he hoped.

"So?" asked Rimble jauntily. "Everything's okay, right? Kelandris and Zendrak are sharing the sheets, the univer-'silsila are beating the crap out of Hennin's holovespa—"

Jinndaven stepped outside the house, pulling the door to him hastily. It was spring at Eranossa. The sweet smell of flowering trees filled the air. Balmy breezes ruffled Phebene's wonderful rainbow robe. Sunlight glinted off the top of Rimble's black hair. Birds soared in gentle ecstasy above them, lifted by the winds that played across the mountain's sheer face. The Greatkin of Imagination gestured at the outdoors, his expression grim. "Don't let all this fool you, Rimble."

"But it's spring," interjected Phebene. "Just look at it," she added, pointing to a cluster of purple hyacinths near her feet.

Jinndaven shook his head. "He's faking everybody out. Only Themyth and I are on to Mattie. The rest of the family thinks we're nuts—"

"I can see why," retorted Phebene. "This is the best imitation of spring I've ever seen, Jinn. You sure you and Eldest haven't been swilling too much wine at dinner?"

Jinndaven groused at Phebene, crossing his arms over his chest. The mirrors on his mauve robe shimmered in the early morning sun. Finally Jinndaven added, "Mattermat is steamed, Rimble—"

"His vegetables, too?" quipped Trickster, suddenly remembering that Mattermat's dish for dinner was a hefty platter of steamed vegetables.

"Of course," snapped Jinndaven. "How do you think I was able to find out what I know? I went into the kitchen, and there on the counter—not on the stove—were Mattie's veggies cooking away. Steaming."

"How's my roast?" asked Rimble with sudden concern.

"Fine, for the moment. But don't think Mattie's through with you, Rimble, because he's not. He's furious with everyone in Neath, too. Especially Troth. As far as Mattie's concerned, Troth doesn't owe you any favors: Zendrak should've stayed dead."

"Well, Troth *does* owe me some favors," snapped Trickster. "Besides, Zendrak's got Mythrrim blood in him. They're the original phoenix prototype, you know. It's almost impossible to kill off a Mythrrim. Only way to do it is to silence the myths they tell. Since that's not likely to happen—"

"Don't bet on it," retorted Jinndaven. "Ever heard of writer's block?"

"What?" asked Phebene.

"I said, don't bet on Mattermat keeping his ill-will away from your project in that Distant Place. Themyth's very worried. You should be, too, Rimble. After all, it is your brainchild."

Trickster said nothing, pulling thoughtfully on his black

goatee. Trickster smiled slowly and slyly. "To market, to market, to sell a fresh tale. Home again, home again, I've just made a sale. In New York, that is," added Trickster. Then he began to laugh.

Phebene and Jinndaven stared at their little brother.

Finally Phebene said, "Rimble, dear—are you all right?"

"Yes, indeed," said Rimble, doing a small jig on the doorstep of Eranossa. "Yes, indeed. I've got Mattie on the run, my sweets. On the run."

Jinndaven gestured helplessly. "Haven't you been listening, Rimble? I'm telling you, Mattie's up to something. Something nasty—"

"Yes. And I've got just the cure for it. Just the remedy. Just the impr*ooo*vement," he said, giggling like a maniac. "May the message of God reach far and wide, guys. Far and wide."

"God?" asked Phebene.

"What's God got to do with this?" asked Jinndaven.

"Plenty," replied Trickster. "At least in Milwaukee."

As Trickster turned to go, Jinndaven caught him by the arm. "Where are you *going*? I mean, we've got an emergency in there and you—"

"Milwaukee," said Trickster.

"Again?" asked Phebene, straightening the pink, wide-brimmed hat she still wore.

Trickster nodded. "By the way, boyo," he said to Jinndaven. "Plant a new idea in Yafatah's brain, will you?"

"*Any* new idea?"

Trickster gave his brother an exasperated look. "No, not *any* new idea. This new idea: nine candles on a long table. One for each *landdraw*. The eighth candle is for the Mayanabi. And the ninth for the Presence."

Jinndaven put his hands on his hips. "That's not a new idea, Rimble. I gave it to the Mayanabi ages ago, remember?"

Trickster groaned. "It's a new idea to Yafatah!"

Jinndaven shrugged. "What's she supposed to do with the candles?"

"Light 'em, you nit! I'm making a correspondence between two universes. Packs a bigger punch. Ooo, won't Mattie be surprised. This is an inner plane double-hitter!"

Chapter Nineteen

RIMBLE ARRIVED IN Milwaukee on a Sunday morning, just in time to cause havoc during the candle-lighting ceremony of an ecumenical service called the Universal Worship. The Obstinate Woman was officiating. Dressed completely in white, she wore only modest jewelry—nothing that dangled or called attention to itself. Her hair was combed neatly, her mood serene. The service was being conducted in someone's living room. A stained-glass window composed of a gold heart with clear wings caught the light and cast its reflection on the white lace altar cloth. Six people sat in a comfortable circle around the altar, some lounging on the sofa, some sitting in a strict meditative posture on the floor. Everyone looked *very* nice. Too nice for Trickster's taste. He decided to liven things up.

Seeing that there was a candle being lit for every major religion in the world, Trickster waited patiently for the Obstinate Woman to honor the tradition of the Native Americans. After all they had given him some of his best names. Plus, the Native Americans had never made a devil out of him. Trickster appreciated this. After a few minutes of waiting, Trickster realized the Obstinate Woman had no candle for the Native Americans on the altar. He was waiting for nothing! Indignant, Trickster yelled, "Hey!"

The Obstinate Woman whirled around, her face pale. Until now, she hadn't realized Trickster was in the room. She said nothing, regarding Greatkin Rimble with consternation. She was certain he meant to disrupt the service.

"Hey!" repeated Rimble, patting the coyote furs on his

legs. "I don't see the Indians up there. I don't see space for Old Man Coyote."

"We don't always light a candle for that tradition," said the Obstinate Woman. "The service was a little long today, so I—"

"So you *skipped* the Native Americans?"

The Obstinate Woman licked her lips, her face scarlet.

Trickster continued his tirade mercilessly. "I mean, it's *their* land you're standing on, kiddo. You gotta honor the ancestors."

The Obstinate Woman coughed, speechless.

"He a friend of yours?" asked a woman sitting on the couch. "We can throw him out—"

Trickster began cackling with wild laughter. The yellow and black paint he had drawn in bold diagonals across his torso rippled with each guffaw.

"You can't," muttered the Obstinate Woman. "I know. I've tried." Taking a deep breath, she turned to Trickster and asked, "So what do you want?"

Trickster grinned, but said nothing.

A spritely, pleasingly plump woman seated on the floor, wearing a pale blue dress and genuine Wisconsin black and white cow slippers, nudged the man next to her and said, "Who *is* this guy?"

"Looks like Rimble to me."

"But he's just a character in one of her books, isn't he? I mean, he's not *real*."

Trickster walked over to the pleasingly plump woman and pointed at the top of her forehead. "What's that?" he asked.

"What?"

"That."

The woman felt around on top of head. She stiffened. Her fingers had touched a strand of hair that was so coarse it reminded her of dog hair. Her eyes widened with astonishment. "I don't have hair like that. My hair is soft and brown and be-y*ooo*-tiful—"

"Must be a hallucination," said Rimble slyly. "Couldn't be *real*."

The pleasingly plump woman stared at Rimble and shut her mouth.

"Rimble," said the Obstinate Woman, "this is a lovely worship service, and you're making a colossal mess of it. I'd really appreciate it if you'd just *tell* me what you want—"

"Patience," replied Trickster. Then he grinned, and vanished.

The Obstinate Woman bit her lower lip. Going to a desk in the living room, she rummaged in its top drawer. She pulled another white votive candle from a box that held twelve. She placed it in a glass holder on the altar. Taking a deep breath, the Obstinate Woman went on with the Universal Worship. Raising her taper, she said, "To the Glory of the Omnipresent God, we kindle this light symbolically representing the Native American Religion."

Thanks, said a voice in her head.

Chapter Twenty

AT THE KALEIDICOPIA, no one knew that Zendrak was again alive. People spoke in low voices, their gestures nervous. For the moment the holovespa wasps had stopped their attack. It seemed the Univer'silsila breed had wiped out Elder Hennin's hive. Still, no one at the Kaleidicopia felt safe any longer. If the two Greatkin in their midst couldn't survive Hennin's poison, then none of the residents of the "K" felt they had much chance of succeeding either.

Himayat and Fasilla tried to dispel the mood of gloom in the house. Although Yafatah was glad to see her mother again, Yafatah was deeply distressed to hear of Aunt's death at the border between Saämbolin and Jinnjirri. She had liked Aunt—maybe even loved her. Aunt had understood the things in Yafatah that her own mother had not. Aunt had encouraged Yafatah to explore and fall down and pick herself up. Above all, Aunt had trusted the young girl to do what was best for herself. This trust had been a priceless gift, and Yafatah sorely missed the giver of it. Especially right now.

"Let me see those stings," said Fasilla, her healer's instincts combining with a mother's natural worry.

"I keep telling you, Ma. I be fine."

"Yes, but *why*?"

"Because I got stung by them other wasps, Ma. Po says they saved me."

"Po?" scoffed her mother. "Now you do be quoting *that* scab at me? Doon't be foolish, child. Po be a pickpocket—"

"Po be a Mayanabi like Aunt!" shouted Yafatah suddenly.

Fasilla's prejudice against the Mayanabi was long-standing. Over the years, Fasilla had tried to prevent Yafatah from meeting the Mayanabi who sometimes accompanied Asilliwir caravans on trading journeys. Any conversation Yafatah had ever had with her mother about this secret order had always ended in argument. Yafatah expected the same outcome now. She would have been shocked to know—had she given her mother a chance to tell her—that while with Himayat, Fasilla had been formally invited to join the Order, and much to Fasilla's own surprise, had done so without hesitation. Fasilla's concern at present was what it appeared to be: Po was a Mayanabi, yes, but he was also a thief by trade. Fasilla didn't believe that Po's spiritual affiliations automatically made him a sterling person. Rather, she suspected his spiritual affiliations mitigated any of Po's less endearing qualities. On this, Fasilla was quite correct.

Yafatah continued her indignant tirade. "Po do be a Mayanabi just like Aunt! And Aunt was your friend. You should listen to Po. He knows things!"

"Po knows only what suits him. Mostly what lies in a person's pockets. You've been living too long in this house. It do be time to take you away from it. 'Tisna a healthy place for you," she added, touching her daughter's swollen face gently.

Yafatah pulled away from her mother abruptly. She ran up two flights of stairs to the second floor of the Kaleidicopia. Coming to her room, she slammed the door and locked it. Two deaths in such a short amount of time was almost unbearable for the young girl. There was also the matter of losing her father, Cobeth, barely three months ago.

"No *big* loss," Yafatah muttered under her breath. Raised by her mother, Yafatah had never known the Jinnjirri. What others told her of him made Yafatah feel ashamed that she had been born of his blood. Cobeth had proved himself to be an out-and-out genius and drug addict—not a happy combination. Yafatah hoped that if it were her misfortune to inherit anything from Cobeth she would err on the side of genius. Her lower lip trembling, Yafatah began to weep as though her heart would break.

She wished she could have attended Aunt's funeral. Fasilla had described the Mayanabi ceremony to Yafatah in great detail. Blowing her nose on a handkerchief, Yafatah looked around the room for a candle she could use to honor Aunt's passing. Finding one in a desk drawer—in much the same way that the Obstinate Woman in Milwaukee had done—Yafatah lit the white votive candle. As she did so, she had the strangest feeling that she ought to be lighting more than just the one. Staring at the candle and the shadows it cast on the wall in her room, she contemplated lighting more. She got up. Reaching into the desk drawer again, she pulled out seven more candles. Arranging them in a crescent, she lit them. Yafatah frowned. Something about the number of candles struck Yafatah as significant, but she couldn't say why. Touching each candle in turn, she spoke the name of a *landdraw*. The seventh candle was for Aunt, she decided. Aunt was Mayanabi, and no matter *what* her mother thought about Podiddley, the Mayanabi were important. They should have a candle. And the eighth? Who was the eighth for? she wondered. She shrugged. When in doubt, light one for the Presence. That could never be a wrong thing to do. Yafatah smiled. She set the candle for the Presence on top of a small wooden box so that the eighth candle would stand higher than the rest. Still mad with her mother, Yafatah separated the seventh candle from the crescent, pulling it slightly forward. That's for you, Aunt, she thought triumphantly.

Someone knocked at the door.

"Who be it?" she asked, her tone of voice uninviting.

"Po."

Yafatah scrambled to her feet. She unlocked the door. Po smiled at the sixteen-year-old girl. "Heard you had a fight with your ma about me."

"Yeah."

"Can I come in?"

"I suppose. Only, doon't let me ma see you, okay? She be ragging on me fierce bad. And I doon't want to hear it."

"Okay," said Po, looking from side to side in the hallway. It was empty. The little thief walked in and shut the door. Seeing the arrangement of the candles on Yafatah's dresser for the first time, he whistled under his breath. "You little Tammi psychic."

"What?"

"Where did you get the idea for this setup?"

"You mean the candles?"

"Yep. The crescent, the number of them, and the color white."

"I doon't know," said Yafatah crossly. "I just thought it up."

Po grunted.

"Why?" asked Yafatah. "What be the big deal, anyway?"

Po sat down on the bed. He patted a spot next to him. Yafatah scowled at the scruffy Asilliwir thief and sat beside him. Po twirled his stringy mustache thoughtfully. "Look, sweetie, I'm going to talk to you real frank now. And I don't want you telling your ma what I say to you. It's not for her to hear, all right?"

"But if me ma asks, I canna' lie to her, Po. She'll know in a second if I lie."

Po took a deep breath. "If you tell her the truth, you'll regret it, Ya. She won't understand. But do what you will."

There was a long pause.

Yafatah stared at the floor in her bedroom, feeling uncomfortable. She knew Po was gazing at her intently. Her Tammirring senses monitored his interest in her silence. Yafatah scowled.

"What do you be staring at?"

"I'm waiting for you to make up your mind."

"About what?"

"About entering into a larger world."

Yafatah kicked her bed with her heel. Conversations with Zendrak popped into her mind. How many times had Zendrak told her Po was a better Mayanabi than thief? And how many times had he counseled her to ask Po about his training under him? And how many times had Yafatah talked to Podiddley about one thing only—the dishes? The young girl shrugged. Maybe she should give Po a chance to be good.

Finally Yafatah said, "So talk to me."

Po pursed his lips. When he returned his gaze to Yafatah, it was intense and very, very sobering. "Ya, you can't have known about putting those candles in just that way without being a Mayanabi yourself. Do you understand? It's one of our most sacred ceremonies."

Yafatah looked at the floor. A single tear slipped down her cheek. "You could've told me anything in the world but this, Podiddley. If this be true, I will lose me ma's love. She canna abide the Mayanabi. She made exception with Aunt because Aunt was special."

"I know."

There was a short pause.

Yafatah swallowed. "Somehow, I doon't be amazed, Podiddley, about me being Mayanabi. When I traveled in caravan, I was always making friends with the Mayanabi Nomads. I just liked them, you know."

"I'm not surprised." Po sighed deeply, his face becoming sad. "It's too bad Zendrak isn't here. He would've liked doing the initiation for you." He swore. "I can't believe he's dead. I just can't believe it."

Yafatah watched Po struggle with his feelings. "You really loved him, didna' you?"

"Sure."

Yafatah smiled tentatively. "Well, seeing as how you loved Zendrak, I would be honored to be initiated by you. Mr. Podiddley."

Po stiffened in surprise. "Me? How about Himayat? He's

been at this path a lot longer than me. He's downstairs in the kitchen making tea."

"You canna initiate me?"

Po licked his lips. "Uh—I mean—I guess so. I mean, I *can*. I just never been asked before." He peered at Yafatah with stupefaction. "See, the thing is, Ya—if I initiate you, then I'm your Mayanabi Elder. Means I'm supposed to teach you things."

"So?"

Po blinked. "Well, I—I just never had a student, that's all."

"So?" Like the others in the house, Yafatah was a natural Contrary.

Po took a deep breath. He got to his feet and paced. Under his breath he muttered, "Where the fuck is Zendrak when you really need him? Dead, that's what."

So initiate her, you big baby!

Po's face paled.

"What's wrong?" asked Yafatah.

"Now I'm hearing voices inside my head! That's what's wrong!"

Yafatah stared at the Asilliwir man. "Doon't you always hear voices? I do. We Tammi always do. 'Tis as natural as having this conversation."

Po scowled, grumbling under his breath again.

"What?" asked Yafatah, starting to think Po didn't like her.

"I said, I wonder who's going to be teaching *who* in this arrangement."

Yafatah shrugged.

Po?

The little thief shrieked.

Yafatah giggled. "What did the voice say?"

"Just my name."

"Oh."

Po?

Po made a grimace and danced across the room, his

hands on either side of his head. "Stop it, stop it, stop it!" He jumped up on the bed.

Po, you little boob—just initiate her, will you? You know the ceremony. Don't scare the poor girl. You're quite right. She's Mayanabi. Trust your spiritual instincts as much as you do your thieving ones.

Po shut his eyes and hopped about in the center of the bed on one leg. He howled and swore vehemently.

Yafatah watched him, her expression puzzled. "Does this mean you're going to initiate me or not, Po? I mean, it do be okay if you think—"

"Silence!" shouted Po, coming to a standstill, his eyes suddenly greedy. "I'm getting messages from inside my head! Know what that means, dearie? Means I must've made it into the next rank." Po grinned gleefully. "At last, at last—out of the scullery and into the real path—"

Po, if you don't shut up this instant, I'll take that rank back. It'll be remedial dishwashing for you. One can go backward on this path.

"I can?" Po said in astonishment. Without further spluttering, Po sat down and attended to the business at hand. He initiated Yafatah into the Order of the Mayanabi Nomads.

What happened between them was a secret, one that Yafatah never told her mother or anybody else.

Chapter Twenty-one

WHILE YAFATAH WAS upstairs with Podiddley, the rest of the house sat downstairs in the kitchen. The group included six of Rimble's Nine and the two Asilliwir, Fasilla and Himayat. Barlimo had just made a large pot of black tea. She poured milk into the cups of those who wanted it.

"Honey?" she offered Janusin.

The master sculptor nodded, his expression as bleak as his blue hair. He held out his ceramic mug for a spoonful of the golden sweetener. He sighed and said, "I've never felt so depressed in all my life."

Tree and Rowenaster nodded their heads in silence. Tree's hair matched Janusin's moody blue. The professor looked as though he had aged ten years overnight. Every gesture he made was stiff and out of rhythm. Himayat peered at Rowenaster intently. *That's* what it is, he thought to himself. This whole group is out of rhythm. But from what? he wondered. The Asilliwir Mayanabi glanced out of the kitchen window. He didn't know what he hoped to see out there. Something. Something that explained the terrible drain he felt being directed at the people seated beside him. Himayat continued to watch the professor, but said nothing.

Rowenaster cleared his throat. "And if Zendrak's death weren't enough," he muttered, "I fear we'll lose the house this week."

Barlimo shrugged. Dressed in layers of wools and mismatched clothing, the Jinnjirri architect made a rude noise with her mouth. "It's an ongoing fight with the Guild. That's all. We just have to remain firm and we'll survive. We always have."

"Things are different now," said Mab softly. "We aren't protected anymore," she added, glancing at the ceiling, toward the upper floor where Zendrak's body had lain. "It's so scary now. We don't even know where Zendrak's body *is*. I mean, how can a body just disappear? Everything's going wrong. Everything."

Timmer snorted. "Mab, just shut up, will you? You're really bringing me down. You're a psychic vamp sometimes. Just sucking away everybody's energy with your fear!"

Himayat raised an eyebrow.

Predictably, Mab burst into tears and ran to the first-floor bathroom to weep over her hurt feelings. No one stopped her. In fact, no one said anything. Fasilla glared at the rest of Mab's housemates and said, "Poor Mab. She just do be sad. You shouldna' judge her so harshly."

Himayat cleared his throat. "Actually, I think Timmer's anger was justified."

There was a short silence.

"What do you mean?" asked Timmer.

"I mean just this: I feel someone or something directing a great deal of rage and despair at this house. Mab's quite sensitive—"

Timmer rolled her eyes. "Yeah. Weeps at everything."

"Yes. And I think she was being used a few minutes ago."

"Used?" asked Barlimo. "By what?"

Himayat glanced out the window again. "It's out there, whatever it is." He stood up. Walking to the window, he watched snow fall lazily from the sky. It was late morning in Speakinghast. Pedestrians wrapped in bright wools and stocking caps trudged through the drifts. Snow melted and froze on the beards of men. It was a raw day. Himayat grunted. "Tell me more about this Elder Hennin person."

"Can't," said Janusin. "We don't actually know that much about her. Po might. He spent more time with Zendrak than any of us. Ask him."

"I will," said Himayat. Before he was able to do so, there was a sharp knock at the front door. Timmer went to open it. Looking out the window before she put her hand on the door handle, she came to a complete halt. Eyes wide, the blond musician came tearing back into the kitchen. "It's Gadorian! He's got an armed escort. Shit, what're we going to do?"

Barlimo got to her feet slowly. "Do? We've done nothing wrong. We've nothing to hide. Go let the guildmaster in, Timmer. Invite him for tea," she added, pulling down a clean cup.

"This should be interesting," muttered Rowenaster.

Guildmaster Gadorian knocked snow off his black boots as he walked over the threshold of the Kaleidicopia. The two guildguards accompanying him did likewise. They were, after all, Saämbolin; they were innately polite. Gadorian greeted Rowenaster and Janusin, who came out of the kitchen after Timmer closed the door after the Saämbolin threesome.

Rowenaster sighed. "You're such a bastard," he said simply.

"Sometimes that's my job, Rowen," retorted Gadorian.

Rowenaster shrugged. "Well, come and have tea, then. Barlimo's making you a fresh cup."

"Thank you," said Gadorian. Turning to the guards, he said, "Relax if you want. But stay in the hall area."

"As you wish," they said, saluting Gadorian, their swords still sheathed.

Gadorian tromped into the Kaleidicopia's cheery kitchen. A blazing fire crackled in the hearth while water boiled over the stove. The kitchen smelled sweetly of some herbs Barlimo and Fasilla had been drying earlier in the morning. Bunches of the dried stuff lay in neat heaps on one of the wooden counters. Gadorian went to sniff the nearest bunch.

"It's all legal," said Barlimo, handing the guildmaster his tea.

He scowled at the Jinnjirri architect and took a seat at the table. Like Mattermat's, Gadorian's body was so large, he spilled out of the chair. Privately lithe Timmer wondered if the chair would support such weight. She decided that if the chair broke with the guildmaster still sitting in it, justice would be served. Every person in the room with the exception of Himayat knew why Gadorian was here. The smug smile on Gadorian's face told them everything.

Barlimo pulled up a chair. Her sex fluctuated for a moment. Gaining control over her emotions, the Jinnjirri said, "So where're the papers? I assume you've come to serve us our eviction notice."

Gadorian pulled them out of the leather purse he wore over his shoulder. He threw the papers on the table. He continued to sip his tea in the intervening silence. Barlimo picked them up. She rifled through them, her hair turning from dark blue to blue-black.

"Seems like everything's in order. Where do I sign?"

Astonished at Barlimo's speedy capitulation, Tree cried, "*Fight* him, Barl! What's wrong with you? What happened to that stuff you were saying earlier? About being firm and all?"

"Yeah," agreed Timmer. "Don't give in to the creep—"

Barlimo cleared her throat reprovingly. "Dear ones, in any battle you have to know when to surrender—"

"Well, how about a hasty *retreat,* then?" retorted Tree. "Forget surrender! He's a Saäm pig. This whole thing is political—"

Gadorian smiled, delighted with the anguish he was causing the Jinnjirri in the room. He continued to sip his tea in silence. Now Janusin spoke.

"And my commitment to the Great Library?" asked the sculptor. "What becomes of all the work I've promised your wife? The Panthe'kinarok Series?" he added, referring to a series of statues he had agreed to create for the grounds of the Great Library of Speakinghast.

Barlimo interrupted here. Handing Janusin three pages

from the sheaf of papers on the table, she said, "They've canceled the contract."

"Great. How will I eat?" muttered the artist.

"You'll manage. You Jinn always do," said Gadorian.

Janusin swore and left the kitchen. The front door slammed.

Without warning, Janusin screamed.

Chapter Twenty-two

EVERYONE IN THE house, including Yafatah and Podiddley, who were still talking upstairs, came running out of the house. The guildguards, who were closest to the front door, were first out. When they reached Janusin's side, they resheathed their swords. They saw no danger. Only a man in green and a veiled Tammirring woman in black. Before either guard could question Janusin, several of the Kaleidicopians behind them also shrieked. There was dead silence.

Yafatah, who was last out, was the first to find her tongue. Tearing through all the adults who had stopped cold on the steps, she ran pell-mell toward the two Greatkin and hugged Zendrak fiercely. Then she turned to Kelandris, tears streaming from her eyes, and said, "You brought him back! Just like you said you would! You brought him back!"

Earlier when Kelandris had stated this was her intention—to go to Neath herself and retrieve Zendrak from the underworld—no one had believed her. Essentially, very few people trusted Kelandris to do what she said she was going to do. After all, she had spent sixteen years being Crazy Kel in Piedmerri. Why trust a madwoman? Yafatah, however, had believed Kelandris. She had trusted the dark Greatkin with the innocence of her youth. Her love for all the Greatkin had not permitted the child to doubt Kel's word. Feeling victorious in her own soul, Yafatah turned around to face the rest of the group on the steps. Speaking to Barlimo, she said, "See? I told you she'd do it! You canna call me daft no more, Barl."

Barlimo swallowed and said nothing.

Podiddley smiled; the girl was a true Mayanabi.

Gadorian scowled at Janusin. "What gives here? You sounded like someone was trying to kill you—"

Gadorian never finished his statement.

Suddenly the guildmaster clutched his heart. Wincing, he staggered. Pointing at something that hid behind a nearby tree, the guildmaster groaned. "The city," he whispered. "The city. Must protect—"

Shocked, the two guildguards drew their swords and ran at the thing behind the tree. Akindo, for it was Akindo, stepped free. As the first guard approached, a mouth appeared on the monster's face. Teeth six inches long glistened with saliva.

"Sweet Presence!" said Rowenaster, horrified.

Akindo slavered. Then, making a hideous whine that rent the air, Akindo attacked the guard. It tore off his sword arm. Blood spurted into the air as the guildguard howled in agony. Akindo hit the guard with outstretched claws and knocked him into a bloody heap into a drift. Red stained white. Then Akindo took a bite out of the man's chest and ate his heart. The man died. The second guildguard blanched with fear. Stepping backward, he turned to run. Before he could do so, Gadorian caught him by the arm and screamed at him to attack Akindo.

Incredulous, the guard said, "Are you mad? Get out of my way—"

"I'll fire you—"

"Do it!" shouted the guard, wresting his arm free of Gadorian's grasp. The guard ran for his life. Most of the residents of the Kaleidicopia backed into the house. Only Po, Zendrak, Kelandris, and Himayat remained outside its protecting walls. Himayat looked to Zendrak for orders. The man in green whistled for Further. Turning to Kelandris, Zendrak said, "Go to Suxonli. Take Po and Himayat with you on Further. Wait for my signal. Hennin draws her power from Akindo. I'll distract the *draw*. Can't kill it."

"Why not?" asked Po indignantly.

"This thing is part of the *draw* of Suxonli. If I kill it, I'll cripple the land of Tammirring itself. The *draw* is distorted through Hennin's will. Dispatch her, and the *draw* will return to its original state. It will be a matter of split-second timing. Think you can handle it?" Zendrak added to Himayat. "Remember, Hennin's gone renegade. And she's a higher rank than you. She's had years of training in psychic arts. She's a native Tammi." Himayat nodded, his expression grim.

As Zendrak finished speaking, Further came thundering into view. Saämbolin pedestrians gaped and shrieked. A small crowd had gathered across the street from the felled guildguard. With Further's approach, the gawkers dispersed in all directions. Kelandris swung to the back of the enormous mare. Zendrak gave Po and Himayat a leg up. There was barely enough room for all three of them. Turning her head to the two men sitting behind her, Kelandris said, "Hang on. This will be cold."

"Cold?" asked Po.

He never received an explanation. In seconds, the mare from Neath plunged them into the Everywhen of the Presence. They rode the lines of coincidence. They would reach Suxonli in minutes.

Only Zendrak faced Akindo now. The perverted *draw* from Suxonli licked its bloody mouth. Its eyes glimmered with a slow, patient intelligence. It was, after all, made of the earth. It could wait until Zendrak made a move. The two faced each other in a terrible silence.

Without warning, Zendrak made a cry like a Mythrrim. It shook the street. Snow toppled off roofs. Horses panicked and ran. Zendrak made the cry again. Akindo remained motionless, its face unreadable. Zendrak opened his arms and waved them slowly like a large bird. Then without warning, he began to shape-shift. Born in Soaringsea, Zendrak had inherited the natural ability of throwing off versions of himself much the same way that the volcanic islands of his native archipelago threw off ash and lava.

Zendrak's clothes began to rip. Wings pushed through his skin. Blue-black feathers appeared sleek and silky on his torso. In moments, Zendrak had exchanged his two-legged form for that of a four-legged Mythrrim Beast. He lifted his ugly head and cackled hyena fashion at the snow.

Akindo hesitated. Feeling the monster's consternation on the other end of the psychic line, Elder Hennin looked through Akindo's eyes. Then, hundreds of miles from Speakinghast, Elder Hennin let out a ferocious curse. Long ago when the Mythrrim had still walked the earth, these beasts had tamed all the *landdraws* of Mnemlith. In fact, the Mythrrim were the ones who had wakened the land from slumber into a keen intelligence. Hennin knew she had to act quickly. In this form, Zendrak would be able to command Akindo. Sending the monster her thoughts, she said, "Kill the Mythrrim Beast. Eat his heart out, Akindo. He cannot live without his heart."

Hennin broke her connection to Akindo, returning Akindo's eyes to Akindo for the moment while she put her full focus on weakening Zendrak's clarity of mind and will to live.

Of course, Hennin didn't know Zendrak was past dying.

Chapter Twenty-three

FURTHER SLOWED TO a walk just outside the village limits of Suxonli. Podiddley, who had been seated last on the dark horse from Neath, sat in a hunched position, his face buried in Himayat's back, his fingers in a stranglehold around Himayat's waist. The little thief also had his eyes closed.

"Uh—Po?" said Himayat gently. "You can get off now."

Po opened his eyes with a start. Seeing that he was again in the "real" world, he let out a tremendous sigh of relief. "Shit. I mean, *shit!*"

Himayat and Kelandris both started laughing. Finally the tall Greatkin said, "Yes, I felt that way, too, the first time I entered the Everywhen. Very scary. And like I said, cold."

"Scary?" exploded Po. "Scary doesn't come close. There was nothing under us, nothing above us, and nothing but wavy colored things streaming at my face. Cold? It was like a lake in winter. Dark and full of unseen ghoulies. Shit. I'm walking back."

Kelandris shrugged. "Assuming we survive Hennin . . . "

Himayat nodded. "There is that."

Kelandris regarded the Mayanabi elder quietly. "Hennin probably knows we're here—unless Zendrak has managed to truly distract her. Anyway, I think we need a plan. I have a lot of power at my disposal, but I have no training. You have training, Himayat."

Himayat nodded. "We'll have to kill Hennin. I see no alternative."

Po nodded. "Me either.

Kelandris bit her lower lip. "It would give me pleasure to do so."

Himayat grunted. "That's not such a good thing. This pleasure."

Po stared at Himayat and then at Kelandris. "Who *cares* about the ethics involved? The woman will certainly take pleasure in killing all three of *us*—"

Himayat cut him off. "These things have to be done right, Po. If they aren't, Hennin can survive death."

Po snorted. "She's as mortal as me—"

"Yes, but she has a lot of psychic power. She can create an accommodation for herself *without* a physical body. From this, she can continue to influence the affairs of the world. She can also possess weak-willed people. It's a fairly simple matter to do any of these things when you reach the level of mastery that Hennin has."

Kelandris narrowed her eyes. "Does she already have a nonphysical accommodation, Himayat? Has she already constructed it?"

Himayat shrugged. "Such construction can be created at the moment of death—especially then. At death, the will to live is particularly strong. All the emotions that would tie one to the world are suddenly unleashed. It's a powerful moment. If she sees that Zendrak is winning with Akindo, Hennin will very likely allow us to kill her. We'll think our problems are over."

"But they'll be just beginning," said Po.

"Right."

There was a short silence.

"Shit," said Po.

"Exactly," replied Himayat.

Kelandris said nothing. Zendrak's insistence that she not go after Hennin alone suddenly made sense to her. She was grateful he had intervened. She smiled slightly. So Zendrak wasn't so spineless, after all. He had simply been biding his time until now. Kelandris reached out to Zendrak in her heart, thanking him. She felt an answering tug on the other end—a gentle acknowledgment of her realization. Kelandris took a deep breath and returned to the conversation with the two Mayanabi. Po was speaking.

"The poison in my akatikki is lethal in seconds, Himayat. I don't see why we can't use it. You have something better?"

"We can't be sure it would kill her—"

"I'm *telling* you, it's lethal—"

Himayat shook his head. "She's immune to some kinds of poison. She handles and trains the holovespa, Po. Think about it. She's been stung and survived it. You can bet on it."

There was a short silence.

"Okay," agreed Po. "So what's *your* plan, then?" he asked Himayat. "I assume you have one"

Himayat shook his head. "I'm still thinking about it."

Po swore. "Look. We ain't got *time* for a *conference* here. We gotta kill this Suxonli maniac before she kills us!"

Himayat glared at Po. "Patience."

Po threw up his hands and walked away. He stopped a few feet away, his hands clasped at his back. Himayat and Kelandris could hear him cursing under his breath. Kelandris took the opportunity to speak to Himayat more privately.

"Hennin draws power from the land itself. I can turn it on her. We'd have to do it at Revel Rock. That means we'd have to get there without being stopped. What are our chances?"

"Depends on Zendrak, I should think."

Kelandris again joined her consciousness with Zendrak. *We have a plan,* she told him. *You have to help me reverse the* draw. Kelandris received no answer. *Zendrak?*

Zendrak lifted into the air, his blue-black Mythrrim wings catching snow as it fell softly in Speakinghast. Akindo craned its head, watching Zendrak carefully, his eyes again belonging to Elder Hennin. Fortunately for Kelandris, Po, and Himayat, Hennin's complete attention was on Zendrak.

When Kelandris got no response from Zendrak, she and the two men started toward Revel Rock, the site of her defeat so many years ago. Zendrak was aware of her decision and lauded it in his heart. At the moment, however, he knew that the safety of Kelandris and the Mayanabi men depended on his ability to confound Hennin. He did not want Hennin to become aware of the three people breaching her psychic fortress. He did not want her to feel him reaching out to Kelandris and therefore telegraphing her whereabouts to Hennin. Let Hennin think she could affect him with her will. This would be a first-rate distraction. Zendrak smiled, his large Mythrrim mouth pulling tight over his enormous teeth. He began to cackle hyena fashion. The sound echoed weirdly in the streets and alleys of Speakinghast. Passersby looked at the sky and widened their eyes.

No one had seen a Mythrrim for several thousand years. Zendrak beat the air with his wings. as he did so, he said:

"In the name of the Presence, we begin.
In the ancient of days when the world was new
The Firstborn race spoke the spell of Once Upon.
The words fell teasingly from our tongues
And what had been real became more than real:
It became True.

"I am a Firstborn,
I speak the spell.
I call the truth:
The land is ill,
I make it well.
Words that twisted
And cursed the *draw*,
Now be removed,
Be free of this flaw.
Be returned to the Presence
From this moment hence,

Be returned to your primal state
Of pristine innocence."

Akindo's mouth slowly closed and disappeared in its smooth face. It raised its hands, its claws tearing at the sky. Then it fell to its knees in the snow. It let loose a mournful cry. Again it raised its hands at the sky. It seemed to be desperately trying to open something. Zendrak watched with interest. Was this some directive of Hennin or some unexpected emotion from Akindo? Zendrak didn't know. Again Akindo howled. The sound of it shook the foundations of the city. An earthquake started. Zendrak snapped at the air. Did Greatkin Mattermat intend to destroy the city if he couldn't have his way? Was he having a temper tantrum in Eranossa at this very moment? Zendrak didn't know this, either. But he suspected Akindo might well be drawing power from Mattermat.

Okay, thought Zendrak. *Okay, big boy—you want to play rough? Fine.*

Zendrak rose in the air higher. Then, diving like a bird of prey, he screamed at Akindo, all seven sets of his vocal cords splitting the air. Thunder and lightning crashed around him. Calling on the power of Trickster and Themyth both, Zendrak fought Mattermat on the earth plane with the power of the spell of Once Upon. He began telling the creation story of the Greatkin that the Mythrrim had recently told Rimble in Soaringsea. With each word, he reminded Mattermat and all of creation that everything answered to Great Being. Nothing acted in opposition to that great will. Anything that attempted to do so would fail in the end. And that end was now, he told Mattermat. Lightning struck the ground. Snow exploded as if it had just been knocked free by a blast of dynamite. Again and again, the lightning struck. Thunder pummeled the air. Buildings shook and crumbled. People screamed. Some ran out into the streets. Others ran into the archways of stone buildings. Animals bolted. Pandemonium increased as the battle raged,

Akindo clawed the air more urgently now. A bolt of lightning hit the monster in the face, boring into the middle of its forehead. Akindo screamed in agony. Suddenly a whirlwind started in a wide circle around Akindo. Zendrak smiled.

Kelandris was turning at Revel Rock.

No sooner had Kelandris started to spin in the center of the monoliths that circled the sacred area known as Revel Rock than Elder Hennin realized she was in Suxonli. Like an ancient fury, the renegade Mayanabi ran out of her house. She grabbed the first saddled horse she found and galloped up the path called the Long Revel Trail. It was steep, the mountains that bordered it sheer and treacherous with snow. Hennin beat her horse mercilessly, forcing it to climb faster and faster. Just as she turned the corner that opened into the large standing-stone circle, she was confronted by an enormous blue-black horse.

This was the beginning of Elder Hennin's nightmare—so to speak.

Further, for it was Further, commanded Hennin's gelding to stop. Glad to do so, the gelding stopped cold. Hennin was so surprised by the sudden cessation of motion that she lost her balance and fell off. The gelding moved away, leaving Further to deal with the woman's cruelty. The mare snorted, her glass eyes wild. Power surged and crackled around Further. Summoning the forces of Neath, the mare stood her ground. Hennin tried to gauge the extent of Further's power. Sensing suddenly that Further drew from Neath and not Eranossa, Hennin began to laugh quietly. Neath was the underworld where all things nefarious were born—so she thought. This was home territory. Feeling more confident, Hennin prepared to do battle with the Fertile Dark.

Without warning, Further charged the Tammirring woman. Striking out with her hooves, she reared and attacked. Hennin concentrated her attention on the emotion of fear. She grabbed at the mare's heart with doubt and horror. The mare whinnied fiercely, still attacking. Hennin jumped out of the way. Then she saw who was riding Further.

It was the Greatkin of Death, Troth.

Staring in shock at Troth—she had always thought he was on her side—Elder Hennin was momentarily caught off guard. Further connected with her skull. And pulverized it with her hooves. Bones caved in, making a sickening sound. Blood and brains spilled into the snow. As this occurred Kelandris spun to the right.

Raising the old bull-roarer she had long ago left in this place, Kelandris sent it sailing in a wide circle above her head. It whined and droned. Calling on Zendrak to steady the power from the land, she brought down the power of the heavens. Kelandris was immediately hit by lightning. Unlike last time, sixteen years ago in Suxonli, Kelandris did not lose control of the *draw*. Himayat and Po grounded her.

As Zendrak pulled the power through Kelandris and used it to finish Akindo, Hennin died, her psyche shattered by the innate goodness of the Fertile Dark. In Speakinghast, Akindo lost its form. Like a ceramic dish suddenly hurled against the floor, Akindo solidified then cracked into a thousand pieces. The diabolic consciousness of Akindo rose in the air to meet Zendrak. Zendrak took a deep breath and blew out the word. "whoooooo" at Akindo. This was the sound Great Being had made when It first released its dreams. The divine sound penetrated and reconstituted Akindo's will with Its own. Forming Akindo into a new pattern, the sound dispersed Hennin's intentions that drove the monster. Suddenly directionless, it hesitated. During that moment of hesitation, Zendrak ate Akindo's consciousness. Greatkin that he was, he absorbed his mistake into himself. Freed of the evil of Hennin's desires, Akindo did not harm him. Now Zendrak spoke to the land, healing it. He sent that healing back to Kelandris. She spun it into the earth at Revel Rock. The door that Hennin had opened sixteen years ago lost its edges and was reabsorbed into the whole of the *draw* of all Mnemlith. There was no scar.

Hennin was defeated.

Troth jumped off Further. He slung the body of the Tammirring woman over Further's withers. Jumping back on the mare, Troth returned to Neath. Hennin would find herself in unpardoned service to him for a long time. Her first task would be to treat Cobeth like the son she pretended he was to her. This time, however, she'd have to muster up the genuine feelings. If she couldn't do it, Troth decided Hennin could clean the stables of Neath for a while until her temper improved. If her temper didn't improve, Troth would make her write the following until it *did* improve.

"All things begin in the name of Presence."

If this took eons, so much the better, thought Troth. The stables of Neath were quite dirty. He'd be glad of a drudge in his service.

Chapter Twenty-four

As SOON AS Zendrak dispatched Akindo, everyone in Speakinghast who had been affected by the steady drain of despair was freed. Through Akindo's death, Hennin's foul desires were thwarted forever. Those who had been stung by the holovespa and lived, now died—with the single exception of Yafatah, who had been saved from Hennin's intentions by the roving univer'silsila breed of wasp.

So Rhu passed away quietly in her home. She joined Cobeth in Neath and was surprised by the change Kelandris had wrought in him. It took much longer for Rhu to forgive Kelandris for making Cobeth unrecognizable to her than it had for Kelandris to jump in the River of Memory and save Cobeth's soul. Rimble-Rimble.

In the city street, all that remained of Akindo was its long gray robe. Faces peered out of the windows of the Kaleidicopia. When Rowenaster and Janusin saw that Akindo was dead, they told the others hiding under various archways and desks in the house. A ragged cheer resounded. People climbed out of their earthquake fortresses and assembled in the living room. Barlimo immediately started checking the walls for cracks. Finding several, she swore. Guildmaster Gadorian laughed at her continued concern over the Kaleidicopia.

"You don't live here. Remember? You just signed the papers."

The rest of the Kaleidicopians, all of whom had been terrified by the earthquake and the sound of Zendrak's Mythrrim screech, just stared at the Saämbolin official, everyone too dumbfounded by his lack of compassion to even reprimand him. Finally Mab broke the silence.

Glancing about herself, she asked, "Where's Tree?"

No one knew. Looking worried, Barlimo went off in search of the twiggy Jinnjirri fellow. Janusin followed her in silence. Both Jinnjirri knew that all of Tree's family had been killed by an earthquake while on a picnic in Jinnjirri one summer. They hoped Tree would come out of hiding when they called him. Barlimo and Janusin investigated every cubby and crawl space they could think of on every floor of the house. They found no trace of Tree. They returned to the larger group, their expressions and their hair color dour.

Mab said, "You didn't find him."

"Nope," said Janusin.

"Try outside," said Himayat. "I can feel him nearby. I just can't place him. Seems he's elevated on something—"

"A tree?" said Yafatah suddenly. "There do be one you can reach outside my window."

"Well, that explains a lot," said Barlimo drily. During Fasilla's absence, Barlimo had been left in charge of the young Tammirring girl. On several occasions, she had found Yafatah's door locked and the girl strangely silent inside her room. Yafatah hadn't been sleeping; she had been out exploring the city streets. Barlimo rolled her eyes, but said nothing more.

Yafatah gave Barlimo a quick hug. "Sorry. Anyway, come on. I bet that be his hideaway."

It was true.

When everyone had piled into Yafatah's small room on the second floor, the sixteen-year-old ran to the open window. Yafatah poked her head out. There on the innermost branch, huddled next to the trunk of the maple that grew beside the Kaleidicopia, sat Tree. His hair was ashen, his eyes shut. He was trembling. Yafatah told the others. Janusin opened the window wider and climbed out. He called Tree's name. Tree said nothing. Swinging carefully to a strong branch, the master sculptor inched toward Tree. Hearing twigs break, Tree looked up. His eyes were wild with fear. He began screaming at Janusin to get away from him.

Janusin licked his lips. "Tree, I mean you no harm. You know that."

"I don't want your help, Janusin. Stay the fuck away!"

Janusin looked helplessly at Barlimo, who now had her head outside the window. Barlimo called softly to Tree, putting all the mothering she could muster into her voice. Janusin felt cheered by her words himself. He turned back to Tree, expecting the younger Jinnjirri to respond in kind.

"Go away! Go away, *all* of you!"

Zendrak, who was still in Mythrrim form, heard Tree's yells. Circling overhead, Zendrak squawked. Tree was so startled that he lost his grip on the trunk. Janusin grabbed his arm as Tree nearly fell off his perch. Feeling the strength in Janusin's hand and seeing the genuine concern in Janusin's eyes, Tree started crying. Janusin, whose arms and back were hard with muscles made powerful through hours of sculpting, pulled Tree toward him roughly. Moving back toward Yafatah's bedroom, Janusin pushed Tree into Barlimo's waiting hands. Once Tree and Janusin were inside, Yafatah shut the window. Tree collapsed in a small, skinny heap on the floor, his face buried in his arms. He made no noise. Now his hair turned stricken blue-black. It frosted with gray. Barlimo sat down next to Tree. She spoke quietly to him.

"Hey, you in there."

"What?" came the muffled reply.

"Life goes on."

"Shut up, Barl."

Barlimo remained undeterred. "Hey."

"*What?*"

"I'm making cocoa. You want some?"

Tree raised his head. "You're not making cocoa. You're in here talking to me, stupid."

Barlimo nodded. "Well, I'd *like* to be making cocoa—"

"So go away. I told you to go away before. So go away."

Barlimo shrugged. "You going to stay inside?"

"Who cares?"

"I do," said Barlimo. A round of voices echoed her words. Barlimo smiled. "Well, will you listen to that? They all care. Must be sick, huh, Tree?"

"Yeah," said Tree, his hair starting to lighten imperceptibly.

Barlimo got up. "I'm going to make cocoa. Anybody who wants any should follow me into the kitchen."

Everybody left the room. Seeing that he was alone—finally—Tree let out a sigh of relief. He glanced at the closed window. He considered going back out on a limb—literally. As the thought crossed his mind, Zendrak pressed his ugly Mythrrim head—teeth, protruding eyes and horns—against the closed window and screeched. Startled, Tree got to his feet hastily and tore down the stairs after his housemates.

Outside the house, Zendrak lifted into the air and flew toward Suxonli.

In the kitchen of the Kaleidicopia, conversation was merry. This surprised Gadorian. After all, he had just served everyone their eviction notice a scant hour ago. The Saämbolin official watched Barlimo throw the eviction papers aside as she readied mugs for cocoa.

Uncomfortable with the good humor in the room, Gadorian said, "Well, I'll be leaving now."

"Why do that, Gad?" asked Rowenaster. "We'll be having lunch soon. You might as well stay."

"*Why* are you being so hospitable to me?"

Rowenaster shrugged. "We're alive, aren't we? Seems like a good moment to act friendly. Even to you. After all, we want the same thing as you. We want the city to survive the Jinnaeon."

Gadorian scowled. "I was going to ask you about those

prophesies the other day at the university. Sirrey said I should."

Rowenaster grinned unexpectedly. "So, *sit*."

Timmer grumbled as she poured milk into a large saucepan. "This isn't going to be *boring*, is it? I mean, this isn't going to be one of your religious lectures, is it?"

Yafatah grinned happily and interrupted before Rowenaster could reply. "They be Tammi prophesies, doon't they?"

"Yes, child. Now, pay attention, all of you. You, too, Timmer. These prophesies affect everyone in this room, this city, indeed, in the whole world. You can close your ears if you dare. Some people like surprises, of course."

Properly chastised, Timmer swore and sat down at the round kitchen table. Tree, Janusin, Barlimo, Fasilla, Yafatah, and Mab soon joined her. Rowenaster stayed on his feet. He was about to give one of his favorite lectures. For this he would pace in his best professorial style. Clasping his hands behind his back, the seventy-year-old man began.

"The Jinnaeon is named for Jinndaven, the Greatkin of Imagination. Jinnaeon is a transition period of creative, imaginative turmoil when doomsday stories proliferate and everyone's worst fears will be realized—"

At Eranossa, Jinndaven started protesting vigorously.

Panthe'kinarok Interlogue

"I AM THE PATRON OF *GOOD* IDEAS!" yelled the Greatkin of Imagination at the top of his lungs. All conversation at the table stopped. Raising his fist in the air and glaring mightily at Rimble, Jinndaven added, "You see what they're saying about me? You see what you did—"

Mattermat roared with laughter as Rimble turned scarlet.

Jinndaven continued his tirade. "I *told* you they'd blame all your chaos on me. The Jinnaeon. Just because you wanted to cause a mutation in a rose gives you no right to bastardize my name, Rimble!" Jinndaven's body trembled with frustration.

"Well, well, Rimble," said Mattermat silkily. "You just lost one of your main supporters here. Feeling a little vulnerable, are we?"

Trickster had just materialized a blanket. He was currently hiding under it. What Mattermat didn't realize was that the blanket was one made by a Native American tribe in a Distant Place. While Rimble hid, he thought. After a few moments—during which Mattermat continued to deride him—Rimble threw off the blanket. Dressed in furs and feathers and mud, Trickster announced, "Fine. You guys don't like me? I don't care. I don't like you, either—"

Themyth tried to interrupt but was unsuccessful.

"Furthermore," said Trickster, standing on his chair, "I don't have to stay here at this blasted dinner. I can leave. I can go live elsewhere."

Rimble paused, delighting at the stunned expressions on the faces of his twenty-six brothers and sisters.

"No one would have you," snapped Mattermat.

"Hoo-hoo, brother dear. You're *so* wrong. I've been marketing. And it's paid off. A new name has been born in a Distant Place. Mine. They've added it to their list. I'm not just Coyote. I'm Rimble. I'm Ubiquitous. I'm National. I'm Dancing in the Streets." Trickster laughed like a Mythrrim.

Hearing the familiar sound, Themyth steepled her fingers on the table. Trickster was up to something, that was certain. Or he had already *been* up to something and the Greatkin were about to find out what it was. She decided the latter was probably the case; Rimble was looking too smug to be bluffing.

Themyth cleared her throat. "What streets are you dancing in, dear?"

"Milwaukee. And D. C. And Pittsfield. And New York. And Boston. And San Francisco. Hey—I'm even dancing in Kenya. I'm not just national, folks. I'm international. Ta-da! My name means Transformer."

"No, it doesn't," said Sathmadd. "It means The-One-Who-Knows-Something-of-Himself. I know. I have it catalogued right here," she added, pointing at her head.

"It also means Transformer," said Rimble.

"Since when?" asked the Greatkin of Organization, her voice skeptical. Sathmadd knew all the names of everything in the known universe. As it turned out, however, the Distant Place was in a universe *unknown* to the Greatkin. Until recently.

Greatkin Mattermat frowned, his burly eyebrows resembling a ridge of briars across his broad forehead. "If you leave this universe, Rimble, you'll cease to 'matter' here. I'll see to it personally."

"I'm sure you will, Mattie," replied Rimble, his voice pleasant.

"You don't sound very concerned," said Themyth. She, on the other hand, felt *quite* concerned.

"Why matter to people who don't appreciate my impro*ooo*vements? Even *I* get tired of hitting my head against mountains," Trickster added, looking directly at Mattermat.

Mattermat smiled. "I'm sure you do, little brother. And we can do very well without you here. If there's another place that needs you more than us—"

Jinndaven interrupted unexpectedly. As much as he felt justified in complaining about Trickster's mutation of a rose into a winterbloom, Jinndaven knew full well what would happen if Rimble left the Panthe'kinarok table for good. Matter would sclerose; ideas would become mediocre; habits would never be broken; life would stagnate. If Rimble did not exist, Jinndaven knew that the world—the universe—would in time cease to exist also. Trickster was the face of the Presence who kept things moving and growing. Entropy and inertia would set in immediately if the little ruffian stopped meddling in reality. Waving his hands, Jinndaven said, "Don't be hasty, Rimble. I'm sure there's plenty of reasons for you to stay here."

"Can't think of a one," said Rimble, and shrugged. Bowing to Mattermat, Trickster said, "It's been a real pain knowing you. Hope things run more smoothly with me gone. I really do."

Themyth stood up. Was Rimble serious? "Rimble? You can't leave here. Without you, everything will go out of balance. We need the tension you create—"

"We do *not*!" cried Mattermat.

"Yes, we do," chimed Phebene. "No one will ever fall in love if you're not here to create the impossible possibility."

Trickster shook his head. "You'll do just fine without me, Phebes. Good-bye," he said to everyone. Then without another word, Trickster vanished.

There was a long silence.

Mattermat peered into the physical space Trickster had just occupied. "Do you suppose he's really gone?" he asked hopefully.

Themyth got up. She walked slowly over to Rimble's chair. She felt the air. She stuck her hand through time and space and grabbed hold of nothing. Her old face paled. The patchwork quilt she had been wearing over her shoulders fell to the floor. Themyth walked into the kitchen.

Rimble's roast was gone.

Chapter Twenty-five

RIMBLE'S DEPARTURE FROM the known universes had immediate consequences. Old habits which one had hopefully discarded or outgrown in youth came creeping back with irritating tenacity. Obstacles that stood between the Guild in Speakinghast and various small interest groups solidified and became unmovable. Lovers lost their creativity and romanticism, breeding contempt and boredom. Artists continued making what they had made before. Surprise birthday parties went out of fashion. So did daring inventions. In short, civilization came to a grinding halt.

Meanwhile, in the unknown universes, specifically the one which held the Distant Place, Trickster's touch created an explosion of New Ideas and Possibility. Trickster, who had been called by many names in the Distant Place, was now recognized as Rimble the Transformer. The old mythology had been given a new infusion by Trickster's recent reentry into that world. He was given a face-lift so to speak. Welcomed by the denizens of the Distant Place, Rimble settled in. Updating himself for the needs of the modern world, Trickster put on new clothing. He adopted a Mohawk on Saturday and Sunday, and a yuppie three-piece suit for the workweek, when he also carried a business card. It read:

IMPROVEMENTS, INC.
Creators of the Impossible Possibility
(800) 999-9999-9
Special Agent: Mr. Rimble

Trickster distributed his business card in every city of the world. People who were in desperate need of radical, irrevocable, and life-giving change in their lives called Rimble at all hours of the day and night. Rimble, who possessed and needed no phone, simply heard their calls in his mind. As soon as the request was made, the power of change was released to the individual. Of course, since it was Trickster answering the calls, change occurred in the most unexpected and fantastic ways. Coincidence knew no bounds. Neither did eccentricity. Trickster loved every minute of his new job. Everyone who requested help from him became *Rimblessah*—blessed by Rimble. And changed forever.

One day, Trickster and the Obstinate Woman took a walk down by the east banks of Lake Michigan in Milwaukee. Even though it was still winter in Mnemlith, it was edging toward fall in Wisconsin. The trees were covered in a pageant of orange-pink and yellow leaves. The air was eager and gusted merrily across the teal-blue water of the gigantic lake. The Obstinate Woman pulled her gray muffler and hat down over her ears. Since it was Saturday, Trickster carried a skateboard under his arm and sported a denim jacket with rhinestones and buttons stuck all over it. His stiff black Mohawk listed in the wind. Trickster turned to the Obstinate Woman and said, "Wonder how things are going in Mnemlith?"

The Obstinate Woman shrugged. "Probably not very well. How long do you plan to abandon them—"

"Abandon them?" interrupted Trickster. "I hardly call it that. 'Tis *they* who have abandoned me, girlie. They didn't know what they had when they had it. Always complaining, always wishing I'd go away. Well, I have. And I likes it much better here," he added with a grin. "People ask for my help, you know. All the time. Day and night. It's quite nice, it is. Quite gratifying."

"You don't think people in Mnemlith need your help?"

"That's not the point. Sure, they need my help. But they don't *want* it. They don't *ask* for it. See the difference?"

The Obstinate Woman grunted.

There was a short pause.

Trickster watched the waves in silence. Finally he said, "You really think I should check up on things?"

The Obstinate Woman nodded. "Yup. You kind of left Kelandris and Zendrak with a mess, you know. You left them in a world that hasn't got the quality of change represented in it. They're your children, yes. But without you being represented at the Panthe'kinarok, how can they activate that side of their nature? You're not there to mirror it back. So what are they to do, Rimble? You've crippled them."

Trickster scowled. "I think you're exaggerating mightily, missy."

"I don't."

There was another short pause.

"Well," said Trickster, wiping his nose on his sleeve, "I *have* been curious about everyone. I suppose I could make a quick return. A weekend jaunt, as it were."

"Good idea," replied the Obstinate Woman drily.

In Mnemlith time, Greatkin Rimble had been gone only three weeks. But what a three weeks it had been. True to his word, Gadorian had shut down the Kaleidicopia, its entrance and first-floor windows boarded up. Rimble's Own, as the members of his ennead were known among themselves, had scattered into the streets of Speakinghast.

In the north, Kelandris, Zendrak, Himayat, and Po remained in Suxonli Village after Hennin's death. The two Greatkin had felt Rimble's departure from the known universes and had been stunned. Unsure what their father expected of them, both Greatkin had sought the counsel of their mother, Greatkin Themyth. Themyth had visited her children appearing as an old crone at the crossroads outside Suxonli on several occasions. She did so now.

Gone were Themyth's playful patchwork clothes. In their stead were drab colors and limp, threadbare materials. Her gray hair was matted, her wrinkles pronounced. Themyth limped toward Kelandris and Zendrak. She used her cane to support her frail body. Her condition had alarmed both her children. They had begged her to contact Rimble, but Themyth had refused. The Greatkin of Civilization preferred to keep her condition secret from Rimble. She wanted him to feel free to do what he felt he needed to do. Kelandris had thought this absurd and spent a great deal of time sending urgent messages to the Obstinate Woman in Milwaukee trying to convince her to tell Rimble he needed to return home as soon as possible. The Obstinate Woman had finally succeeded down by the shores of Lake Michigan. Rimble made his first appearance in Mnemlith at the crossroads outside Suxonli moments after Themyth appeared there.

Sleek and happy himself, Rimble stared open-mouthed at the Greatkin of Civilization. He had expected Themyth to react negatively to his disappearance, but he had never expected her to waste away. "Themyth," he said softly, "why didn't you tell me this was so hard on you?"

The Greatkin of Civilization shrugged. "You needed to leave. Why should I stop you from doing that? You're an independent sort, Rimble. Always have been. From the moment you freed us all from Great Being, that's been your nature. Your freedom *is* your being. I understand this and would never cage you here."

Rimble swallowed. He felt awful—for once. He put his hands out and touched Themyth gently on the cheeks. "You're so very dear to me. More than any of the others, you matter most to me," he said with uncharacteristic affection. "I would've returned for your sake. Always."

Kelandris, who was standing nearby with Zendrak, raised an eyebrow. She leaned toward her brother and whispered, "Seems the Distant Place has softened his heart a bit."

"Yes," agreed Zendrak. "How unexpected. Somehow I never figured Dad for a paragon of compassion. Suppose it's a trick?"

Kelandris shook her head. "Feels to me like he's really upset about Themyth's health. I think he really loves her."

"Phebene is getting through to Dad, after all."

"Yeah."

Rimble put his arm around Themyth. He guided her away from their children, measuring his quick step to Themyth's labored ones. Out of hearing of Zendrak and Kelandris, Rimble said, "You want to make love?"

Themyth shook her head. "You always make me pregnant."

"I don't have to make you pregnant."

"No tricks?"

"No tricks."

Themyth smiled slightly.

Rimble grinned. "I saw that. I saw that smile there, girlie."

Themyth started laughing. As she did so, she lost years off her apparent age. Her eyes twinkled as she thought of the happy prospect of bedding Trickster. "Remember that position where you hang from the ceiling and I—"

Trickster shrieked with giggles.

Kelandris looked at Zendrak. "What do you suppose they're talking about?" she asked.

Zendrak kissed her playfully on the mouth.

Chapter Twenty-six

WHILE RIMBLE AND Themyth made love, the world of Mnemlith was transformed. Civilization prospered—albeit eccentrically—and Rimble's Nine found their footing again. Rowenaster, who had always been independently wealthy (and quite tenured), bought a house in the Asilliwir section of Speakinghast and invited the rest of the Kaleidicopians to come and live there. Friends with some of the most powerful and influential merchants in the city, Rowenaster was able to buy the house for practically nothing. Located on Bazaar Street, the house was symmetrical and not quite as large as the Kaleidicopia. Made of old brownstone, it was studded with stained glass and marble archways. The house had a central courtyard and was surrounded by a walled garden that had been meticulously cared for by its previous tenants. Here was a place of great privacy. The Asilliwir merchants who prospered on this well-to-do street allowed the Guild little interference in their lives. Many of these merchants were the ones who kept the Guild solvent. Rowen knew it.

And so did Gadorian.

Guildmaster Gadorian stared moodily into his coddled egg which nestled inside a floral porcelain container on the kitchen table. Master Curator Sirrefene bustled about squeezing oranges on the counter and browning toast on a rack over the open fire in the kitchen hearth in their Saämbolin residence. Seeing Gadorian's expression, she said, "Cheer up, love. The Asilliwir will keep the Kaleidicopians in line—more or less."

"It's the *less* I'm worried about."

"Well, at least the house on Bazaar Street is attractive."

"True."

Gadorian groaned. "What's *wrong* with Rowenaster? Why does he *insist* on living with those people?"

"Maybe he likes them."

Gadorian rolled his eyes.

Sirrefene put a glass of fresh juice on the table next to her husband's dark-skinned hand. "You know, Gad—the Kaleidicopian's got *rid* of that gray thing. Akindo, I think they called it. No one at the 'K' wanted it in the city any more than you did."

Gadorian pursed his lips. "There were reports of a Mythrrim in the sky, Sirrey. And these reports all originated inside that house. Those people are rumormongers. They're dissidents. They make havoc of city rules. They should be kicked out of Speakinghast altogether. And there's a new mood, Sirrey. Have you felt it? All in the last week or so. Members of the Saämbolin Guild are saying we're looking at a more relaxed time now in the city. They're even considering starting a scholarship fund for artists over at the university. They're going to *pay* the Jinn to go to school!"

Sirrefene smiled. "Maybe our time in the city is past, Gad. Maybe there's a new age acoming. If so, we'll have to make room for it, won't we, my love?"

Gadorian grunted.

In the north, Kelandris and Zendrak began the long process of straightening out the distortions they found in the rituals the Mayanabi had given to Suxonli Village centuries ago. It seemed that the person who had done the original telling of the Mythrrim for Greatkin Rimble had added a few things of his own to the storytelling. Since Rimble was such an eccentric Greatkin, it had been difficult to even *see* the distortions, much less correct them in the original.

Needless to say, the old guard in Suxonli—all those who had been loyal to Hennin—complained bitterly of the changes Zendrak and Kelandris brought to their village.

When they also discovered that Kelandris was indeed the same person they had judged akindo sixteen years ago, there were midnight meetings and talk of enacting the Ritual of Akindo a second time. When Zendrak found out about these meetings, he laughed. Calling the entire village together, he informed them that he was Trickster's son and emissary. Pointing to Kelandris, he told them she was Trickster's daughter.

"In other words, folks, you're looking at a direct line of transmission. Greatkin to Greatkin. You want to twist my father's rituals into something unrecognizable? Fine, but you do it on your own time. And you do it far from Suxonli. Centuries ago, Suxonli was a sacred spot—so designated by the Mythrrim Beasts of Soaringsea. You will keep Trickster's Hallows exactly as they are handed down to you, or you will leave."

Zendrak paused while the villagers muttered among themselves.

Hennin's best friend, Village Elder Rigga, spoke harshly. "Rituals change over time. Stories are embellished. Accounts are changed to suit the needs of the people. If Greatkin Rimble were here, I'm sure he wouldn't impose rules on his followers. He's the *breaker* of rules, not the maker of them. You've been living in Saämbolin too long. We don't like your attitude. And we're not going to accept it."

Zendrak smiled. Turning to Rimble, who presently sat at his feet in the guise of a pied-eyed brindle dog named Pi, Zendrak said, "Your turn, Father. They don't think I'm representing your wishes."

Trickster grinned, pulling his lips back over his teeth. Standing up, Trickster changed form. He appeared to the villagers of Suxonli as a middle-aged skateboarding punk. Chewing a large wad of gum, Rimble blew a pink bubble. It popped.

The sound of it was deafening.

People put their hands to their heads. A few cried out in

pain. Rimble watched their discomfort with a glacial expression. When the noise and complaining in the village council room had died down, Rimble said, "Now that I've got your attention, I have this to say: This village isn't special in the least to me. It's only a physical place, folks. If you had kept my Hallows intact and not read into them what you wanted to see, *then* this place would've been special. As it is, I could blow it off the face of the world and not miss it one whit." Trickster let his words sink in. "And I may yet do that. Themyth and I are discussing your fate, you see. She's your champion. Not me. Personally, I don't think you deserve to be given a second chance with my Mythrrim. You've proved yourselves grossly incompetent as it is. I gave you my daughter, and you tried to *kill* her? And now you'd run my son out of town? You know what that says to me? Says you're blind, deaf, and stupid." Rimble's eyes blazed as he warmed to the task of telling Suxonli what he thought of them. "Either you accept Zendrak and Kel's rule, or you get out. *Now*."

There was a short pause.

During the silence, Rimble went up to several people in the front row. "You leave. And you. You, too."

"But I—" began one of them.

Rimble slapped the woman on the face. "You think I can't read your mind, lady? You think I can't read your ugly thoughts? They're like a quadraphonic stereo blaring in my ears!"

"A what?" asked the man next to the unfortunate woman. Of course, no one in Suxonli had ever heard of a stereo, much less a quadraphonic one.

Greatkin Rimble ignored the question. Pushing through the chairs, he told several more people to leave. When they hesitated, he began to blow at them. They lifted into the air and slammed against the back of the council room. Those who shared these people's opinion of Zendrak and Kelandris got to their feet hastily and ran from the room. They didn't want to wait until Trickster read their thoughts as well. Only a handful of people were left in the room—approximately twelve, some of them teenagers over the age of seventeen. Trickster put his hands on his hips. Looking down at one young girl, he said, "You want to turn for me this autumn at the revel?"

The girl blushed, and nodded vigorously.

Looking at Himayat, who was still in Suxonli with Po, Trickster said, "You train her, will you?"

Himayat nodded, and bowed slightly to Trickster.

"Po?" said Trickster. "You've got a choice. You can either stay up here and keep this village in order, or you can come back to Speakinghast and keep order there."

Po peered at Rimble. "You sure you're talking to *me*?"

"Yeah. Why?"

"Keeping *order* isn't my favorite thing—"

"Well, bud," interrupted Trickster, "it's your favorite thing *now*." Trickster bowed to the little thief. As the Greatkin did so, he clunked Po on the forehead with his own head. Po staggered backward, swearing. When the little thief had gotten his balance back, he said, "What the fuck did you just *do*, Rimble?"

Trickster cackled. "Change or be changed, asshole."

Po winced. He felt like taking a bath. When he realized this, he panicked. Until now, it had been against Po's principles to bathe more than once every two weeks.

"So?" asked Zendrak. "Staying. Or going home?"

Po rubbed his forehead gingerly where Trickster had hit it. Po shrugged. "Yafatah needs me."

Zendrak raised an eyebrow. "Commitment? Responsibility? Consideration? All in one clunk on the head?" Zendrak turned to Trickster. "We should all be clobbered on the head by you, Dad. What a time-saver."

"Okay," said Rimble, speaking to the few who remained in Suxonli. "Kelandris, Himayat, and Zendrak will remain here to guide you." He waved good-bye to his children, who both bowed to him. Grabbing Po by the back of the neck, Rimble and Po disappeared into thin air.

Kelandris and Zendrak burst into laughter. When Rimble had grabbed Po, the little thief's expression was one of sheer contrariness. Grinning, Kelandris said to Zendrak and Himayat, "What an evenly matched pair those two make."

Chapter Twenty-seven

ON THE WAY to Speakinghast, Rimble dropped by the Feyborne Mountains—literally. The punk Greatkin and Po appeared on a snowbound, craggy mountain ridge. Blowing on the snow as he had done to the recalcitrant villagers in Suxonli, Rimble cleared away the snow in a matter of seconds. There, under the snow, were the winterbloom. They were alive and growing.

Rimble slapped his thigh. "See? An idea whose time has come." Looking heavenward, Trickster yelled, "Take *that*, Mattie. I won. Na-na-na-na-na," he added, doing a little jig in the snow. Without warning an avalanche started in the peaks above them. Rimble's eyes widened. Grabbing Po's hand, he said, "He's got a bad temper, that Mattie. Come on, before he buries us in this muck!"

Po and Rimble disappeared from view again. When they reappeared, they were in Speakinghast just outside the new residence of Rowenaster and the rest of Rimble's Nine. Po stared at the immaculate, pale yellow door. He peered at the sparkling clean windows and the tidy front walk.

"It's even got matching drapes," said Po, his voice incredulous.

"Just your style," Trickster said. "Remember?"

"Oh, yeah. I'm supposed to like this sort of thing now." Funny thing was, in Po's heart of hearts, he found that he *did* like the clean appearance of the place. Had he felt this way all along? The little thief wasn't sure. Nothing was as it seemed.

"Welcome to Jinnaeon," said Rimble gaily. "Nothing is as it *was*. Not even you, kiddo."

Po grumbled under his breath. Catching sight of smoke issuing from a neat, brownstone chimney on the slate-blue roof, Po said, "Does this place have a name?"

"Yeah," said Rimble. "Bazaar House. 99 Bazaar House, to be exact."

"Figures," muttered Po, looking at the brass numbers on the front door that read 99. Po took a deep breath. "Might as well go in, I suppose."

Before Podiddley could put his hand on the shiny brass knob of the house, the door opened. It was Themyth. Gone were her rags. Instead, she wore her fantastic coat of tails, her hair neatly coiffed, her age not more than sixty now. She welcomed Rimble and Po graciously. They entered the house and were instantly met by the sound of Janusin lugging a box of sculpting tools out of the kitchen and into the hallway. The master sculptor looked up. Amazed to see Po and Rimble, Janusin yelled, "Hey, look who's here. Po and Rim—"

Po cut him off. "You're going to scratch that nice hardwood floor if you drag the box that way, Jan."

Janusin stared at the frumpy little thief. "Did you say what I think you said? I mean, since *when* have you ever cared about any floor?"

Before Po could reply, people poured out of the kitchen. Mab, Tree, Rowenaster, Barlimo, Yafatah, Timmer, and Fasilla made a ring around Po and Rimble. Questions and answers flew back and forth.

Finally Barlimo announced that it was time for high tea.

Po's eyes widened as he walked into the sparkling clean kitchen of Bazaar House. Counters were made of blond wood that had been covered by some kind of newfangled wood protector. The icebox was large, the goods inside neatly packaged and labeled. The pantry was well stocked, Barlimo's herbs hanging in tidy, easily identifiable bunches that hung from the rafters. Not a dish was to be found in the pink marble sink.

"And we aim to keep it that way, Po," said Timmer crisply.

"Of course," replied Po, and meant it.

No one believed him at this time, of course.

Yafatah sidled up to Po. "So you came back. I thought you mightna' do so. Thought you might run."

"From teaching you?" asked Po. "Nah. Never entered my mind."

Themyth interrupted here. "It's time for a little holiday. A little festival," she said warmly. Then without further warning, Themyth shut her eyes and called the Mythrrim Beasts of Soaringsea out of their seclusion. No one save Trickster knew she had done this, however, for Themyth called her children in silence. When Themyth opened her eyes, she found most of the people in the room staring at her expectantly.

Trickster and Themyth burst into laughter.

Fasilla said, "This doon't be a holiday, you sitting with your eyes tight shut."

Themyth began to hum to herself.

"What's she doing?" Timmer asked Mab.

"Don't know," replied the plump Piedmerri, offering herself and Timmer another helping of brown bread with dark honey and butter on it. "Maybe she's playing a trick. After all, Trickster and she *did* share sheets a week or so ago."

Timmer nodded and munched in silence on her sweet.

Far to the north, on the roof of the world, said some poets of old, the Mythrrim Beasts of Soaringsea heard their mother's call. The gigantic creatures organized themselves briefly with a great deal of squawking and laughter. Then, one by one, they rose into the air, their wings making a thundering noise that traveled for miles. They circled slowly, effortlessly, and wheeled toward the mainland, their direction due southeast.

The Mythrrim Beasts of Soaringsea would arrive in

Speakinghast by dawn the following morning. Once there, they would confront staid Saämbolin with their impossible existence until the city itself capitulated and admitted that the Mythrrim were in fact real.

As were the Greatkin.

Chapter Twenty-eight

KELANDRIS AND ZENDRAK slept that night, wrapped in each other's arms. Kel's face was relaxed, the terrors of her previous years in Suxonli finally laid to rest. Zendrak's breath rose and fell lightly next to her face. All of sudden, Kelandris sat bolt upright. Thinking his sister had just dreamed one of her habitual nightmares, Zendrak started to comfort her. When he saw the wild joy on Kel's face, he stopped.

Then he heard them.

The Mythrrim reached Suxonli at two in the morning, their voices cacophonous and joyful as they conversed on the way to Saämbolin. Grabbing a yellow blanket, Kelandris threw it over her naked body and ran outside. Zendrak covered himself, too, and followed her. They looked up. Large silhouettes veiled the sky and made strange shadows on the ground in the moonlight. The few villagers who were left in Suxonli came pouring out of their homes. No one screamed in fear; no children cried in horror. In fact, every heart was lifted by the sight of these legendary beasts come home once again.

The Mythrrim were the first teachers of the two-legged races. Memory of the Mythrrim stirred in the generational consciousness that each person inherited from his or her respective *landdraw*. Smiles became radiant as the creatures passed overhead. People danced and turned for joy. Standing close, Kelandris snuggled next to Zendrak. He kissed the top of her head and murmured, "Won't Speakinghast be surprised."

Rimble-Rimble.

* * *

The Mythrrim Beasts of Soaringsea flew into Speaking-hast in silence at dawn. They landed on the grounds of the Great Library, folding their wings neatly beside them. They tucked their ugly heads under their wings and slept. The Mythrrim were so motionless in their sleep that they resembled the black glass statue of a Mythrrim that lay in the heart of the Great Library Maze. Indeed, when early morning students cut across the snowy grounds, they thought the Mythrrim were inanimate. Hearing student conversation, the eldest Mythrrim of all, Kindra, lifted her head. The Saämbolin and Dunnsung students present shrieked and ran. In no time at all, word of the sleeping Mythrrim spread about town. Hundreds of people flocked to see the great creatures, keeping a safe distance as they ogled. The Mythrrim paid the students and residents of the city no attention. Instead, they began their morning toilet, cleaning and ruffling their splendid feathers and striped hides.

As the morning before—Gadorian loved routines—the guildmaster was eating a coddled egg when a guildguard knocked sharply on his door. Sirrefene went to open it, her face puffy from crying. Sirrefene and her husband had been arguing since daybreak over Gadorian's action against the Kaleidicopia. The guildguard bowed to her awkwardly and hurried into the kitchen, where Gadorian sat hunched over the table.

"The Mythrrim are here, sir."

Gadorian yawned. "More rumors from the Kaleidicopians?"

"I don't know what you mean, sir." He paused, licking his lips nervously. This conversation with the guildmaster was going to be more difficult than he had imagined. "But I do know this, sir—the Mythrrim Beasts of Soaringsea are sitting on the grounds of the Great Library."

Sirrefene smiled, her expression unexpectedly relieved.

Gadorian stared at the guildguard. "Have you been sipping ale this early in the morning, Captain?"

The guildguard stiffened. "I certainly have *not,* sir. Well, suit yourselves. I've just come from the grounds myself. So I'm giving you a firsthand report. Don't say you weren't told." He bowed to both and left the opulent residence of the guildmaster and master curator.

Sirrefene regarded her husband steadily. "It's not like Captain Besredd to drink or lie, Gad. What do you think he saw?"

"Don't know," replied the guildmaster, taking a bit of egg. "Don't care, either. One thing's for sure—the Mythrrim are beasts of fantasy. Not of fact. Maybe Besredd had a bad dream—"

"Don't you think we should investigate?"

"You can if you want, Sirrey. Me, I'm going to have my breakfast in peace."

Master Curator Sirrefene reached for her woolen maroon cape which hung on a peg in the hallway. "The library and its grounds are my responsibility. See you for lunch," she added coldly.

Then she left the house.

As Master Curator Sirrefene walked outside, she was buffeted by a cold blast of winter wind. Pulling her cape close, she trudged through last night's snowfall and turned right. As she hurried along the city streets, she saw hundreds of people running toward the Great Library.

"Presence alive," Sirrefene muttered to herself. "Has my time finally come? Imagine that."

By the time Sirrefene arrived, the sun had already risen and Professor Rowenaster was well on his way to classes. Also seeing hordes of people running and jumping through the snow to get to the Great Library, he was perplexed. He decided to pay the Great Library a visit himself.

An extraordinary sight met his eyes.

Several hundred Mythrrim were ringed by several thousand people. Everyone stood or sat in silence, even the baby Mythrrim. Rowenaster put his hand to his heart in wonder. Here were the teachers he had always longed to see. Zendrak's brief shape-change into a Mythrrim several weeks ago had only whet the old man's appetite for knowledge of ancient things and ways. Tears rimmed his eyes as he crept forward. Students made way for the old man. Several of them thought Rowenaster might be responsible for bringing the beasts to Speakinghast; the old man had been known to employ wild teaching methods in his classroom during the past few years. Rowenaster approached the Mythrrim cautiously.

Kindra eyed him. When he was within ten feet of her, she said, "Welcome, Professor. We were told to look for you. And now we see that you're here. Please, don't be afraid. We ate before flying last night. And we don't eat two-leggeds, anyway. Only horses and the occasional bear."

The crowd murmured, clearly shocked at Kindra's clear speech.

Kindra, who was as tall as a medium-sized dinosaur, looked out over the heads of the people gathered around the Mythrrim. Seeing the rest of the members of Bazaar House approaching—including Themyth and Rimble—the Mythrrim Beast began to purr. It was a deafening sound, rumbling and echoing throughout the streets. The crowd backed up.

Kindra's tail thumped the ground in doglike greeting to her Greatkin mother and father. Her own biological parents were among the Mythrrim present. She grinned at Trickster.

"And now we make *kinhearth*."

Trickster prodded Yafatah to the front. The young girl's eyes were wide and full of awe. Trickster pointed to a small sack she carried carefully in her hands. "Take out the candles," he told her.

Yafatah did as she was bid. Slowly she pulled out eight candles. Kindra watched her do so with great interest. When all the candles and candlesticks had been accounted for, Kindra spoke with surprise.

"Where is the candle for the Mayanabi, child?"

Yafatah held up the seventh candle. "Here."

"Well, you can't have forgotten the Presence."

"Oh, no," agreed Yafatah, holding up the eighth candle for Kindra to see. "Here it be."

Kindra squawked. "Have you a candle for each of the *landdraws*?"

"Yes. Here be the six—"

"Six?" said a chorus of Mythrrim voices.

Kindra bent down, her large mouth close to Yafatah's head. "Did you forget *us,* child?"

Yafatah swallowed. "The Mayanabi ritual only calls for eight candles. Not nine. At least, that do be what Po told me—"

"Po?" asked Rowenaster, starting to laugh. "Po doesn't know—"

At this point, Podiddley cut in. Putting his hands on his hips, he yelled at the Mythrrim and at the rest of his housemates. "The Mayanabi ritual called for eight candles. Not nine. *I* don't know when it got changed. Maybe centuries ago. Alls I know is that *I* didn't fuck with it."

"He's quite right," said Themyth quietly. "The current Mayanabi ritual of light calls for eight candles." Themyth sighed. "See what happens when people toy around with a perfectly good ritual? Leaves out things. Important things." Themyth held her hand up. Instantly another candle and candlestick appeared in her palm. She handed it graciously to Yafatah.

"Thank you," said the young girl, her face solemn.

Satisfied, Kindra directed Po and several other people to make a kind of table out of snow. Yafatah put the candles on the table and lit them. The last candle for the Presence she placed on a handful of snow near the back. Like the candle to God in Milwaukee, this candle also sat a little higher than the rest.

When Yafatah had finished arranging and lighting the

candles, she turned to Kindra and said, "Why do we be doing this?"

"We're making *kinhearth,* child—two-legged fashion. In our own land, we sit around a blazing pit fire. Here on the mainland, we do it differently for all your sakes. Here we honor each *landdraw.* We light a candle for that *draw* and place it on the same table. This is for peace, child. Do you understand this word 'peace'?"

"Of course!" retorted Yafatah. "I doon't be a baby! I be *sixteen*!"

The Mythrrim roared and cackled with laughter. Their average life span was three to four thousand years. A girl of sixteen was a newborn to them. Kindra flapped her wings with hilarity. When she had regained control of her humor, she smiled at Yafatah and said, "You're very bright for one so young. And so we shall test you, yes?"

Yafatah hadn't expected this. She shifted weight uneasily, stuffing her gloved hands deep inside her scarlet cloak. "I didna' know I was in school," she grumbled.

Rowenaster interrupted here. "We're all in school in the presence of the Mythrrim Beasts of Soaringsea."

"Shit," said Po. "That's no mistake."

Kindra cocked her head to the side dog fashion and said, "Tell me what peace is."

"It be the opposite of war," said Yafatah.

"Is it?"

Yafatah pondered the question. "Peace be when you feel all comfortable and friendly. When you doon't wish to fight or fuss."

Kindra shook her head. "Peace is accommodation. It is the stretching one makes to understand one's friends and one's housemates. It is not weak or spineless. Peace is a quality of the Presence. It is a Greatkin who is seldom invoked in this turbulent time, this Jinnaeon. Would you care to hear this Greatkin's name?" asked Kindra.

Rowenaster smiled. He knew the name.

Yafatah nodded.

Kindra spoke softly. "She dresses in beauty, she walks in harmony, and she offers a tolerant love to all she meets. Her name is Universalima. And as we speak her name, she comes."

Themyth and Rimble watched the approach of their silent sister with smiles and whispers. This Greatkin had sat through the whole Panthe'kinarok dinner without saying a word. While Mattermat and Rimble had quarreled, she sat in utter stillness. Now that an accommodation for her was being made in the world of Mnemlith, she responded by appearing to all present on the Great Library grounds. Universalima wore white furs and a crown of gold, her dark skin and dark hair startling against the white of her furs. Like Rimble and Troth, Universalima was a resident of Neath. She was also a resident of Speakinghast.

Rowenaster's jaw dropped. He could barely say the word that came to his stunned lips. "Sirrefene?"

Master Curator Sirrefene smiled at the open-mouthed crowd in front of her. "Yes. It's me. The real Sirrefene died some years ago. Gadorian had been sweet on Sirrefene since childhood. Before he was able to ask the real Sirrefene to marry him, she contracted Hatter's Disease from a Jinnjirri hat she bought here in the city. She died from it." Turning to Rowenaster, Universalima said, "This was before the fateful 'affair' with the Jinn artist. See, *I* was the libertine. Not Sirrefene. Not that I slept with the man, mind you. But I was different in temperament than the good guildmaster family's daughter. People felt that and thought what they wished. but I digress. Anyway, at the time of Sirrefene's death, Gadorian was so distraught, he tried to kill himself. I appeared to him before he was able to do so. I offered him peace. I have remained by his side ever since that day. He has forgotten the real Sirrefene's death. He doesn't know who he lives with."

Janusin spoke for the first time now. "No wonder you wanted me to do all those statues of your family." He paused. "Why did you cancel the contract for the Panthe'-kinarok Series?"

"I didn't. Gadorian did. I like your work, Master Janusin."

Janusin blushed. "Shame I only got to do one statue, then."

Universalima laughed. "You've made one more, I believe."

"You have?" asked Barlimo, who like everyone else was dressed for winter with woolens and mufflers in layers around her neck. "Where is it, Jan?"

Janusin shuffled his feet in the snow. "Well, I hid it in the Great Library Maze. It was just a small thing, really—"

"But, oh so exquisite," replied Universalima. "And it helped, you know. It helped bring the two of them together. Art does that. You create an accommodation on the plane of imagination and eventually it will find its way into manifest reality."

Tree turned to Janusin. "What in the world did you create, Jan?"

"I made a tiny statue of Kelandris and Zendrak kissing. She was so upset when Zendrak died that I thought I would try to immortalize their love for each other in stone. Something romantic like that."

"Well, it worked," said Universalima.

There was a short pause.

Fasilla stared at the master curator turned Greatkin. "You've been in this city all along?"

"Yes, dears," said Themyth. "She has. Only we've all been making so much noise, who's had time to listen to the Greatkin of Peace? Much less recognize her," added the crone drily.

Timmer let out a big sigh. "How you could stand living with that lout, Gadorian, is beyond me."

Universalima inclined her head. "Everyone deserves peace. Even guildmasters."

"And the city?" asked Rowenaster. "Does it deserve peace, too?"

"That will be up to you. All of you. With the return of the Mythrrim, you may again learn the ways of peace. If you do, this city will know a great flowering. Out of the worst winter will come the perfumed bloom."

"No problem," said Trickster. "The winterbloom is growing in the Feyborne Mountains again. So is Kelandris." He grinned. "I keep telling 'em patience. Keep telling all the worlds that. Everything comes in its own time. Especially civilizations," he added with a naughty wink at Greatkin Themyth. She blushed.

Kindra cleared her throat. Calling all the other Mythrrim to form a perfect circle around her, she said to Podiddley and the rest of the Mayanabi in the crowd, "What is your purpose?"

"To serve the Presence."

"By doing what?"

"By keeping remembrance."

"And how do we do that?"

"By keeping *kinhearth* among ourselves. By lighting the candles for all. By including all. By loving all."

Kindra nodded her ugly head. "And so we end this tale by beginning a new Mythrrim. It will be called the *Mythrrim of Universalima*. And you will have to tell it among yourselves. You may start now."

Panthe'kinarok Epilogue

GREATKIN MATTERMAT SLOUCHED in his chair. He didn't want to admit it, but he was desperately glad to see Rimble again. The weight of his own gravity and inertia had almost overwhelmed *him*. Now he knew how the mortals felt when they spiraled downward into entropy and procrastination. Mattermat poured himself another glass of wine, his hand shaking. When Rimble finally made his reappearance at the table, his smile victorious, the rest of the family—all save Mattermat—got to their feet and cheered. Trickster sidled over to Mattermat and asked, "You *still* holding a grudge?"

Mattermat shrugged. "Not exactly."

"Yeah? Well, that avalanche of snow in the Feyborne was convincing. You nearly buried my friend, Podiddley."

"Well, *you* were rubbing it in, Rimble. Singing that stupid song. You deserved to be buried."

Rimble considered the situation from Mattermat's perspective. "I can see how you might think that."

"I *did* think that."

Rimble sighed. "Miss me?"

Mattermat rolled his eyes. "Maybe."

Trickster grinned. Announcing to the rest of the family, he said, "Mattie missed me."

Mattermat put his elbows on the table and his head in his hands. His expression was dour. Trickster whispered something in the big fellow's ear. Mattermat's face immediately brightened. "Really?" Mattermat asked Rimble.

"Yup."

"What?" asked Jinndaven uneasily as he watched this interchange.

Mattermat smiled secretly and wouldn't say a word.

Greatkin Themyth, who was looking younger and younger by the hour, pointed her cane at Rimble and said, "Tell, Rimble. Tell us what you're hatching."

Trickster looked at Mattermat. "Think we should tell them?"

Mattermat shrugged. "It's up to you."

Trickster grinned. "I'm pregnant."

There was a long silence.

"By who?" asked Themyth, her voice indignant.

Rimble smiled. "An obstinate woman."

Jinndaven started swearing. "You can't get pregnant by a *woman*, Rimble. It doesn't go that way!"

"Rimble-Rimble," said Trickster.

Afterword

Trickster as Transmitter of Mystical Teaching

by
Arifa Goodman

In stories, legends, myths and dreams spanning all cultures and all traditions, there is one figure who is ubiquitous: Trickster. There's no mystery in this figure's popularity and appeal; we all need a little comic relief, a break from the serious and often agonizing dramas that unfold throughout life. And if Trickster comes along and mocks or pokes fun at the Hero of the story (with whom we certainly identify, whether that Hero is the protagonist of a story or the leading character in our own life), we are bound to feel some relief at the resulting deflation, excruciating as it may be. Sometimes, the Hero is the Trickster, and the story, or life, becomes one long, circuitous misadventure of the absurd. When we're through laughing (or frowning in indignation), we may scratch our heads in perplexity and bewonderment, and marvel at Life itself which not only allows, but is rooted in paradox. For Life always does manage, sooner or later, to defy our most precious intentions, expectations, and conceptions.

It is just this paradoxical quality of Life that suggests a more profound role for the Trickster figure, quite aside from the comic relief—a role which no other character can play. In fact, it is Trickster who can bring us face to face with the truths which the mystics and prophets describe. Trickster embodies an understanding which is beyond words or explanations or logical thinking, and so the reality of the ineffable comes to us direct. Trickster might shock us, might outrage us, might tickle or amuse us; however it happens, we'll be knocked right out of the familiar and comfortable perspectives and assumptions that we all have about ourselves and the nature of this life. Suddenly, somehow things appear differently than they had before.

Trickster actually embodies several different types of characters, and all of them can be catalysts for catapulting us to a new level of understanding. Trickster can appear as a Fool, a Magician, a Deceiver or, at the very deepest level, a *Madzub*. As Fool, Trickster can show a simplicity and naïvete almost beyond belief, or can exemplify the height of vanity. With no sense of societal mores, no conception of good and evil, the Fool is purely instinctual, driven mostly by appetites and desires. So as the Fool wanders through life, getting in trouble, finding a way out of trouble, getting hooked again by his or her vain desires, we can see our own foolishness reflected. We too are led—indeed, ruled—by our vanity and our self-interest. We fall, get hurt, suffer pain. We moan and lament, and say, "Oh, why did this happen to me?" and then we'll get caught again by our vanity and appetites. When we laugh at the Fool, we are laughing at the fool that our little ego-self is.

Trickster as Magician shows us the ephemeral, transitory nature of Life. The Magician questions the consensus view of reality. Rather than seeing only what appears on the surface, the Magician will peer beyond the veils of this illusory world. By accepting ambiguity and rejecting a static view of the world, he or she can, at an elemental level, catalyse change, mutation, transformation, which is why Trickster is called "shape-shifter." Thus, things will appear differently than we thought they were. We'll think we are here, and we are there; we'll expect a certain outcome of our well-laid plans, and something entirely different will happen; we'll be locked in a certain perspective, and a hole will be blown through it revealing a new way of looking. And all the while, Trickster will be laughing at our feeble attempts to make sense of it all within the framework of conventional human comprehension. If we can manage to let go of our logic and see Life through Trickster's eyes, we will find ourselves in a different world—the magical realm of Creativity—where the unexpected and the unpredictable are allowed to emerge out of the rigid structures of a sclerosed mentality. It takes a certain audacity to defy 'the facts' or 'the rules' and give birth to a fresh, novel approach to Life and to ourselves.

It is in the role of Deceiver that Trickster's trickery comes into full play, and it is through this aspect that we can be led into the inner sanctum of the Great Mystery of Life where, to our utter astonishment, our eyes are finally opened and we behold . . . the Grand Hoax! For, as mystics of all traditions have been telling us throughout the ages, this Life isn't what we think it is; we aren't who we think we are; and God isn't who we think "He" (or "She") is. It is here that Trickster shows himself or herself to be the quintessential mystical guide, but very few seekers will follow Trickster to the depths he or she leads us to. Most often we valiantly resist all challenges to our established notions and conceptions; we don't want to get thrown into the chaos of uncertainty; we won't risk stepping off the edges of the parameters of our comfortable self-image. So we cling to what we've been conditioned to believe, and whenever the boat is rocked we cry out, "Deception!", not realizing that the deception arises from within. We think we're tricked by other people, by circumstances of life, etc. It is a courageous person who acknowledges with Goethe: "We are never deceived. We deceive ourselves." Trickster is the Master of the illusory world because Trickster realizes that *maya* does not mean that the world is illusory; it rather refers to our self-deception whereby we delude ourselves into thinking the world is a certain way. With this realization, Trickster rises above the snares and pitfalls that come from falling into this delusion. He or she is then free to play with this illusory nature and not get entangled in it, and even use it for transformation. By not resisting or scorning Trickster's tricks, we loosen up the cement of the towering walls we have constructed of How Things Are Supposed To Be, and open ourselves to a larger vision of life, above and beyond the field of our self-interest and self-conception. When Life then plays a trick on us, rather than bemoan our cruel fate, we can smile and say, "Ah yes, it's Trickster again," and welcome the demise of the old and cherished situation or belief so that a new revelation or breakthrough can arise. This is why the Sufis particularly have stressed shattering: shattering the conceptions, shattering the beliefs, shattering the ego-image. "Shatter your ideals upon the rock of Truth." (Hazrat Inayat Khan) By continually masking, then unmasking and remasking the hoax—making us acutely aware of the deceptive nature of life—Trickster ultimately leads us to Truth. As the Sufis say, the veil over the face of the Beloved both conceals and reveals what it covers.

Trickster at this developed stage of realization can be seen in the Madzub [who is the wandering Sufi madman or madwoman, drunk on the ecstasy of God]. The Madzub dwells in the Valley of Perplexity, the Valley of Bewilderment, a stage every seeker must pass through in the path of spiritual awakening. At this point, all human logic and reason totally break down before the staggering vision of The Way Things Are. Here, all human structures, codes and behaviors are so absolutely meaningless that the one lost in this vision becomes an anomaly of human experience. His or her words and actions are a mystery and defy all human convention. The rules just don't apply, because he or she has stepped outside the framework. Trickster in this guise has only to throw us a glance, blow us a kiss, or shine on us a smile, and our universe will be created anew.